LOST IN PERDITION

Lost in Perdition

SHANA MAVOURNIN

IngramSpark

In dedication to my dad.
I hope you found your peace and are no longer lost in perdition.

Chapter 1

As soon as Jack entered the Starbucks on O Street he felt as if he had just walked into a private club in which he didn't know the secret handshake. All the people lounging in the plush chairs, gazing deeply into their MacBooks, seemed to belong there. They blended into the background like the pop-art paintings on the walls. Jack had more of a Grant Wood look about him than a Jasper Johns. He felt out of place and ill at ease. Jack's long, scruffy, salt-and-pepper beard might as well have been a big red sign around his neck exclaiming "I am a McDonald's coffee drinker! I do not belong here!" Not a single patron actually took notice, but he felt as if all eyes were upon him.

Instead of walking directly up to the counter, he loitered around the display stand which held over-priced bags of coffee beans and gigantic mugs the size of soup bowls. Halfway down the shelf he spotted something he could actually use, a thermal insulated travel mug. *That*, he thought, would be useful. He was forever guzzling his coffee in the thin paper cups the shelter handed out. He hated cold coffee more than anything and the cold winter air chilled his coffee too quickly if he didn't drink it fast. It was hell living on the streets, but the winters were especially brutal.

Jack grabbed the travel mug and waited patiently in line while the young barista behind the counter made a grande-mocha-whatever or a skinny-caramel-whatchamacallit. While he waited, he pulled out the shiny plastic gift card he was given by one of the kinder passersby earlier in the week. She had a warm smile that actually reached her eyes. That was a rare trait these days in Jack's opinion.

As he stood in line, Jack noticed the young woman in front of him smelled strongly of patchouli. He stared at the back of the woman's dreadlocked head without really seeing it. His mind wandered back to his days at Penn State. The parties, the booze, the frantic cramming after sleeping off a doozy of a hangover, and the drugs. Always the drugs. Jack remembered how his roommate (Toby? Tony? He couldn't recall his name anymore) had joked that he should take stock in incense burners until they either graduated or Jack moved out. He always burned patchouli. It was the only smell that covered the skunky odor of pot that lingered wherever Jack went.

He remembered, all too clearly, the day his father showed up at his apartment. It was still two months to graduation, and it was neither a holiday nor Jack's birthday, so the visit was entirely unexpected. He had frantically tried to fan the smoky haze from his last joint out the window while simultaneously spraying the room with aerosol deodorant and tossing his stash into the opened dresser drawer full of holey underwear and mismatched socks. He needn't have gone to the trouble. As it turned out, his father had known for quite some time that his son was a pothead. He had just chosen, in his typical tight-lipped way, to ignore it. Jack was, after all, a grown man. Winston Harper was not there to berate his son, nor was he there to console him. He was there to simply let Jack know his mother had passed. Winston loathed the telephone, so he drove the two hours to campus to tell his son the news. That was the day Jack's life changed. That was the day Jack Harper, honor society member, straight-A student, occasional stoner but all-around good guy, had become Jack the junkie.

A familiar scent is one of the strongest memory enhancers. That was one memory Jack wished never to relive.

"Can I help you?" the barista asked.

Jack stood rooted to the spot, thermal mug in hand, lost in his memories.

"Dude, you're next."

He turned slowly around to face a young man, no more than twenty. The boy had nudged him in the back with his elbow, not wanting to get his hands dirty on Jack's grungy coat. Jack stared at the boy as if he were a new breed of human.

"You gonna order man?" the boy asked, "cuz I got a class to get to."

Jack blinked hard and took in his surroundings. He wasn't in his college apartment. He was in a Starbucks on the strip. He didn't belong here.

"I'm sorry," he told the barista as he put the mug on the counter. "I've changed my mind."

He turned to the college kid and handed him the gift card. "Here kid. Make sure you get to that class on time."

Jack pulled up the collar of his coat, shoved his hands deep into his pockets, and trudged out into the cold January air. He made his way slowly down the street making instinctual turns here and there until he ended up at the counter of McDonalds where he ordered a large black coffee. He dug out the correct change and quickly counted what was left. He had a mere buck twenty-five to last him the rest of the day and it wasn't even noon yet. He hadn't had a snort of coke, a drop of acid, or a hit off a joint in nearly two decades, but he was still a junkie. He had to have his coffee.

Jack lingered in the warmth of the restaurant as long as he dared. He knew the manager of this particular McDonald's didn't have a problem with his sort coming in off the street to warm themselves, but he also knew the man didn't like them to dawdle. Men like Jack unwittingly scare away the stay-at-home moms and their runny-nosed brats and that was bad for business. They were the money makers.

His coffee was half gone, and his nose had thawed so Jack decided it was time to leave. On his way out, he saw a young woman hand in hand with a little kid so heavily bundled he couldn't tell if it was a boy or a girl. He held open the door for the pair and nodded a cursory "hello." The woman smiled briefly but it barely reached her sad eyes. The kid, on the other hand, gave him a big toothy grin; the kind reserved only for small children and the mentally challenged. He watched amusedly as the youngster waddled after his mother in his bulky snowsuit, still beaming at Jack with an innocent openness only a child could muster.

"Don't stare Jacky," she scolded. "It's not polite."

Jack looked at the lady quizzically until it dawned on him that the child's name must be Jack as well. It *is* a rather common name he thought on his way out the door.

The gutters and the edges of the sidewalks were filled with gray slush from last week's snowstorm, but the streets were plowed clear. Jack walked to the corner and, misjudging his stride, stepped into a deep puddle of icy water. He hobbled another dozen steps, cursing under his breath, until he reached an enclosed bus stop and sat down. There was a time, long ago, when Jack would have bought himself a monthly pass and just ride the buses all day. He told himself it was the best way to search for "help wanted" signs without wearing holes in his shoes, but if he were to be honest, he did it simply to stay warm. Now he didn't even bother. The cold winter streets of Lincoln were his penance for a lifetime of misdeeds, and he intended to face them.

He took a quick look at the clock on the bank across the street then checked the bus schedule posted up on the plexiglass wall. He still had about twenty minutes before the next bus came. Enough time to sip his coffee and try to warm his frozen foot. He sat and sipped and watched the passersby. Jack was a people watcher by nature. He always enjoyed making up stories for the people he saw.

As he sipped his coffee, he imagined the man across the street in the tartan wool coat, methodically tapping his caned umbrella in the center of every paver, had driven his wife mad with his obsessive-compulsive behavior. As he was thinking what it must be like to live with such a person, the man stopped, took two steps back, and firmly tapped the previous sidewalk square in the proper place. Once satisfied, he went on his way, around the corner and out of sight. There was a middle-aged woman on the corner where the tartan wool coat man turned. She was absentmindedly spinning her wedding band around her finger as she stared blankly across the street. Jack imagined she was contemplating having an affair, possibly with her next-door neighbor, to get back at her cheating ass of a husband. She stopped playing with her ring when the "walk" light turned green and, she too, was on her way.

It was too cold for most people to be out and about so his entertainment was sorely lacking. Jack's mind wandered to the young mother he saw at McDonald's. He pictured her and her young son in a small apartment, just the two of them as the father had recently walked out. It would explain the sadness in her eyes. He pictured the two of them having a weekly lunch date at the little Jack's favorite restaurant, even though she shouldn't spend the money. Jack felt for the pair and a lump rose in his throat.

"Excuse me," came a soft voice to his right.

Jack looked up and smiled at the young mother he was just thinking of. "Yes?"

She held her son close against her leg. "Please don't take this the wrong way, but my son wanted to give you this." She held out a Happy Meal bag.

Jack looked from her to the bag to her son. He knew she had to be on a budget; her coat was rather old and didn't look overly warm, and she wasn't wearing a hat or gloves. Her son, however, was bundled up with layers of insulation. He felt a tad guilty taking a hot meal from her, but he figured he would feel much worse seeing the proud smile fall from her son's face if he refused the offering.

"Thank you," he said with a smile.

"Can I please have the toy mister?" the little boy asked politely, breaking away from his mother's grasp.

"The toy?"

"Happy Meals comes with a toy," the young Jack informed him. "See? I gots this one already!" He showed Jack what appeared to be a small plastic mammoth.

Jack dug into the paper bag and pulled out a small plastic bag with a funny looking animal with wide set eyes and handed it to the boy.

"Look mommy! I gots Sid! Thanks mister!"

The woman looked down at Jack and smiled. "Thank you."

Jack shook his head. "No, thank *you*."

He couldn't help but notice, this time the woman's smile reached her eyes. The couple turned back down the street, his small hand in hers, his other hand clutching the little toy Jack had given him.

Jack's stomach rumbled loudly at the smell of food. He pulled out a lukewarm cheeseburger and a small pack of soggy fries from the bag, held the food up to his scruffy face and inhaled the wonderful, greasy aroma. Before he knew it, the small meal was gone, and his hunger had hardly abated. He began to crumple the bag to put in his pocket as it would make good kindling for later, but was struck with a better idea. He removed his icy, wet sock, stuffed it deep in his coat pocket and slid the paper bag over his bare foot. He then slid his bagged foot into his boot and tied up the laces. It surely wasn't the most comfortable thing in the world, but it was better than trudging around with a wet foot all day. It was funny, he thought, that a few years ago, if he had seen someone doing what he just did, he would have laughed rather than applauded the person's ingenuity. Some things you just can't learn from higher education.

As Jack saw the bus round the corner, he decided he had better be on his way. He groaned as he pulled his old bag of bones off the metal bench, stretched until all his joints loosened, and got moving. He made his way back to Carter Park; haven to hobos, drunks, and runaways when night fell, but during the day it was all but deserted. Parents stopped bringing their kids there sometime after the younger Bush left office. There was something inherently creepy about abandoned playgrounds. Jack thought of it as the land of lost souls.

He made his way over to the large cement tubes at the edge of the playground and crawled into the one on the far left. Snow covered the other end of the trio of tubes, and, in mid-February, the snow drifts piled up as high as the cylinders, blocking them from most views. Without the snow, the tubes looked like large sewage pipes, just tall enough for a small child to stand up in. As Jack was no small child, he had to crawl from one tube to the next. It was a tight squeeze, but it kept him out of the cold wind.

Jack had found this place a little over two decades ago. Shortly out of rehab, still craving a hit, he had wandered into Carter Park one night after walking too far from his temporary home. He was tired and his feet ached, and he didn't want to spend any money on the bus or a cab. Back then, the playground was still somewhat shiny and well used. He crawled into the cement tubes and almost instantly fell asleep, only to be woken by a hardnosed patrolman who ushered Jack out of the park. He hadn't stepped foot in the park again until last year. He came back to the little playground by mere chance one spring day and was astonished by its dilapidated nature. The swings were rusty and hanging wonkily, the teeter-totter was broken in half, and the slides were covered in rust. It was unfortunate to see a once colorful place in such a state of disrepair. He felt an instant kinship to the park. He, too, was rather shabby. The only thing that appeared the same was the set of cement tubes. He crawled in, cleared out the debris, and called it home.

He crawled to the far-right tube where he kept two big black garbage bags filled with his meager belongings. Jack pulled one of the bags to him and pulled out a stray sock. It was stiff and cold and had seen better days, but it was dry. He took off his boot and his makeshift paper sock and slipped on the dry one. As soon as his foot hit the floor it chilled to the bone. The cement kept the wind out like a charm, but it did nothing to keep out the cold.

Jack shuffled backward, carrying the paper bag until he reached the middle tube. He placed the bag on a charred spot just below a small round opening in the top of the cylinder. He punched at the hole with a gloved finger to clear away the snow then lit the McDonalds bag with the small Bic lighter he kept in his pocket. He added a few twigs he kept for kindling and, once the flames had caught hold, he backed out to gather a few pieces of wood he kept under a tarp in the undergrowth on the edge of the playground. Within a few minutes the concrete drums were filled with a cozy dry heat. Jack laid his wet sock next to the fire to dry, climbed into his battered old Army surplus sleeping bag, and quickly dozed off.

His last thoughts before drifting off to sleep were always the same. He figured every bum on the street had similar thoughts when they let their minds wander. He thought of the life he had, the life he has, and the life he hopes to have someday. Jack no longer had the delusion he was better than anyone else. He no longer believed he was invincible. He no longer believed the world to be his playground, oddly enough since he now *lived* in a playground. The old Jack had believed all those things. He had a great job, a beautiful home, a beautiful wife, and a beautiful girlfriend. The old Jack believed he had his life, his future, and his drug habit in complete control. As he drifted off, he thought the same thing he always did: how had everything, once so perfectly perfect, gotten so ugly so fast?

Chapter 2

Jack Harper was not born a man of simple means. With the proverbial silver spoon in his mouth, he had never wanted for anything. The best schools, the best clothes, the best cars; all were at his disposal. All he had to do was say the magic word, and that word was "mommy." It wasn't until his Intro to Psych class at Penn State did Jack theorize his mother gave into his every whim as a way of overcompensating for the sadness she felt at the loss of Jack's sister.

Jack and Elizabeth were born three minutes apart in the spring of 1962. Elizabeth's arrival was a welcome surprise as their mother, Kathryn, had always longed for a little girl. Although the twins were almost a month premature, they both left the hospital in good health by the time their due date arrived. Jack and Elizabeth were the joy of the Harper household. Kathryn dressed them in coordinating outfits and took them everywhere she went. People ooh'd and ahh'd over them on a daily basis. From day one, Jack was attached to his twin sister. He would cry if they were apart, so much so that Kathryn took to putting both babies in the same crib just so Jack wouldn't cry all night. Elizabeth, it seemed, never cried.

When the twins were nearly a year old, Elizabeth came down with measles. Jack cried incessantly at the removal of his sister from his side, but Kathryn couldn't bear the thought of both of her babies becoming sick. Jack never got sick. Little

Elizabeth never recovered. They buried her in the family plot on her first birthday.

After the initial shock of losing her little girl wore off, Kathryn devoted all her time and energy and money on Jack. Shortly after they laid Elizabeth to rest, Winston suggested to his wife that they could always try for another child at some point. Kathryn refused. She considered it an insult to Elizabeth's memory. Winston, a lion in the courtroom, was a lamb at home and knew better than to argue with his bride. They both knew who the boss was, and it wasn't Winston. Kathryn was born into a great amount of wealth. Her family had flourished during the great Susquehanna log boom of the late nineteenth century and her grandfather had invested wisely.

While Kathryn grew up with the best of everything, Winston Harper spent his youth working his fingers to the bone. He was born to a farming family from Nebraska in the midst of the Great Depression and knew the value of hard work. He knew how it felt to be cold and hungry, and he vowed to never let his own children feel that ache. Growing up on a mid-sized farm in the heartland of America, Winston was expected to take over the family business, so when he told his parents he was going to college back East, they were less than pleased. In the summer of '48 his mother succumbed to heat stroke and passed away. Rather than yielding to his father's plea to stay and help tend the farm, Winston bought a bus ticket and travelled the thousand-plus miles to Pennsylvania, where he would excel in his classes and, eventually, become a lawyer. The year Winston took the bar, his father, Jack Harper, died of a massive heart attack while plowing the back forty. Their pastor found him three days later.

Winston had met Kathryn at a college mixer his junior year at Pitt. They had an old-fashioned courtship that lasted more than two years. As soon as he passed the bar, Winston got down on one knee and proposed. Kathryn's family was less than pleased, so they skipped the elaborate wedding and went to the local justice of the peace. After their brief honeymoon in a motel off route 80, Winston convinced his new wife to move back to the small town in Nebraska. He painted such a lovely picture of rolling wheat fields and neighbors that would give you the shirt of their backs, Kathryn got swept up in the romance of it all. Less than a month later, they were back on his family homestead. He had come home with a college degree, a new wife, her family's disapproval, no money, and no family.

It had only taken a year for Kathryn to put her foot down and insist they move back East. Winston couldn't find a paying legal job and they couldn't pay the back taxes on his family's property. Kathryn called her father and secured a job for Winston in his legal practice if they came back to stay. Winston had discovered two things about himself that year. One, he truly did love his wife more than anything in the world, and two, he most definitely *did not* wear the pants in his family. Needless to say, within the month they had sold off the farm, packed up their belongings, and headed back to the central Pennsylvania town in which Kathryn had grown up. Kathryn was welcomed back with open arms. Winston was given a job and the cold shoulder.

After eight years of marriage, Kathryn and Winston got pregnant with twins. Her parents were less than thrilled as they had hoped their daughter's marriage to the farmer's son would fail. However, after holding their new grandchildren for the first time, all disapproval had been forgotten. They spoiled Elizabeth and Jack with more toys and clothes than any baby could ever need. The loss of Elizabeth had just strengthened their resolve to spoil their only remaining grandchild as much as possible. Along with the clothes and the toys, Jack had a sizeable trust fund set up shortly after his birth. Elizabeth's trust was transferred to Jack's and the entire amount was to be managed by Winston and Kathryn.

While Jack was busy being pampered by his grandparents, Kathryn had taken to attending church after Elizabeth died. She found a faith she never knew existed. She also discovered the depths of her husband's love for her and a strength she never knew he had. Winston was always by her side when she needed him. This newfound strength and tenderness did not go unnoticed by Kathryn's parents. They saw how Kathryn, always so stubborn and headstrong, had leaned on her husband when no one else could comfort her. Less than a year after laying baby Elizabeth to rest, Kathryn's father did two things he never thought he would do; he made Winston a partner in his firm, and he hugged his son-in-law.

The Harper family learned to live without their little girl and doted on their only son. Everyone agreed that Jack was a beautiful child. He was the blonde-haired, blue-eyed little boy everyone adored, and those traits helped him get out of a fair amount of trouble. Jack, since the day he could walk, had a proclivity for mischief. When he was seven, he fell out of the hundred-year-old elm tree in his grandparents' backyard and broke his arm. By the time he came back from the emergency room, that beautiful old tree was cut down. When he was nine, he flipped his bike over on a crack in the sidewalk and re-broke the same arm. His grandfather had the entire block repaved. For his sixteenth birthday he asked for a 1952 Mustang so he could spend the summer restoring it. Instead, he got a brand-new Mustang. His parents and grandparents all agreed he would be safer in a new car. Jack's interest in working with his hands was falsely taken as humility. He crashed the Mustang into a tree after a party later that summer, landing himself in the hospital for a week with several broken bones. When he returned home, the '52 Mustang was in the garage along with *almost* all the tools and parts needed to fix it up. This was his mother's way of keeping him from getting behind the wheel again for as long as possible.

For as much as Jack was given everything he ever needed or wanted, he was not necessarily a happy child. Of course, he was thrilled with the mountains of toys under the Christmas tree every year and he was well known in school for his over-the-top birthday parties in which every child in his grade attended, but he always felt as if he had no control over his own life. His parents were so afraid of losing him that they never really let him live. He supposed that was why he turned to drugs at an early age; it was something he believed he could have some power over. Jack had never been more wrong. It didn't take long for the drugs to dig their sharp talons into the soft core of Jack's being.

The four years Jack spent on the campus of Penn State were a blur of parties, cramming, and classes. He made the dean's list every semester and even graduated with honors. Even at his lowest, Jack was still exceptionally bright. His professors liked him enough to remember him but not one of them tried to stop him from spiraling out of control. Not even his friends attempted to talk him out of the harder stuff. They all smoked a joint on occasion, but Jack was the one who sought out the next great high. Only one person in those four years had the ability to steer Jack out of the path of self-destruction.

Claire Simmons was a year Jack's senior but in the same graduating class. She had spent a year in Europe "discovering herself" right out of high school. Later in life she would look back and realize she never really discovered herself until well into her forties. Jack and Claire had met at a homecoming party during their senior year. While Jack did not participate in any sport himself, he never missed out on a chance to party. This particular celebration would forever be imprinted in Jack's memory. He was lounging on a beat-up old couch in a classmate's apartment halfway to feeling good and baked when someone unceremoniously plopped down next to him, pulled the joint from his mouth, and stomped it out under a well-worn Birkenstock on the end of the most perfectly formed leg Jack had ever seen.

"Those things will kill you," Claire said.

Jack's eyes wandered from her long, shapely leg, over her pleasantly curvy body and up to her heart-shaped face surrounded in layers of auburn hair.

"I'll take my chances," he replied with a sly grin.

"It'll peter out your sex drive," she told him with a wink.

"Pun intended?"

"Now what do you think?"

Jack shifted in his seat. He was accustomed to flirting co-eds, but this woman was something special.

"Maybe you should ask peter himself?" Jack replied, instantly regretting the bold cheesiness of the line.

Claire threw her head back and laughed. "Is that an invitation?"

Jack leaned into her, inhaling the sweet aroma of Chantilly Lace and VO5 shampoo. "Well, that depends?"

"On?"

"On you."

Jack looked deeply into her dark green eyes and instantly felt a connection. He had no reason to know Claire had been attracted to him as soon as she laid eyes on him. It was the shroud of smoke that had kept her away, and somehow, he sensed it. It was in her eyes. Her eyes pulled away from his long enough to spot the baggie of marijuana on the coffee table. She narrowed her eyes, ever so briefly, in a look of disdain before returning her gaze to Jack.

He placed one hand on hers and, with the other, grabbed the baggie. "This isn't mine," he lied. "It's my roommate's."

Claire sized him up, trying to decide, through the four shots of tequila, if she could trust him.

"Ok, I admit, I *have* partaken on occasion, but mainly at parties and never more than a joint or two." Another lie. "Is that what you wanted to know?"

Claire nodded, wanting to believe him but not entirely trusting him. She stood up, took Jack's hand, and led him down the hallway to an empty bedroom. They were all over each other before the door closed. Just when things were reaching the point of no return, Claire pushed Jack off of her and ran to the adjoining bathroom where she, not so discreetly, got sick. Jack wasn't quite sure what to do so he just sat on the edge of the bed and waited. After a few minutes he slipped on his boxers and went to the bathroom door.

"Are you okay in there?" he asked.

"Go away," Claire groaned.

"I'm not going anywhere until I know you're okay."

There was a flush, a splashing of water, a gargle, and a spit. Claire tentatively stepped out of the doorway. She walked past Jack without looking at him and began gathering her clothes.

Jack handed her a shoe that slid under the bed. "You don't have to go ya know."

"Yes, I do," she stated without looking at him.

"Why?" Jack asked. "Just because you got a little sick? Believe me, if every girl who threw up she saw me naked left, I'd still be a virgin!"

His crack at a joke diffused the tension enough for Claire to smile. She sat back down on the bed, holding her clothes to her, and looked up at him. "It really had nothing to do with you. I just... well, I just never do anything like this is all."

Jack sat down next to her. "Like what?"

"This!" she motioned to the bed. "I'm not a virgin, please don't get me wrong, but I'm just not the type to get drunk and pull a complete stranger into bed."

Jack slid his arm around her shoulders and kissed the top of her head. "Tell ya what," he started. "How about we get out of here and head over to the Diner for breakfast?"

"It's two in the morning!"

"It's never too early for pancakes," Jack surmised. "You definitely need to get some food in you, and it'll give us some time to get to know each other. Names would be a good place to start."

Claire got dressed and walked over to the door. She picked up Jack's pants from the corner and tossed them over to him. "Claire."

"What?"

"My name," she clarified. "It's Claire."

Jack smiled at her as he pulled on his pants. "Claire... that's a pretty name. I'm Jack."

"It's nice to meet you Jack," she smiled shyly. "I'll wait outside."

"I'll be right down."

"Oh, and Jack?"

"Yes."

"No girl in her right mind would ever get sick from seeing you naked." She winked and closed the door.

Jack looked down at himself and chuckled.

Pancakes and coffee gave them the perfect opportunity to get to know one another, although after three hours, they had no more interest in either the pancakes or the coffee. Jack ended up spending the rest of the weekend in Claire's apartment. They were all but inseparable since. Jack found himself falling in love but, under her watchful eye, it was difficult for Jack to get his fix. He still found ways to get high, but now it was done in secret and that made him feel dirty and miserable. That feeling of betrayal pushed him to stronger drugs and, by the time he clumsily got down on one knee after graduation, he and Claire were both fully aware of just how far Jack had sunk. Still, Claire said yes. She believed her love could save him. She believed wrong.

Chapter 3

Jack landed himself a substitute teaching job at a local elementary school shortly after graduation. A year and a half later he finished his master's and married Claire. Just a month after the wedding, Winston Harper died in his sleep. The doctors told Jack his father had a massive heart attack, but Jack knew he died of a broken heart.

Orphan life did not sit well with Jack and his drug use quickly escalated. With both of his parents gone, Jack felt accountable to no one, not even Claire. One particularly rough morning, as he was getting ready to shave, Jack noticed his hand was shaking so badly he was sure to cut himself. He barely recognized his own face in the mirror as he looked at least twice his age. He decided a change of scenery was in order. He knew too many people in that town, and he knew who to contact when he needed a hit. He thought if they moved far enough away, he could get himself clean. When he suggested to Claire they move west, she agreed without hesitation. She loved her husband and wanted him away from the poison that, she feared, would eventually tear their life apart.

Jack grew up listening to stories about farm life from his father. Although farming had never been a remote consideration for a career, Jack was always amused by the stories of skinny dipping, corn husking, and cow tipping. He had never been west of Pittsburgh in his life, but he had very clear visions of how it would be. He wanted to see the rolling fields of wheat and corn dancing in the breeze, the endless horizon with nothing in the way, and he wanted to see for himself the way the sky transformed from blue to purple to green before a big storm. He wanted to get himself clean and what better place to do that than in the heartland of America, where the air was clean, and the people were cleaner. So, in the early summer of '86, Jack and Claire packed their tiny one-bedroom apartment into a U-Haul hooked to the back of Claire's aging Duster and headed west.

They took a good week to make the trip, stopping along the way to take in the sights. They spent two days in Chicago where they gorged themselves on deep dish pizza and discovered a new love for jazz during a street festival they happened upon. Jack hadn't had a hit the entire trip and actually felt pretty good about it, until they made it to the city limits of Lincoln. He was amazed, and somewhat crestfallen, at the sight of the city. It was nothing like he had imagined. It was an actual city and not the fields and acres of farmland he had pictured, but for better or worse, it was home now.

While Jack was out job hunting, Claire was busy looking for a place to call home. The little efficiency out by the airport they were staying at would not suffice. Claire wanted to start a family and the rumble of jetliners wouldn't go well with a baby's sleep. It took less than a month for Claire to find the perfect place. Pretty little ticky-tacky houses lined the streets where kids of all ages rode their bikes and ran through sprinklers. The three-bedroom ranch was nestled in the middle of a cozy little housing development in the northwest corner of town and was the perfect place to raise a child. With the money Jack received from his father's life insurance policy, they were able to buy the house outright. They signed the papers on their second wedding anniversary. That same week, Jack was offered a position teaching American Literature at a local high school. He was two months clean. Claire noticed the change in Jack, and she was happier than ever. That night she threw out her birth control and ravaged her husband with a fervor she hadn't had since their honeymoon.

Nearly a year went by, and Jack stayed on the wagon, always under the watchful eye of his bride, but he didn't begrudge her one bit. He was happy sober and wanted to keep it that way. Jack loved his job and quickly became a favorite teacher among the students and the faculty of Lincoln High. He and Claire quickly made friends with the other young couples on their block and regularly had barbecues, dinner parties, and general get-togethers where they could bullshit about sports, politics, music, and the like. Life was just about as perfect as it could be. Then Claire became pregnant.

Claire was so excited she could barely contain herself. She broke the news to Jack over a dinner of baby back ribs, baby potatoes, and baby carrots. Jack, totally oblivious to the clever menu, devoured the meal with relish as Claire watched in amusement.

"What did you think of dinner daddy?" she asked him coyly.

"Delicious" he said through a mouthful of potatoes. He had completely missed the moniker she gave him.

"How about dessert?" she asked, as she got up from her seat.

"None for me, thanks babe. I don't think I could eat another bite."

Claire walked out with a small plate with two cupcakes, one frosted in blue, the other in pink; a slip of paper was tucked underneath. She sat the plate down in front of Jack, took her seat, and watched as he figured out the puzzle.

"What is this?" Jack asked with amusement.

"Just dessert."

Jack pulled the envelope out from under the cupcakes. "No, this?"

"Open it and see."

He licked some of the blue frosting from his finger as he opened the envelope. Jack skimmed the paper, looked up at Claire, and then read it again.

"You're pregnant?"

Claire nodded, a grin spreading across her face.

Jack looked from the note, to Claire, back to the note again. "You're pregnant!" he exclaimed, jumping out of his seat. He picked her up in a great big hug and spun her around the room, covering her face with kisses.

"Jack! I'm gonna get sick!" she squealed through tears of laughter.

Jack put her down and kissed her gently on the lips. "I'm gonna be a daddy!" he exclaimed, tears in his eyes. He knelt down and kissed her belly. "I'm gonna be a daddy" he whispered again.

Jack wasted no time in preparing the nursery. Every evening after work he came home, kissed his wife, changed into his paint-covered blue jeans, and headed straight into the bedroom next to theirs. On an average night, he would work for two or three hours before breaking for dinner. He already had the room painted a pale yellow and had built floor to ceiling bookshelves he had painted in a soft green. He told Claire he intended to fill the shelves with every children's book he could find. While he worked, Claire was usually sitting in the antique rocking chair Jack had found at a pawn shop, knitting and humming lullabies while she watched him work. She fell in love with her husband all over again in the first couple months of her pregnancy, and as short lived as it would turn out to be, she relished every second of it.

Three months after she found out she was pregnant, Claire had her first visit with her OB/GYN. Jack took the day off to be with her. According to the books they both avidly read in bed at night, Jack knew they should be able to hear the heartbeat by now and was anxious to do so. As they sat in the waiting room, they bounced baby names off each other to kill some time.

"If it's a boy I think we should name him Jack," Claire stated with a smile, leaning her head on Jack's shoulder. "After his daddy."

Jack kissed the top of her head. "I'd like that."

"Okay, that was easy. Now what about a girl's name?"

"What do you think of Kathryn?" Jack asked. "After my mother."

Claire mulled it over. "Kathryn. I like it."

"Kathryn Elizabeth," Jack added.

"Elizabeth?"

"After my sister."

Claire sat up and looked at him. "You never told me you had a sister."

Jack shifted in his seat and cleared his throat. "Didn't I?"

Claire just shook her head.

"Well, to be honest, I never really think about her. She was my twin. She died of the measles when she was a baby, so I don't really remember her. I guess she stuck with me though to come up with her name like that."

Claire didn't know what to say. She thought she knew everything about her husband, but now, after all this time, she found out he had a twin sister. She was torn between feeling hurt and sad and angry, then she looked into Jack's eyes. She could see he had not meant to keep anything from her. He surprised even himself with the acknowledgement of his sister.

She took his hand in hers and agreed. "Kathryn Elizabeth it is."

Jack squeezed her hand and smiled.

"Claire Harper?" a voice called from across the room.

"Here we go," Jack whispered to her.

Claire changed into the flimsy hospital gown and waited on the exam table for nearly half an hour before being joined by a very young, very frazzled-looking doctor. He introduced himself as Dr. Tscheski and Jack secretly wondered how long it would take him to spell the name right on the payment checks. Dr. Tscheski asked Claire to lay down so he could see how far along she is. He poked at her belly while making an annoying sucking sound through his teeth. Jack, already irritable from waiting so long, found himself clenching his fists tighter at every suck.

"Can we hear the heartbeat?" Jack asked, preemptively stopping the doctor from starting another sucking sound.

"Well..." the doctor proceeded to measure Claire's belly with what looked like a seamstress's measuring tape, "it might be a bit early."

"I'm about four months along," Claire piped up. "All the books say we should be able to hear the heartbeat by now."

"Four months? Really?" the doctor asked.

"Yes. Why? What's wrong?" Claire asked.

"Oh, nothing really. You just might be carrying small," Dr. Tscheski assured her. "Let's listen for that heartbeat."

He pulled out a device that, to Jack, looked like a toy microphone on a phone cord. The doctor squirted a jelly-like substance onto Claire's still-flat belly and proceeded to spread it around with the microphone. A few minutes went by before a worrisome expression grew across his face. Jack was becoming so concerned he didn't even notice the sucking sound anymore.

"Is there something wrong?" Jack asked.

The doctor shook his head. "I can't find the heartbeat."

Jack and Claire looked at each other, stunned.

"It's probably nothing," the doctor assured them. He held up the heartbeat monitor. "These things fizzle out all the time. Let me grab a different one and I'll be right back."

Jack held Claire's hand tight. Neither of them spoke in his absence, both afraid of vocalizing their fears.

The door opened and Dr. Tscheski came in followed by an older, equally frazzled-looking doctor that looked as if he could be his father. "Okay," he announced. "Let's try this again."

He repeated the whole performance again with the same results. No heartbeat. The elder doctor took the monitor from him and tried himself. He had the air about him that he needed to show the young doctor how it's done, and Tscheski did not look pleased. Jack would normally have sympathized with the young man, but his thoughts were only on hearing the heartbeat.

The elder doctor shook his head and walked out of the room, never saying a word.

"What does that mean?" Jack asked irritably.

"Well," Dr. Tscheski began, "it could be any number of things. You could have misjudged your conception date and you're not as far along as you originally thought."

Claire shook her head, unable to speak without crying.

"The baby could be underdeveloped or just hiding from us today."

Neither Jack nor Claire understood this as an attempt at levity.

"Or?" Jack prodded.

"Or," he let out a deep breath, "you could have an ectopic pregnancy, but you would have been in quite a bit of pain by now."

Claire shook her head again.

"There is a possibility the baby wasn't viable."

Jack stared at the man. "Wasn't *viable?*"

"She could have miscarried."

Claire squeezed Jack's hand tightly as tears streamed down her face.

"How can we be sure?" Jack asked.

"I'll set you up for a sonogram as soon as possible."

"Today," Jack insisted. "Now!"

"Of course," the doctor agreed. "Absolutely, today."

As soon as Dr. Tscheski left the room, Claire let herself openly weep. Jack wrapped his arms around her and mumbled words of comfort, how everything would be okay, how it was all just a big mistake. He didn't even notice when his tears fell into hers.

The sonogram confirmed the doctor's worst diagnosis. Their baby didn't make it. Claire's body still hadn't realized there was something wrong with the fetus and, therefore, didn't miscarry on its own. She was scheduled for an immediate D and C to remove the baby. Neither one of them wanted to know the sex of the baby. Losing it was hard enough without knowing if it was Jack Junior or Kathryn Elizabeth.

Jack waited impatiently in the reception area while they took his wife down the hall. He paced back and forth, driving the elderly volunteers crazy. They suggested he get a breath of fresh air or a cup of coffee and pointed him in the direction of the cafeteria. The sound of his footfalls in the empty corridor echoed in his ears and the mingling odors of disinfectant, cafeteria food, flowers, and death permeated his nose. He didn't want a breath of fresh air and he didn't want a damn cup of coffee. What he wanted was to get high. He *needed* to get high, but he still bought the cup of coffee, sat out on the patio, and let it get cold.

A fresh breeze tousled his dirty blonde hair and stung at his eyes. He took a deep breath, and the crisp fall air cleared his head enough for the dam to break. The pain was a sucker punch in the gut, and he exhaled the most excruciating sob a man could let out. Jack's heart broke into a thousand pieces that day and he felt as if he would never be the same man again. He fell to his knees and cried openly until the tears ran dry. He didn't care who saw him or what they thought. He was in his own private hell, and he didn't see a way out.

Jack slowly began to pull himself together when he thought of how he would be expected to comfort his wife. He felt like a heel. He knew, no matter how much pain he felt, Claire's pain would be much worse. The bracing air that punched him in the gut now slapped him in the face and energized him. He wasn't quite ready to go back into the stale hospital, so he walked around the building and into the parking lot. He trudged over to their little car, got in, and popped the glove box open. Inside was a beat-up copy of Irwin Shaw's *Rich Man, Poor Man*. It was one of Jack's all-time favorite novels and Claire hated it, which made it the perfect place to stash enough weed for a joint or two. He had almost forgotten about it over the past year, and he was certain it would taste like shit, but he needed *something* to dull the pain enough to be able to comfort Claire.

Jack sat behind the wheel and methodically rolled the old weed into one of his cigarette wrappers, twisted both ends, and, without a second thought, lit up. He was right about the flavor, but it still had the required effect. He wasn't too con-cerned about Claire noticing the smell; she would be too upset to notice and the dingy upholstery was already soaked with the fumes of joints long past.

After his second joint, Jack dragged himself out of the car and headed back to the entrance of the women's wing of the hospital. His head felt clearer than it had in ages and the pain, while still there, had dulled to a low throb. One of the little old ladies at the desk informed him that his wife was in recovery and she would be ready to go home within the hour. Jack thanked her and took a seat in the corner of the room where he buried his face in today's issue of the Journal Star. He read and re-read an article about a pumpkin growing contest up in Wahoo about half a dozen times before Claire was wheeled out to him. Her face was puffy from crying, her eyes were glazed over from the drugs, and she looked as if she had aged a decade in the last four hours. Jack went to her, popping a mint into his mouth just to be safe, and knelt down beside her.

"How ya doin' sweetie?" he asked.

She just shook her head and began crying again. Jack got up, walked around to the back of the wheelchair and began pushing her out to the car.

"Let's get you home, ok?"

Jack left Claire with the orderly while he went to get the car. He rolled down the windows to air out some of the fumes. The orderly helped Claire out of the wheelchair while Jack came around and opened the passenger door. She wrapped her arms around his neck and he kissed her forehead.

"Everything's going to be alright," he told her. He placed his hand under her chin and lifted her face to meet his. "I promise."

She kissed him lightly on the lips, pulled away, and looked at him quizzically.

"What," he blurted out, a bit more defensively than intended.

She furrowed her brow and shook her head once, left, right, center. She knew. Jack knew that she knew. That one small gesture, the furrowing of her brow, stirred up a self-righteous anger deep inside him. Fine then, he thought. He figured if they both knew what he did then there was no reason for him to hide it and he sure as hell wasn't going to go through the hassle of quitting again. It would be a welcome reprieve not having Claire always riding his ass, second guessing what he was doing. He knew he couldn't get through this without the comfort of his old friends, and he didn't intend to try.

Chapter 4

The next year was a blur for Jack and a constant head-ache for Claire. Jack's re-acquaintance with his old habit had progressed quickly from pot to acid (which he didn't care for) to cocaine. After one particularly nasty fight with Claire, he even ventured into heroin, but regretted that decision when he literally woke up in a dumpster behind a frat house.

In addition to re-discovering his old friends, Jack had also found himself a buddy who shared his fondness for narcotics. He had developed a rather inappropriate adulterous relation-ship with a female student from his twelfth-grade honors Literature class. That affair continued through her first year at UNL. As far as Jack was concerned, Claire was blissfully unaware of his infidelity, and he only felt brief pangs of guilt whenever his current high wore off. Whenever he felt any guilt creeping in, all he had to do was look his wife in the eyes. The lack of love he saw there was enough to quickly change his mood from one of regret to ambivalence.

The day Claire had lost the baby was the day her love for Jack had started to die. When she smelled the pot on his breath, she had known she hadn't just lost her child, she lost her husband as well. The drugs had completely taken over every aspect of Jack's personality. Instead of being attentive and caring he had become aloof and withdrawn. Claire had some experience with his moodiness while he was using in college, but now, as his addiction dug its claws in deeper and deeper, she had no idea what to expect from day to day. If it was just the marijuana, she could have let it slide like she did all through college, but when he got back on the harder stuff, it scared her.

The nights that Jack didn't come home had become nights to relish rather than worry over, and his eminent arrival was a thing she grew to dread. He had never gotten violent in his drugged state, she wasn't afraid of that. What scared her most was the emptiness she felt when he was near her. He had become a shell of the man she had once known and loved. It was like living with a ghost and that frightened her beyond all realm of comprehension. She could feel the cold hollowness of him when he sat beside her in the evening on their battered sofa. They'd watch reruns of MASH or Three's Company together, munching on popcorn or, sometimes, sharing a bottle of Coke, but she could tell he wasn't paying attention to the lighthearted comedy on the tube. He was in another place. Although his body remained, his mind, his soul, his very *being*, was a million miles away. She would try to catch his gaze on numerous occasions when he was wandering through the house, a blank expression on his face. On those rare occasions when he looked her in the eye, she would see a fleeting look of sorrow, quickly replaced by uncertainty.

When Jack was lightly buzzed he would wander through the house, beer in one hand, cigarette in the other. He always ended up in the same place. The unfinished nursery at the end of the hall had become less a place of warmth and comfort and more of a morbid shrine. It was a place for Jack to go and wallow in his own greed and self-pity. However much Claire hated him using their baby's room as a hiding spot, it gave Claire some respite from Jack's hauntings. Ultimately, Jack would come out of the room, his eyes red-rimmed from crying, get in his car and leave, sometimes for days. As soon as he left, Claire would always go into the room and scrub it clean before sealing it up again. She couldn't bear looking at the cheery yellow walls or the creaky old rocking chair with the half-finished blanket sitting on the table next to it. It was a room she truly hated, and she couldn't understand why Jack insisted on going in there.

For Jack, that room had a deeper meaning. The day he had brought Claire home from the hospital he had gone directly to the nursery and just stood there, in the center of the room, eerily spinning in a slow-motion circle, taking in every square inch of the empty nursery. Claire had stood in the doorway watching him for a few minutes before crawling into bed for a much-needed nap. As she slept and dreamt of a baby girl with her flaming red hair and her daddy's bright blue eyes, Jack went out to find himself a new supplier. It wasn't as hard as one would imagine. He was, after all, a high school teacher and had picked up and retained a few names over the past year.

He knew better than to bring the drugs into their home. Claire soon figured if Jack wasn't home by the time she got home from her job, he was out scoring his next high. She didn't know where he got the drugs, she didn't know who, if anybody, lit up with him or where they did it, nor did she know where he got the money for his habit because their joint account was always spot on. Claire didn't care about any of those things, as long as she didn't see it happen. All she cared about was staying as far away from Jack as possible until she figured out whether she wanted to try to salvage their marriage or not. Every day that passed pushed her closer to the "not" option.

There were times when she looked at him and saw a shadow of the old Jack. Those were the times that he came home, passing as sober, and sat down to dinner with her. He'd tell her about his day and ask her about hers and, occasionally, they would fall into bed together as if there had never been any bad blood between them. The kind, sweet, poorly misguided Jack she fell for in college was still in there somewhere and she could clearly see him on those days. But sometimes he was buried so deep she couldn't find him at all. Those were the days, more often than not, when he came stumbling in at god-awful hours of the morning, stinking to high hell of reefer or stale beer or vomit. Those were the days when she was ready to pack a bag for him and toss him out on his rear, but something always stopped her. Whatever they had become over the years, Jack was familiar. His presence, his body, his quirks, even his sickening habit were all familiar and predictable and, strange as it may seem, safe. Claire was not one for variety and leaving Jack would be the biggest change of her life. Sometimes she thought she should get out of it while she was still young. She was still at an age and a stage of her life where she could easily start over. They had no children to fight over, and she had a good job of her own. All they had was the house and she honestly didn't care whether she kept it or if he did. All she knew was she had to decide before she was stuck for good. What finally made up her mind for her was the appearance of the two little blue lines.

Jack had been on a sober streak over the holiday break, and they had gotten along better than they had in years. Claire wasn't under the delusion that he had called it quits; it was more likely that being out of school had kept him away from his supplier. Whatever the reason, she wasn't about to complain. It was like having the old Jack back. They had even decided to take Claire's bonus and go on a mini vacation down to the Florida Keys to get away from the brutal Nebraska winter. They had gotten rather intimate on the trip and, for the first time in a very long time, Claire wasn't the least bit disgusted with the act the morning after. Their holiday was the most tranquil time they had ever spent together. Walking on the beach, watching the sunset, sipping drinks with little umbrellas in them; it all added up to a romantic reattachment to one another. Claire had forgotten all about her ideas of starting over without him and just enjoyed being in Jack's company.

She forgot how funny, and smart, and sweet he could be, and, in turn, she forgot how spontaneous and lively and relaxed she could be. It had been so long that neither one of them had remembered who they really were, they both felt like they were newlyweds again. At least, they did, until they had gotten back home and into their daily routine.

Shortly after they returned from paradise the drugs came back full force. Jack had disappeared for three days over a mid-February weekend and Claire was genuinely concerned for his wellbeing this time. She supposed it was the lingering feeling of serenity she brought home from the beach, but it could have been the fact that Jack had never vanished for more than a night or two before. It was during that weekend that Claire had taken one of those home pregnancy tests they sold in the drug stores. She was three weeks late and was horribly afraid that it would come out positive. As much as she wanted to be a mother, the last thing she needed right now was a baby thrown into the mix with a drug addict husband and her own insecurities.

The five minutes it took to wait for the result seemed to take an hour. The old adage, *a watched pot never boils*, kept springing to her mind every time she caught herself peeking at little window in the plastic pee-stick. When the kitchen timer she set went off she had to force herself not to run down the hallway to the bathroom. Two lines. There were two lines, clear as day. She was pregnant. Claire fell to her knees and vomited into the toilet, and she was quite sure it was not due to morning sickness. She spent the next half hour sitting on the bathroom floor, her knees pulled tight to her chest, crying and wondering just how she was going to handle this.

Claire never doubted that she was meant to be a mother. As a child she would spend hours playing with her dolls, changing their little diapers, feeding them bottles and pretend baby food. It was in her nature. After the miscarriage she had all but forgotten her dream of having a child. Staring at those two little blue lines had awoken all those old feelings again. She wanted this baby more than anything in the world. She was also completely certain that she didn't want Jack to have anything to do with it. As happy as he was at the announcement of her first pregnancy and as sweet as he was to her during those first few months, she couldn't forget how he had handled the stress of losing their baby. The first thing he turned to for comfort wasn't his wife. It wasn't even his friends. It was his precious drugs. Claire had no reason to believe he would get himself clean in time for the birth of this child and, even if he did, she couldn't convince herself that it would last. What if she lost this one as well? She didn't think she could handle another tragedy like that again, especially if it made her husband sink deeper into the abyss in which he was already floundering. She had made up her mind, she just had to act before she lost her nerve.

When Jack came back home Monday afternoon he came home to an empty house. All of his belongings were still in place, the furniture was still there, and it basically looked identical to the day he had last seen it, but, without Claire, it was no longer a home. Her side of the closet was left with only two dozen or so wire hangers and the side of the bureau in which she kept her various sundry items was empty. The only things missing were her clothes and a few toiletries. Lying on the pillow on Jack's side of the bed was a sealed envelope with his name scrawled across it in her delicate script. If Jack had looked in the wastepaper bin, he would have found about a dozen balled up drafts of the letter he sat down to read.

"Dear Jack," he read aloud without realizing he was doing so, *"I have no idea when you plan to come home so I have no idea how long I'll have been gone when you read this. Please believe me, this is the hardest thing I have ever had to do but we both knew it was coming. I always thought you and I could conquer*

anything as long as we had each other, but I was wrong. Over the past few years, I have come to realize that there hasn't been an 'us' in quite a long time. There has been a 'you' and there has been a 'me' and then there was that unmentioned problem. Your addiction has gotten out of control, and I just can't handle it anymore. I am willing to take some of the blame. I never pushed you to get help or even asked you for that matter. I just accepted it as a part of you. I owe you an apology for that. I'm sorry Jack. I'm sorry I never loved you enough to get you the help you needed. Maybe if we hadn't lost the baby, we'd be okay, but I sincerely doubt it. Our time together has come to an end. Part of me is ashamed of myself for ending it like this, in a letter, but I just don't have the strength to face you anymore. You should be expecting divorce papers in the near future. I don't want the house or anything in it but what I have already taken. Please Jack, don't come looking for me. If you have any love for me just let me go. I will always love you sweetheart, just not enough to stop loving myself. Always, Claire."

Jack read the letter over again and then once more for good measure.

He wandered around the house half-heartedly looking for anything that was missing. Other than her car being absent from the garage, nothing looked out of place, until he got to the bookshelf in the spare bedroom. Their wedding album was gone.

She had left all the framed pictures of that summer day hanging on the walls, but she had taken the big white book with all the snapshots their friends and family had taken.

He didn't know what to think. He wasn't sure if the joint he smoked in the school parking lot before he came home was dulling his senses or if he was in shock. Probably a little of both, he surmised.

Again, he found himself standing in the center of the closed-off nursery he had worked so hard on what seemed an eternity ago. He had done this so regularly that every square inch of the room was permanently etched into his mind. The fading yellow paint, the unfinished shelving unit he planned on filling with toys and children's books, the refurbished rocking chair Claire would sit in and knit while he worked on the room. When, he wondered, had things gotten so bad between them that they couldn't work it out? Jack sat down where he stood, leaned his elbows on his knees and pressed the heels of his hands into his closed eyes until he saw stars. He was alone. Never in his life had he been so alone, and it scared him more than anything. For the first time since Claire's miscarriage Jack had allowed himself to feel the pain he had tried so hard to dull with the drugs. In that moment he realized how much Claire had meant to him. He never let her know how much he appreciated her or how much he loved her and now, it was too late. How had he not realized that before now? How had he let his selfishness get so out of control? The drugs, the affair... he would gladly give it all up if he could just have his wife back. He felt the tears prickling the back of his eyes, but they never came. He felt dead inside, and dead men shed no tears.

Jack pulled himself up and trudged to the bathroom where he splashed cold water on his face. A half-empty bottle of Claire's Nivea lotion was on the edge of the sink next to the hand towel Jack reached for to dry himself off. He stared at the big blue bottle for an unknown length of time before he shifted his gaze to the vanity mirror. There was a stranger looking back at him. A haggard old man with bags under his eyes and a permanent five o'clock shadow stared back at him. He looked at least ten years older with his sallow skin and yellowing teeth. This man was a far cry from the young gentleman in the wedding photos hanging in the hallway. Looking at himself in the mirror gave Jack the answer he was subconsciously looking for. He knew right then and there what he had to do. He had to let her go.

Chapter 5

Jack woke from his dream with a start. It had been ages since Claire crossed his minds and he wasn't overly surprised to find tears freezing on his cheeks and in his scruffy beard when he wiped the sleep from his eyes. Claire was the one and only love of his life; letting her go had been the hardest thing for him to get over, harder even than getting clean. Jack closed his eyes and tried to get back the quickly fading pictures of his wife. It was decidedly inconvenient, Jack surmised, that on those rare occasions he was blessed with a good dream, he could never get that feeling of joy back as easily as he could reach the fear when awakening from a nightmare. His bad dreams left him feeling cold and alone and jonesing pretty badly, and that feeling usually stayed with him for the remainder of the day. Oh, what he wouldn't do to keep with him all day that feeling Claire gave him. After trying, and failing, to get that sensation back, Jack decided it was time to start the monotonous drudgery of his day.

It snowed at some point during the night. Not enough to cover his entrance, just an inch or so of optimal ski powder, but it was enough to be a nuisance. Jack crawled backwards out of the tunnel, shoveling a path with his knees as he went. He stretched his aging body and grimaced up at the blinding early morning light as the knots loosened and his joints creaked and popped. Spending his nights in a three-foot wide cement pipe was most certainly not the optimal condition for a man in his fifties, but, he figured, this was the life he had made for himself. It was the life he felt he deserved. Could he be doing much better? Most definitely. But this is where he told himself he belonged. For better or worse, Jack was now married to the streets.

Morning chores consisted of sweeping out the ashes from the previous night's fire with a new branch of pine needles, gathering kindling for later that evening, and making his bed, which was nothing more than shaking out the old army sleeping bag, rolling it back up and pushing it to the back of the last tube with his other belongings. After Jack had finished his chores, he walked across the playground to the timeworn restrooms that still stood, unused by anyone but himself and a few other street people that occasionally stumbled upon the tiny brick building. Even though no one had cared about maintaining the park for years it was still passable for clean. Once a week Jack would clean the sinks, sweep the floors, and pour disinfectant down the open toilets. He may be homeless, but Jack was no animal. His routine was the same every day. No need to worry about shaving but he did keep a toothbrush and a box of Arm & Hammer on hand to brush his teeth every morning. He splashed icy cold water on his face with a tattered washcloth and then gave a once over to his under arms. This was about as clean as Jack got in the winter months. If it were warmer out, he could be found in the tiny duck pond scrubbing himself down with that same washrag and a bar of Ivory soap. Always Ivory. It was cheap and it was the only soap that floated, a characteristic that was especially handy when one bathed in an open body of water. This was a fact he had learned the hard way.

After his morning ritual, Jack would dig to the bottom of one of his trash bags and pull out two dollar bills without looking. Depending on what he grabbed that day he could have enough for a decent hot meal and some basic necessities, or he would end up panhandling on the street to supplement his meager two-dollar allowance. Today he happened to come up with a five and a one. Not bad, but not great either. It was, at least, enough for a decent cup of coffee from Dunkin Donuts three blocks down. No matter how much Jack came up with each morning he always made a beeline for a cup of coffee. Which direction he turned out of the park depended on how much money he had in his pocket. If he had pulled a mediocre amount, he made a left and headed to Dunkin Donuts. If he only had two ones, he would turn right and head toward the shelter for a free Styrofoam cup of the sludge they passed out to other bums like him. If he happened to head straight, which had happened only once, it meant he had a good twenty bucks in his pocket and would walk the five blocks to Starbucks.

This morning, as he turned left at the park entrance, he had wholeheartedly wished he hadn't given that Starbucks gift card to the college student behind him in line. Jack was a peculiar man. He lived on the barest of means, occasionally went days with nothing to eat but the stale Saltines he kept in his pocket for the pigeons, but he was still the first man to give away what little he had. The gift card, for example. Jack had no idea how much money was on the card; it could have been two dollars, it could have been twenty, and he had just given it away without a second thought. He had no way of knowing that the woman who dropped the festive looking plastic card at Jack's feet the day before had filled it that morning with fifty dollars, specifically to give to him. What Jack could never know is that that young woman had lost her brother to the streets and had a soft spot, and an open wallet, for the unfortunate of Lincoln. In this case, what Jack didn't know probably *would* hurt him.

The other peculiarity of Jack was, no matter how much money he had left in his pocket at the end of the day, be it a penny or a dollar, he always left it in the donations box in the lobby of the Children's section of St. Elizabeth's hospital. Every day, without fail, he would walk quickly, head down, past the suspicious gaze of the security guard and the quizzical stares of the ladies at the information desk and drop his loose change in the clear plastic box at the far end of the brightly lit Children's entrance. He would just as quickly walk out. No one ever stopped him or questioned why he was there, but the whole place made him feel uncomfortable. The only time he strayed from his ritual was on one day of the year. Every year on the anniversary of the day he and Claire had lost their child, he would drop a check into the box instead of change or crumpled bills. But as it was now the end of January, Jack had a good ten months before he would have to get out his battered old checkbook again.

The smell of sweet rolls and bagels and coffee permeated Jack's nose as soon as he opened the door to the donut shop. He hadn't paid any attention to his surroundings on his walk down the street. His thoughts were turned inward to his former life and his sweet young wife. Why did she have to haunt his dreams the way she did last night? It was bad enough when she invaded his waking thoughts. When he saw a young red-haired woman on the street, when he heard the unmistakable puttering of the engine of a Volkswagen Beetle (the car Claire had bought herself when she got the bank manager job, she had worked so hard at), when he caught a whiff of Chantilly Lace perfume; any of these things brought Claire to the front of Jack's mind. But he rarely, if ever, dreamed of her at night.

"Can I help you?" came a rather snooty and exasperated voice, jolting Jack out of his reverie.

"Oh, yeah," Jack retorted. "Large coffee. Black."

"That'll be two-fifteen," the young cashier told him.

Jack laid down the crumpled five and tried to smooth it out for the girl. She grabbed it before he got the chance, possibly afraid he'd try to snatch it back before she could take it. She pushed his coffee and his change across the counter, not wanting to touch him in any way, shape, or form. As Jack turned from the counter he saw her, out of the corner of his eye, squirt antiseptic gel into her hands and rub them together vigorously with a wrinkled sneer on her face. Jack couldn't care in the least what germs she may, or may not, have thought he had.

The coffee was hot and strong and just the thing he needed to cut the chill of the day. Jack wandered through the streets making footprints in the powdery snow and watching the cars go by. He sometimes thought about the people in those cars. He wondered where they were going, where they came from, what they did for a living. Mostly he thought about where they lived. When he saw a well-suited young man in one of those luxury sedans, he pictured a swanky loft apartment with art on the walls and a fridge filled with imported wines. Wines he used to impress the women he brought up after a night of clubbing, knowing, if they were sober, his inadequate libido would send them laughing out the door. When he was passed by a minivan with all the bells and whistles driven by an uppity soccer mom, he envisioned one of those McMansions on the outskirts of town; the ones with all the lawns perfectly manicured and landscaped to give the illusion of the perfect life when the family inside struggled with enormous debt, borderline alcoholism and chronic adultery. If a young kid behind the wheel of a third or fourth-hand junker passed his way he would immediately see himself; a sarcastic, smartass, pothead kid passing his college classes without really trying but struggling to keep his day-to-day life from catching up to him. Those were the cars he sometimes envisioned himself jumping out in front of, if only to grab the attention of the kid behind the wheel and wake him from his delusion that life would go on forever and he always had time to fix his mistakes. Jack knew, all too well, what a lie that was.

Ah, but the coffee... the rich aroma from a steaming cup, that blissful first sip on a cold winter day, the way the caffeine sent a jolt through his body and awakened, however temporarily, all of his senses. That, my friend, was truth. Naked, unabashed, brutally honest, beautiful truth. Jack had to believe that. It was the only thing he had left.

So, this was how Jack spent his days. Drinking coffee, walking the streets, watching people passing by. Occasionally, when his feet began to ache from the chill, he would sit down near a steam grate or in a doorway that was frequently open so he could warm his tired old bones for a while. Sometimes people would drop coins or even dollar bills into the empty coffee cup he held between his knees. Other times he would get nothing in his cup but wadded up gum wrappers or slips of paper telling him to 'get a job' or 'find Jesus,' as if the discovery of these clichéd sentiments would cause him to jump up on the spot, shave off his beard, rejoin the workforce, get married, buy a house and a car, start a family and live happily ever after. When he got those little reminders that he was, in fact, a bum he nonchalantly balled them up and tossed them in the corner garbage cans. He couldn't allow the opinions of others to dictate his choices. That was another sentiment he had learned the hard way.

As he sat and watched the world go by, Jack spotted a young woman with a limp that took him back to another time. It was almost five years ago that Jack had found himself on the outskirts of the University of Nebraska campus. It was nearing graduation time and the hustle and bustle of the students brought back such vivid memories he had to take a seat on one of the park benches placed around the quads. The trees were in bloom, the birds were singing their little hearts out and the occasional chipmunk would dart out of the bushes to snag a stray acorn. It was one of those Disney-perfect days that most people took for granted or completely ignored, but

Jack no longer let a day slip by him without finding something for which to be grateful. As he was watching a particularly chubby-cheeked chipmunk try to shove another grain of food into its mouth, Jack was joined by a well-dressed woman with a briefcase. Not many people would just casually sit down next to a man like Jack and start a conversation, and of the few who have swallowed their pride long enough to realize he was just another human being who might like a friendly ear, none of them had been professional, well-bred women. To say Jack was caught off-guard was a bit of an understatement.

"I once had a teacher," the woman began, "who told me the best way to learn about human nature is to get yourself good and lost."

Jack looked quizzically at the woman.

"The theory being," she continued without prompt, "one can only fully find one's inner self when left on one's own."

"Smart teacher you had there," Jack replied cautiously.

"That's what I thought. He was the most brilliant man I had ever known. He was the reason I became a teacher" she confided. "After I graduated high school, I took a trip. I sold everything I had, bought a bus ticket to California without telling anyone and got myself good and lost."

Jack returned his attention to the rodent with bulging cheeks, not liking where this conversation was going. His companion let her gaze shift from some random spot across campus to where Jack was looking and then to Jack.

"I think I misunderstood what he meant," she revealed. "I was seventeen when he gave me that little kernel of wisdom. I was young and stupid and, to be honest, quite smitten with this man. I took his words way too literally and got myself into more than one bad situation. When I finally got home almost a year later, I was a completely different person. Do you want to know something?"

Jack reluctantly looked at the woman next to him. She had the deepest, warmest, and saddest brown eyes he had ever seen. Her mocha skin was flawless, save for a nasty looking scar that ran the length of her jawline. He shook his head. He didn't want to hear what she had to say, but still asked. "What?"

"I learned more about human nature than I ever wanted to learn. I learned that under every beautiful act there is an ugly reason. I learned that no matter how bright and shiny the penny is, the other side is tarnished. I learned that telling a stupid kid to get 'good and lost' is a very irresponsible thing to say."

She got up to leave and slipped a twenty-dollar bill into Jack's hand.

"Some things Mr. Harper," she said, "we are never meant to learn."

He watched her walk away, briefcase in hand, small limp in her step, and he could almost catch a glimpse of the young girl he had taught more than two decades ago, but his memory was bad, and he couldn't quite place her in his own personal history. He remembered giving all his honors Lit classes that same message, thinking it deep and thought-provoking at the time. Now he wondered how many other misguided students he had sent off on a wild goose chase. That was the first time in roughly fifteen years he had wanted to find a quiet corner and get good and high. Instead, he got up off the bench and headed as far away from campus as he could get. It was the first (and last) time he had skipped his detour to the Children's Hospital before he turned in for the day.

It's funny how the human mind works. Jack was finding his thoughts were becoming increasingly random as the days went on. He woke up this morning thinking of his wife whom he hadn't seen in over twenty years and now, for no apparent reason, he was thinking about some student he had run into five years ago. Maybe, he thought, life on the streets was finally taking its toll on him. Or maybe it was a delayed reaction to all the drugs he took decades ago. Whatever it was, he thought it best if he just headed back to the park for the day.

When Jack wandered the streets, he never had any particular place in mind, he just walked wherever his feet took him. As he turned to go back home, he noticed for the first time where he was. He was standing in front of the McDonalds where he met the nice lady and her little boy the day before. Realizing he hadn't eaten anything yet today he decided to grab a bite to eat. He had just enough money left over after his morning coffee to buy a hamburger happy meal. Jack had never bought a Happy Meal in his life, but the brightly packaged, funny looking little creatures that were that month's toy inspired him to purchase one. He ate the burger and fries on his way home and pocketed the crumpled bag for kindling later that evening. The plastic baggy with the toy in it was shoved deep into his other pocket and quickly forgotten.

Jack made his usual detour before he finally got back to the playground just before dusk. Within minutes he was curled up in his sleeping bag, toasty fire crackling by his side. He rolled over and felt something hard poke at his side. He had forgotten all about the little toy in his pocket. In the firelight it looked like a cat, but as it was wrapped in plastic, he couldn't be certain. He stared at it awhile before he shoved it deep into his inside jacket pocket.

The light in his little cubby hole was perfect for reading and since Jack wasn't the least bit sleepy, he decided to pull out a well-worn paperback copy of Stephen King's *The Stand*. It was one of his all-time favorite books; one of those fictional wonders he could read over and over again without it losing any of its original intrigue. He was at the part where Larry had decided to walk through the Lincoln tunnel to get out of New York. That part had always caused his imagination to run away from him and this time was no different. Suddenly, Jack felt there wasn't enough air in the cement tube. He started to hyperventilate. Getting out of his bedtime wrappings and backing out of the opening seemed to take an eternity and his vision was starting to blur. When he finally made it out, the crisp night air was the most delicious thing he had ever tasted. The chill in his nose made its way icily down his throat and filled his lungs with frosty fingers causing the real world to snap back into focus. The night sky was filled with stars but the ambient light from the city overshadowed their cosmic beauty. The moon was full and high in the sky which told Jack he had been lost in the terrifying words of Stephen King for well over two hours. No wonder his body had started to play tricks on him. His eyes ached from the strain of reading without the glasses he so desperately needed, and his chest was tight with ash from his makeshift fire.

After a few deep breaths he got up and walked over to the line of trees outside the perimeter of the playground and relieved himself. When he got back, he saw something small lying on the ground between his snowy knee prints. It was the plastic wrapped toy from his breast pocket. It must have slipped out in his struggle for fresh air. In the moonlight he could now see it was clearly not just a cat, it was a saber-toothed tiger. Funny toy for a kids' meal, he thought, but what did he know? He placed it back in his pocket, crawled back into his sleeping bag and, after adding a few sticks to the fire, drifted off into what he hoped would be dreamless sleep. Instead, his dreams were plagued with little plastic toys chasing him and a small boy in a heavy winter coat through the Lincoln tunnel.

Chapter 6

Jack sometimes sat in front of the train station terminal and reflected on his life. The building itself was nothing special. It was a simple, squat brick building on the outskirts of town that had seen better days. The structure wasn't what intrigued Jack; it was the trains. Ever since he was a small boy, he held a deep fascination for trains. He wasn't sure if it was the size of them, the sheer power they seemed to portray or the dependable schedule they kept. Today, as he sat on one of the creaky, paint-chipped benches at the end of the platform he decided what attracted him to the trains were the people inside. They were free to choose any mode of transportation out there and yet they chose to take the train. Sure, it was more convenient than driving if it was a decent length trip and it sure as hell beat the crowded smelliness of the bus, but they could have chosen to hop on a plane and been to their destination in a few short hours instead of spending a day or more on a rumbly, bumpy train. Then again, if Jack had chosen at that moment to travel to any other place in the country, he most likely would have also chosen Amtrak over Delta, if only to divulge in his own childhood fantasies. He was lost in his thoughts when the station manager approached him.

"Time to get going Jack."

He looked around at the voice and saw Edgar sitting next to him holding two steaming cups of coffee. Jack took the one held out to him and thanked the elderly man. Unlike most people, Edgar didn't have a problem with Jack's presence. He didn't bother anyone, didn't smell bad like some of the drifters that came through, didn't beg for food or money, and he was always polite to anyone who passed by. Unfortunately, Jack was still bad for business and the train station's commodity was the whole city. The last thing they wanted to convey to the passengers who stopped there was that their fair Hamlet was filled with bums and ne'er-do-wells.

"Thanks Ed." Jack tipped his cup of joe in Edgar's direction, got up and wandered around the side of the building back to the street.

The sun shone bright that day and Jack enjoyed every moment of much needed warmth. It turned out the sunny day was nothing but a tease. The next week, weather-wise, proved to be a doozy and Jack had come down with a flu bug at some point, which kept him stuck in his makeshift bed for three days. He tried to pull himself out of it on the first day long enough to make his way to the corner drug store for a bottle of NyQuil but after becoming drenched in sweat by simply trying to get out of the sleeping bag he thought better of it.

So, Jack spent the next seventy-two hours in a rotating hell of fever and chills, vivid dreams of trains taking him nowhere, and the inability to tell what time it was, let alone what day. He had bouts of bone rattling coughs, waves of nausea, and a headache strong enough to take down an elephant. He hadn't felt this awful since he was going through withdrawals in rehab. He slipped in and out of fretful sleep, unaware of whether he was conscious or not and only forced himself to leave the warmth of his bed to get more firewood or to relieve himself, which he dreaded every time as it felt like he was pissing fire. On the fourth day Jack woke up feeling better. Not great by any means, but better. His fever had broken sometime in the night and the pain in his chest had loosened enough so he could breathe without shuddering in pain. He ventured out into the cold air of a new month and slipped in the slushy mud outside his entryway.

February promised to be a damn sight better than January, if the weather that day proved a useful measurement. Although the air was cold and crisp, the brightness of the sun was visibly melting the icicles hanging on the rusty, abandoned swings, and patches of snow were falling from the barren branches of the oak trees lining the pond. He could hear the soft *whoosh-plop* of their descent from the lower branches as he headed toward the restrooms. His legs were still a bit shaky, and a charley horse threatened to take him down with the slight-est misstep, but he made it to the tiny cinderblock building without trouble and, by the time he emerged, refreshed and removed from the sticky sick-sweat, Jack was feeling more like himself. He held a newfound respect for the normal, everyday workings of his body. When it was functioning as it should he took it for granted as, he imagined, most people did, but when he was ill, he longed for the everyday aches and pains of simply being human.

Jack decided to cheat a little today when it came to his daily allowance. He was ravenous, having not eaten for days, and he felt like a big breakfast to go along with his coffee this morning. He rummaged through the black garbage bag and pulled out a crumpled twenty from the bottom of the bag, shoved it into his pants pocket and backed out through the cramped tunnels into the sunlight once more.

Today, rather than being a Starbucks day, as it should be due to the amount of money in his pocket, was going to be a McDonald's day. More than anything he longed for a couple of egg McMuffins and about three or four of those crispy, fried hash browns. It took Jack a good hour to amble down the sidewalk to the fast-food restaurant a mere half mile from the park. He was taking his time, lost in his thoughts, and enjoying the warmth of the sun on his face. By the time he sidled up to the counter to place his order, the emptiness in the pit of his stomach had grown exponentially. He ordered four egg McMuffins, four hash browns and a large coffee.

"You just made it," the young cashier told him as the breakfast menu rolled over to the lunch menu.

"Good thing," Jack said with a wink. "Sometimes only a McMuffin will do."

"Or four of them," the girl said with a pleasant giggle.

He took his loaded down tray over to an unoccupied booth in the back corner of the restaurant. He wasn't concerned about being asked to leave because he was an actual sitting down, food purchasing patron today. He devoured the first of the muffins and two hash browns faster than he had intended and almost had to run to the restroom, thinking he was going to be sick. Instead, he gave himself a few minutes to let the food settle on his empty stomach. He took a few deep breaths and felt much better. He took his time to savor the remaining food on his tray, not knowing when he'd have another feast such as this again. The view from the window looked out upon the hustle and bustle of downtown Lincoln. People were walking quickly, heads down against the breeze instead of looking up into the brightness of the sun. He pitied those people as, he assumed, they would have pitied him if they had seen him out on the streets. They were missing one of the undeniable joys of life, the simplicity of just soaking in basic warmth. Instead, they were chatting on cell phones or dodging slush puddles, not wanting to ruin their designer loafers or slip in their four-inch heels. If only they would slow down and enjoy life, Jack thought, how much happier the world would be. He was totally absorbed in watching an elderly lady across the street trying to steer her toy poodle away from the icy slush in the gutter that he didn't notice when the young woman with the small boy from last week entered the establishment. His last sandwich was in his hand heading toward his mouth when he heard a tiny voice next to him.

"I know you," said the heavily bundled little boy. "You gave me Sid!"

Jack put down his breakfast and looked from the boy to his mother. She passed a glance between the two of them and nodded her assent to Jack.

"I know you too," Jack leaned down and told the boy. "You gave me a hamburger."

"It was a Happy Meal," the boy corrected him.

"Yes, it was," Jack agreed. "It made me very happy."

The little boy smiled at that and started to laugh. It was a good laugh, Jack thought; hearty and full and completely genuine. At that moment he decided to throw caution to the wind and introduce himself.

"I'm Jack," he said as he held out his large, weathered hand toward the boy's small one.

The little boy looked from Jack to his mom. "Mommy! He has my name!"

The mother glanced nervously at Jack's hand, most likely inspecting the cleanliness of it before allowing her son to accept the handshake. He must have passed her inspection.

"This nice man is offering his hand for you to shake Jacky," she informed him. "Be polite and introduce yourself."

"My name is Jack too," the boy told him, placing his small, warm hand in Jack's, "but my mommy calls me Jacky even though I don't really like being called Jacky and I wanna be just Jack."

Jack laughed heartily. "Well, 'Just Jack', I think that's a fine name you have there," he said with a wink.

He turned his hand to the young mother. She looked extremely pale, especially so with the frame of deep brown hair around her tiny haggard face. She stared at Jack uncertainly. He knew she was weighing the decision heavily in her mind, wondering if she should give this stranger, this man of the street, her name or should she just keep to herself. He knew she was already somewhat regretting her decision to sit near him at her son's request, but her heart must have won over her head in the end because she held out her hand to meet Jack's.

"I'm Kate," she introduced herself.

"It's a pleasure to meet you Kate," Jack replied. "That's a fine boy you've got there. He even looks like a Jack." He tossed young Jack a little wink.

Kate smiled at her son. That smile was filled with such a huge amount of love the energy from it nearly bowled Jack over, but there was also a sadness in that stare that he couldn't quite place.

"He's named after my father," she told him.

"Then your father is a very lucky man to have such a wonderful young man named after him."

Kate looked down at her own tray and contemplated her salad with more interest than was needed for a bowl of vegetables. Little Jack kept looking from his mom to the bearded man that shared his name.

"My grandpa's dead," Jacky blurted out.

"Jacky!" Kate admonished.

He turned his tiny face down to the table.

"I'm sorry if I said anything to upset you," the elder Jack apologized.

She shook her head. "No, you didn't. Jacky just likes to talk a lot, don't you Jacky."

"I don't like being called Jacky," the boy mumbled under his breath.

"Eat your lunch honey," she told him with a sigh.

As Jacky pulled out the little plastic toy bag from his Happy Meal, Jack remembered the toy he had gotten just the other day, still shoved deep in his breast pocket.

"Hey there young master Jack," he started. "If it's okay with your mommy there I just happen to have something I've been saving in case I saw you again."

Jack showed Kate what was in his pocket without letting the boy see. He had no intention of upsetting this young mother by undermining her authority, even if it was just a little plastic toy from a fast-food restaurant. Her pale face broke into a huge grin that, for the second time Jack could recall, met her eyes. That smile lit up her face and truly showed the beauty she possessed and somehow made her look familiar. For a brief moment he saw Claire sitting across from him. He supposed it was a cross between his recent dream in which his former wife was in and the feverish state from which he had just recovered. Whatever it was, it didn't last long. As quickly as the flash of his past came to him, it was gone.

"What toy do you have there Jack?" he asked the child.

Jacky turned the baggie over in his hand. Brow crinkled, tongue sticking out to the side, he proceeded to tear open the package and out fell a weaselly-looking creature with an eye patch.

"It's Buck!" he exclaimed. "Look mommy! I didn't have Buck yet but now I do!"

"I see that honey, that's great!"

He proudly showed Jack his new prize. "See mister Jack too? Now I have almost alls of 'em. I just need Day-go."

"Diego," his mom corrected him.

"Yeah, him," Jacky agreed. "He's a saber-tooth tiger and he's really cool but I don't have him yet but maybe next week when mommy brings me back to Mickey D's."

"Maybe you won't have to wait until next week," Jack told the boy.

"Yeah, I will. Mommy says junk food is only okay once a week. I guess nuggets and fries are junk food."

Jack pulled the toy out of his pocket and placed it in front of his new young friend. Jacky's eyes grew to the size of saucers when he saw the tiny form of Diego the saber-toothed tiger staring back at him. He snatched it up in his pudgy little hand and held it up to his other new toy and then turned to look at Jack. He eyed him suspiciously, his bright blue eyes boring into Jack's head like fire.

"Mister?" he implored as he inched closer to Jack and beckoned him forward with a curve of his finger.

Jack leaned in closer. The boy laid one hand on top of Jack's own hands and the other he cupped around his tiny mouth, leaned in toward Jack's ear and whispered his question.

"Are you Santa Claus?"

Jack let out such an unexpected laugh it startled the poor boy right back into his seat.

"Oh, Jack, I'm sorry kiddo," he apologized for scaring him. "I didn't mean to scare you like that. It's just, well... no one's ever asked me that before."

Jacky looked at him thoughtfully. "Well, you have a beard," he pointed out. "And you're nice and you give out toys so you must be Santa, right? It's okay. I won't tell anyone. I promise."

The sincere belief that Jack was really Santa Claus was written all across the little boy's face and he didn't have the heart to contradict the boy's faith. But, then again, he didn't want to say anything to upset his mother. He tried to convey his feelings to her without words, but she was too busy trying to keep her pent-up laughter under control. Jack was on his own.

"Well," Jack carefully began. "What do you think? Do you *really* think I'm Santa?"

Jack sat back as the boy got up out of his seat and sat down across from him. He leaned his little body over the table so far, he was almost lying on top of it as he studied Jack's features with the complete bluntness only a four-year-old could get away with. After a full minute of eyeing Jack over, a look of dawning comprehension crossed Jacky's little face.

"Yes," Jacky whispered to him. "You *are* Santa!"

Jack looked at the boy and simply winked. That response must have been good enough for the child because he practically skipped back to his seat where he contentedly ate his lunch with a look of smug knowing on his face.

Kate watched the whole scene play out in between bites of her salad and was secretly impressed with this strange man's interaction with her son. She was usually a very guarded individual, even more so after her husband had just up and left them six months ago, and she was especially overprotective of her only child. But there was something about this man that put her at ease. She couldn't put her finger on it, and she knew it was crazy, but she felt as if she knew him.

The trio chatted lightly as they finished their meals. None of them were in any hurry to leave the warmth of the restaurant as the sun of the day had taken refuge behind the clouds, hugely pregnant with an upcoming snow squall. Nearly an hour had passed before the manager came over to their table.

"Time to get going there," the man told Jack without even looking at the mother and child he was clearly conversing with.

Jack, who never made a fuss when told to vacate any premises, grabbed his tray and started to get up.

"Excuse me," Kate piped up, "but why does this man have to leave? I didn't see any sign on the door stating there was a time limit for your patrons."

"He's not a patron ma'am," the burly man calmly explained. "He's a bum. I let him come in from time to time to get out of the cold but..."

"But nothing," Kate admonished warningly. "It looks to me like Jack here had purchased himself a rather large meal and, if I'm not mistaken, that constitutes being a patron, doesn't it?"

"You can't kick out Santa Claus!" Jacky stood up on his seat and yelled at the manager.

Jack was still gripping the edges of his tray, but he had settled back down into his seat, trying not to laugh. Clearly flustered by the situation, the manager conceded to Kate's argument and left the three of them in peace. Kate continued to sip her coffee as if nothing had happened.

"Thank you," Jack told her quietly.

She shook her head. "He was wrong. Men... *people* like that are used to getting their way. I just gave him a little taste of reality. I can't help it if he didn't like the taste."

"You told him mommy!" Jacky exclaimed and planted a ketchupy kiss on her cheek.

"So did you sweetie."

She gave Jack a little wink over her cup and smiled coyly at her and her son's impertinence. Jack let out another hearty laugh. He hadn't remembered the last time he felt so happy.

"I really should be getting out of here though," Jack told them as he tidied up his mess. "I have a couple of errands to run before the snow hits."

"Yeah," Kate agreed. "I should get this little guy home for his nap."

"I don't need a nap," Jacky yawned.

The two adults chuckled and smiled down at him.

"It was a pleasure meeting you Mister 'Just Jack.'" Jack bent down to shake the boy's hand again. He was met instead with a surprisingly strong hug. The boy's little arms barely wrapped around Jack's neck, but it instantly warmed him from the inside out. Jack was even more shocked when the kid planted a big kiss on his scruffy cheek. He was certain Kate would freak out about it, but she just stood back and smiled at the pair. When Jacky let go of his big bear hug, Jack stood up and offered his hand to Kate.

"It was a pleasure meeting you as well ma'am."

"Call me Kate," she insisted as she took his hand.

"As you wish, Kate,"

The two Jacks, young and old, held the door for their lady companion on their way out into the cold. Kate bent down to adjust her son's mittens and Jack turned up his own collar. The wind was picking up and he was seriously considering taking the bus across town to the hospital to make his daily donation. He pulled out a well-worn bus schedule because he couldn't remember which line took him directly to the Children's hospital.

"Where are you headed?" Kate motioned to the bus schedule in his hand.

"Oh, um," Jack stuttered. "Saint Elizabeth's."

"Is everything okay?"

Jack was touched by the sincere concern in her voice. "Yeah, it's just there's something I have to do there. Something I do every day."

"You go to Saint E's *every day*? That's quite a distance."

Jack shrugged. "I have to. Especially today. I've been sick and missed a few days, so I really have to get there today."

Kate nodded as if she knew exactly what he was talking about. "Okay then. The car's this way."

She and Jacky started walking down the street hand in hand. Jack stayed glued to the spot. The boy, realizing Jack was not walking with them, let go of his mother's hand and ran back to get him.

"Come on Jack," he tugged at his overcoat.

Kate was waiting a few feet away, watching the scene play out with a mixture of amusement and exasperation on her face.

"I can't," Jack told them.

"Sure you can," Jacky told him. "Just move your feet."

Jack chuckled. "No, I mean I can't accept your offer. Thank you anyway."

Kate walked back to them; her hands folded tightly across her chest. "Yes, you can. Just don't expect me to take you every day. I have a job, you know. Now come on, it's getting cold."

From experience, Jack knew when to argue with a woman and when it would be an effort in futility. This was the latter. He trudged up the street with Kate by his side and Jacky between them holding each of their hands. Not since his childhood, had Jack felt like he was part of a family. He knew feeling this way was bringing him into dangerous territory. He was almost certain to have his heart broken when he never saw these two again, but the moment was now and that was good enough for him. It was kind of his motto, having lived on the streets for so long; "live for the moment" was permanently etched in his brain.

"We can listen to my Raffi CD in the car," the young Jack informed him excitedly. "Do you like Raffi?"

Jack, having not a clue who, or what, Raffi was, smiled down at the boy. "I *love* Raffi."

Chapter 7

Kate's little Honda Civic had most definitely seen better days but, as she stated, it was paid for and it got her from point A to point B without any major problems. She bought it for five-hundred dollars cash from her old neighbor just after her husband left her for another woman. He had taken as many of their belongings as he could fit into their brand new Suburban and cleaned out their savings to boot. She planned on trading it in for a brand new *anything* just as soon as she finished her degree and got a decent paying job. As it was, she was a mere half-semester away from graduating with her LPN. She had been perusing the want-ads every Sunday readying herself for the professional workforce, but she had yet to submit her resume anywhere. When they pulled up to the hospital, she parked her car in the visitor's lot rather than leaving Jack at the entrance.

"You could have just dropped me off at the doors," Jack told her.

"I know, but I want to run into the HR department and grab an application. Besides, it looks like mister man back there isn't the slightest bit tired."

Jack turned around and faced the little guy in the back seat. He had almost forgotten Jacky was back there; he had been so quiet on the ride across town. The menagerie of Happy Meal toys in the back had kept him merrily occupied and he was obviously lost in his own little make-believe world.

"Ready bud?" Kate asked her son.

"Can I bring in my toys?"

Kate got out of the car and opened the back door to un-buckle the boy. "You may bring *one* toy."

Jack walked around to the back of the car, completely enthralled at watching their little family dynamic play out in front of him.

"But mommy," Jack explained without a trace of normal preschool whining in his voice. "Manny and Diego and Sid are bestest friends, and they like to play together."

"I know that kiddo, but you only have two hands and there are three of them. How are you going to carry them all?"

Jacky stayed in his seat and pondered his mother's question. "I know! I'll put Manny in my pocket. It can be his cave!"

Kate sighed and smiled down at her son, conceding to his request. He took her hand, hopped out of the car, grabbed his toys, and carefully placed the largest of the three in his pocket. The trio then walked into the Children's entrance together. Jack liked to think if anyone had given them a second glance, they would have simply assumed that they were three gener-ations of the same family. He quickly shook that thought away as dangerous territory. He could not allow himself the luxury of daydreams anymore.

The familiar, antiseptic odor that greeted them when the doors slid open was never a pleasant welcome to Jack. It brought back too many painful memories. Perhaps that was why he forced himself to make the trip every day. There were hospitals much closer to where he lived but it had to be this one. Jack had punished himself daily for over two decades now and would continue to do so until he felt his penance was over. He didn't think many people would understand why he did what he did, why he lived on the street when he could easily have gotten a job and a house and a car. For now, he had no intention of explaining himself to anyone. His life was his business; no one else's.

Kate and Jacky walked over to the room directory while Jack made his way over to the donations box. She pretended not to watch what he was up to, but when she saw him pull out a wad of money and shove it bill by bill into the container, her curiosity got the better of her. She watched as he made his donation then mumbled something under his breath. She assumed it was a prayer because his eyes were closed. She kept an eye on him with a scowl on her face during his head-down walk back to the entrance and didn't even bother to pretend she hadn't noticed what he had just done.

"What was that?" she asked him.

"What?"

"Is this what you do here every day? Shove money into the donation box? I thought you were broke... living on the street."

"I do live on the street," Jack explained.

"Well maybe you wouldn't if you saved the money you got off of people instead of putting it in there!" Kate realized she was raising her voice and took a deep breath to calm herself.

Jack wasn't sure what to say to this woman. They had just met, and her kindness today meant more to him than she could possibly realize, but he wasn't about to tell her his whole life story. He had to make her see that this was something he had to do without going into too much detail.

"Kate," he started, choosing his words very carefully. "A long time ago my wife lost our baby here in this hospital. Back then, well, I did a lot of things I'm not proud of and I messed up pretty badly. This is just my way of atoning for some of my sins. I don't expect you to understand, but it's something I need to do."

Kate mulled his explanation over and must have let it pass because she apologized for her attitude.

"Just so you know," Jack continued, "I don't always put in that much money. It's usually just a few cents. Whatever I have left in my pocket by the end of the day goes directly in there."

"I need to go upstairs to grab an application," Kate told him.

Jack nodded. "Are you a nurse?"

"Not yet. I've been taking night classes for quite some time now and I'm due to graduate in May. I thought I'd get a start on the job search."

"Good idea," Jack said as he turned toward the door. "Well, good luck to you Kate. Maybe I'll run into you again one of these days."

"Where are you going?" Jacky asked him.

"Yeah," Kate chimed in. "Where do you think you're going?"

"Umm, the bus stops here in about five minutes. I'm going to go wait for it."

"And how exactly do you plan on paying for the bus if you just dropped all of your money in that locked box over there?" Kate inquired.

Jack didn't think about that. The excitement of the day must have taken more out of him than he thought. Kate saw that he didn't think his day through as much as he should have and she gave him a decidedly mom-like stare; one eyebrow raised, small smirk on her lips.

"I guess..." Jack started.

"You guess nothing," Kate scolded. "Just wait right here and I'll drive you home. I'll be down in a few minutes. No arguments."

Jack was dumbfounded. He felt rooted to the spot, not wanting to disobey this young woman, and possibly hurt her feelings. Even though she had offered him a ride and she clearly meant to follow through, he still felt like he was somehow taking advantage of her. He stayed there and kept his head down to avoid the stares of the hospital patrons. He was staring so intently at the unusual pattern on the swirled marble floor that he almost didn't notice his companions had returned until Jacky tugged at his overcoat.

"Ready to go mister?" he asked Jack.

"Ready when you are young sir."

"Here," Jacky said. "You can hold Manny. He doesn't like it in my pocket. It's too dark in there."

Jack took the toy mammoth and held it up to his face. "He kinda looks like me, don't you think?" he asked the boy.

Jacky laughed that earnest little kid laugh again that Jack had quickly become addicted to hearing.

"He does!" the boy agreed.

"Jacky!" Kate admonished him. "That's not nice!"

"But mommy, he said it first," he pointed out. "And look, they're both big and hairy..."

"Jacky!"

"And they both have happy eyes!"

Kate looked at Jack and tried to silently apologize for her son's frankness. Jack wasn't offended in the least. He did, after all, put the idea in the child's head.

There were flurries in the air as they made their way across the parking lot and back to Kate's car.

"Dammit," Kate mumbled under her breath as she took her place behind the wheel.

"Is there something wrong?" Jack asked her.

"No, not really. It's just I hate going to work when it's nasty out."

"I thought you took night classes?"

"I do," Kate said. "I also have to work. On Wednesdays and Sundays I'm off from my regular job but those nights I tend bar down at the Isles. Bad weather makes for bad tips and pretty much a waste of my time."

"Oh."

Jack had noticed she wasn't wearing a wedding band, but the tan line was still there. When he first saw her the week before, he guessed that she was a newly single mother. He didn't want to scare her with too many personal questions, but he was sincerely concerned about her and the child now.

"What about Jack?" he asked, motioning toward the backseat.

"My neighbor watches him for me. She has twins about Jacky's age, and she doesn't charge me anything for the night, but I usually give her what I can. He goes to preschool during the day when I work though and he loves it there, don't you Jacky."

"Umm-hmm," he agreed as he dozed off in his booster seat.

"See?" Kate said. "Told you he needed a nap."

Jack chuckled quietly, not wanting to disturb his sleep.

"So, where exactly am I headed?" Kate asked.

"Oh, yeah." Jack realized he hadn't told her where he lived. The thought kind of scared him, to be honest, but he wasn't about to lie to this nice young woman. "Carter Park."

"You got it."

They made idle chit-chat on the drive back across town, mostly about the weather and how much longer winter was bound to last. They discussed the Huskers' chances of ever becoming a viable team again and how the city has expanded so fast it was hard to keep up with where the city limits were anymore. They were almost at the entrance to the park when Kate turned to Jack and, somewhat shyly, asked him if he made his trip to McDonald's a regular thing.

"To be honest Kate," Jack told her, "I don't have much of a scheduled life."

"Oh, ok. I just thought, maybe, well, since Jacky seemed to have taken such a shine to you, that maybe you'd like to join us next Wednesday. I take him every Wednesday, kind of a lunch date we share."

"I'd hate to crash your date," Jack said with a smirk, "but I think I can squeeze you in."

Kate let out a deep breath. "Good. Jacky will be so happy to see you again."

"As will I," Jack said. "That's a fine boy you've got there Kate. But I'm sure you know that."

She pulled up to the entrance and turned around to look at her sleeping son.

"Oh, I know," she agreed.

Jack got out of the car and leaned back in to thank Kate for the ride. As he headed toward the playground and his make-shift home, he heard her car pull away and head off in the unknown direction of her home. He shoved his hands deep into his pockets when the wind picked up and felt the hard plastic mammoth Jacky had given him to hold. Not that Jack needed an excuse to see the duo again but holding the child's toy in his hand had reaffirmed his decision to meet them for lunch in a week. He kept patting his pocket as he went about his evening chores to make sure he didn't lose the toy. He wouldn't forgive himself if he'd lost something Jacky had given him to look after. What kind of Santa would he be if he let down such a sweet kid?

Chapter 8

The next week seemed to drag by. Jack tried to busy himself with his daily chores, which had never felt so mundane. He never thought much about how boring his life was before, but now, having something to look forward to, he realized the tediousness of it all. The snowstorm that had threatened the previous Wednesday amounted to nothing more than a brief squall that added less than an inch of accumulation on top of the muddy post-January slush. There hadn't been an ounce of precipitation since. In fact, it had been unseasonably warm; a veritable Indian summer.

The break in the weather gave Jack a chance to do a bit of cleaning around the park. He dug out the bottle of antiseptic from one of the garbage bags and scrubbed down the outhouse as much as humanly possible. As he scrubbed at the permanent water stains, Jack found himself lost and wandering in his thoughts. Nearly half an hour had gone by before he realized his hands were burning from the harsh chemicals and he hadn't even made a dent in the filth of the park restroom. He couldn't even recall what he was thinking about so deeply when he came out of it. Jack decided the fumes were getting to him and gave up the futile effort of cleaning the un-cleanable.

By the time Wednesday rolled around again Jack was so excited to see his new friends again he woke up earlier than usual. During the previous night he mulled over the idea of cheating again with his daily allowance. His argument with himself was not a hard one to win. If he showed up with only two dollars in his pocket, he would only be able to buy himself a cup of coffee which might make Kate feel sorry for him. From what he learned of her last week, she was likely to spend her own hard-earned money to buy Jack a meal, and he just couldn't let her do that. He knew she was on a fixed income, a single mother working two jobs; she needed to save all the money she could. His decision was made. He would no longer leave Wednesdays up to chance. He would have to peek into his stash of crumpled bills to make sure he had enough to cover his meal. Twenty years of routine thrown out the window, so to speak, all because he befriended a small boy and his young mother.

Jack woke up that morning with a spring in his step even though he got close to no sleep the night before. He felt like a child waiting for Christmas morning. He was sure to change his clothes and wash up as much as humanly possible with a washrag, a bar of soap, and icy cold water. He didn't want to give the manager any reason to approach him again today. After he cleaned up and put away his meager toiletries, he grabbed ten dollars out of the garbage bag and backed out of the cramped tunnel. Almost forgetting the most important thing, he climbed back in to grab the little plastic mammoth. He had slept with it by his side the past seven nights and had even found himself talking to it as he dozed off. That was something he never intended to tell another living soul, afraid that it would be considered grounds for commitment into the nearest psychiatric ward.

Jack decided to head down to the fast-food chain early to catch the breakfast hour before it switched over to the greasy burgers of lunch. Whatever else Jack Harper may be, he will always and forever be a breakfast man. He could eat bacon and eggs morning, noon, and night without complaint. Breakfast wasn't the only reason Jack wanted to get there early. He didn't want to risk the chance that Kate would offer to buy his meal. He got to the counter with a good five minutes to spare, ordered up a big platter meal with his usual large coffee and took his place in the back corner booth he had, in the space of a week, considered 'their spot.'

His coffee was hot and the meal smelled heavenly, but he didn't touch it. Somehow, he thought it would be rude to eat without his company. About ten minutes after Jack got there, Kate and Jacky walked in the door. It wasn't until he caught the boy's eye and got a glimpse of that wide, toothy grin of his did Jack realize he was afraid they wouldn't show. He gave himself a quick once over as they ordered their meals, to make himself as presentable as possible. Jacky was bouncing up and down, holding onto his mom's hand and pointing toward Jack with his free hand, which happened to clutch one of his precious Happy Meal toys. The next thing Jack knew, the boy ran over to him and tackled him with the biggest bear hug his little arms could manage.

"Hi Jack!" he squealed.

"Hi Jack!" the older man copied.

The fact that they both had the same name struck the younger of the Jacks deliciously funny and he doubled up in gales of laughter.

"I think this belongs to you," Jack said as he held out Manny the mammoth in his chapped, but clean, hand.

"Manny!" he cried. "I was looking for him you know, all over the place because Sid and Day-go missed him and so did I. Mommy said maybe I'd get a new one today but when we got here all I saw were Hot wheels cars in the window and those are neat too but I was sad because I thought I lost my Manny but you had him the whole time didn't you!"

Jack was amazed at the speed in which this little man talked and how he didn't seem to take a single breath. He simply nodded because he was afraid if he opened his mouth he'd start laughing and he didn't want the boy to think he was laughing *at* him.

Kate joined the duo moments later with Jacky's Happy Meal and her salad.

"I'm so glad you could fit us into your schedule today," she joked with Jack.

"I moved a few things around," Jack replied with a wink.

They spent the next hour enjoying their meals and their conversation, which was nothing more than your basic idle chit-chat, but to Jack it meant the world. In fact, it seemed to stop the world. Inside the cozy warmth of the restaurant booth, they were the only three people left on the whole earth. All their problems and worries and fears seemed to melt away and they just *were.* An outsider might look at them and think Jack had some hidden agenda; that he had an unnatural attraction to this young, kind, and pretty young lady. That person would be terribly, terribly wrong. Jack did not look at Kate like that at all. In fact, if he felt anything unnatural, it was his sense of responsibility toward the two of them. Something about them made him want to take care of them, but, of course, that would never happen. Hell, he could barely take care of himself. But still, the feeling was there.

Jack talked with the boy about his favorite cartoon character (SpongeBob) and his favorite book (Goodnight Moon) and learned all about the mean kid at preschool named Keith that liked to flick his boogers at the girls and spit in Jacky's hair. They played with the toys that he brought with him, shoved in each and every pocket of his oversized coat and even found a way to add his new Hot wheels car into the mix. Kate regaled him with tales about nursing school and her day job cleaning rooms at the Cornhusker Inn.

After an hour or so Jack noticed the manager glaring at him and decided it was time to go. Kate looked at her son and said she should take him home before he fell asleep at the table. On their way out she asked him if he would like to meet the following week and, of course, Jack happily agreed.

Kate and Jacky headed to her car parked at the corner while Jack started off in the opposite direction. He had to run some errands before his daily hospital stop and he wanted to get a good distance away before Kate offered to give him a ride again. He almost made it to the far corner before he heard his name being called.

Kate was running up the street with Jacky in tow, desperately trying to keep his toys from slipping out of his pockets; his snow boots clunking on the sidewalk as his little legs scurried to keep pace with his mom. She was waving a blue bag in her free hand and handed it to Jack when she finally reached him.

"What's this?" he asked.

"I noticed you had a big hole on the palm of your glove when you got out of the car last week."

Jack pulled out a pair of very heavy, fur-lined, brown leather gloves.

"I can't accept these," he sadly told her. "They must have cost a fortune!"

Kate just shook her head. "Not as much as you might think."

"Kate..."

"Seriously, they didn't cost a thing. They were my ex's," she explained a little ashamedly.

Jack was about to put them back into the bag when Kate reached out and placed her own gloved hand on his arm.

"I'm not leaving until I see you put them on your hands."

He looked cautiously at Kate, shifted his gaze to the gloves and then down to her small son.

"She means it mister," Jacky informed him. "She won't let me watch cartoons until I clean up my toys and she stands there just like that and watches me do it and, trust me, she can stand there an awful long time."

Jack smiled down at him and slipped off his old gloves. He hadn't really noticed the hole in the palm of the right one before. It must have been made from gathering his firewood at some point, but he'd be damned if he could remember it happening. Slipping on the new gloves felt like plunging his hands into a pile of fresh, hot laundry, straight from the dryer. Back in his old life, laundry had been the one chore he never complained about doing, especially on cold winter nights. The simple act of pulling on those new gloves brought back memories of helping his mother fold towels, writing his term papers in the dorm laundry room, and sitting on the floor sorting socks with Claire in their cozy little ranch home before everything had gone to hell.

"Thank you," Jack choked out, trying to keep the tears at bay.

Satisfied that Jack would keep the gloves, Kate turned and walked back to her car with her young son in tow.

Jack shoved the old pair of gloves into his pockets and vowed only to use them to gather firewood; his new pair just wouldn't do for such a dirty job. Although he made his way down the street with tears freezing on his cheeks, he walked with a spring in his step he hadn't had in ages. He couldn't remember the last time anyone had cared enough to give him a gift, especially one with so much heart.

As he meandered down the sidewalk his thoughts eventually turned inward as they nearly always did. He thought what a mad world we lived in. It was beauty and misery and pain; it was hate and love and discovery; it was random acts of kindness and seemingly random destruction; it was heaven and hell and everything in between and Jack had taken it for granted for too long. But no more. He wasn't sure how much time he had left on this earth and, be it a day or a year or twenty years, he was going to live each day to the fullest.

The sad part was, Jack had given himself this same lecture at least once every year, sometimes every month, and he had never stuck to it. Life just seemed to take its toll on him more heavily than usual after these epiphanies and the light-heartedness of the moment was quickly forgotten. That was also part of the madness we lived in if Jack were to look at it honestly. The human will changes every day. Some people were just better at realizing it than others.

That could be why Jack continued to live in the middle of Carter Park instead of in a nice home anywhere in town. The fact of the matter was, Jack truly *could* live the life of a normal human being, he just chose not to.

Chapter 9

Some might think it peculiar for a man who lives in cement tubes, bathes in a pond or a restroom sink, and wanders around all day looking for a decent cup of coffee he could buy with pocket change, to have *chosen* that way of life. But Jack didn't care what other people thought of him. What he did care about was karma.

After his wife had left him over twenty years ago, Jack had gone into a deep downward spiral. He had respected her wishes and stayed away no matter how much his heart ached when he thought of her. On more than one occasion, usually when he was completely sober, he had picked up the phone to call her. He would sit on the floor of his bedroom and hold the receiver to his ear until the recorded operator's nasally voice came on the line explaining to him that if he wanted to make a call he had to hang up and try again. He didn't know Claire's number but holding that phone in his hand like he was going to make the call made him feel better.

Within a month of her departure, Jack had sold most of the furniture from the living room and bedroom. Claire's eclectic bohemian style was all around him and it was too painful for him to walk in every day and not have her there to make sense of it all. The bed was the first thing to go. He slept on the couch until he sold it for drug money. After sleeping on the floor for three nights he broke down and bought himself a thin mattress he put in the guest room that was supposed to have been his office.

Three months after she left, Jack received the divorce papers by certified mail. He signed them without even reading them. He was stoned out of his mind at the time, but to be honest, he would have done the same thing if he had been sober. He had reached a point where he just wanted the pain to be over and he thought, in his almost always altered state of mind, that making the divorce final would heal all his open wounds. He was wrong.

Less than a year had gone by before he lost his job and two months later, he walked out of his house, leaving the keys on the kitchen counter. He showed up at his girlfriend's house one midsummer night looking for a place to score a hit, grab a quick lay and crash for the night. Unfortunately for Jack, she had already had the same idea, and it wasn't Jack she was interested in that night.

Having a place to lay his head had never been an issue for Jack. Even when he was on one of his binges, he always found a friend to take him in for the night, but now it seemed like everyone had turned their backs on him. He was completely on his own.

Jack made his way down First Street in his little Volkswagen and stopped at the seedy liquor store on the corner. He knew from experience that they would cash his personal checks for him for seventy-five cents on the dollar, so he wrote out a check for two hundred. It was their cash limit and the remainder of the money he had in his account. The cashier handed him the hundred and fifty bucks and Jack turned back out into the night. He found himself about half a mile away at a dingy, no-name motel off Cornhusker Highway. Fifty of his dollars paid for a week's stay in a depressing, grubby room with peeling wallpaper and mice scurrying around behind the walls, but the television worked if he moved it near the window and the bed was passably comfortable.

After settling himself in his room, Jack picked up a couple of pizzas and a case of beer from the strip mall down the block, hoping it would last the week. He stopped at the front desk for a toothbrush and some extra towels and, on his way back to his room, he met Linda. For twenty bucks or a hit of coke, Linda would do just about anything a man asked of her. She followed Jack into his room, carrying his case of beer for him as she fidgeted with her bra strap that kept slipping down her bony shoulders. Jack figured she couldn't be more than eighteen at the outside, although he really believed she was closer to sixteen, but in his state of mind he just wouldn't admit to himself that he was about to bed jailbait. She wasn't pretty in the slightest bit, but, hell, sex was sex, and she was available.

Linda came out of the room ten minutes later, twenty dollars richer. Jack stayed in the bed guzzling his second beer, officially broke and feeling less like a man than he ever had. He was barely in his thirties and yet he failed to perform, with a teenage hooker no less. She didn't seem to be overly upset by the ordeal. After all, she got her money, and it was just enough to score a hit if she went to the right place.

That night was the first time in a very long time that Jack had seriously considered getting himself clean. He saw what the drugs were doing to the young girl that just left his room more clearly than he saw what they did to him. That was the funny thing about addiction. The person with the problem was usually the last to know.

Jack trudged into the cramped bathroom to splash some water on his face and saw his reflection in the mirror. The grizzled old man staring back at him scared Jack to death. He nearly jumped out of his skin as he spun around to see who had broken into his room. Of course, there was no one there but him and the hidden mice in the walls. He checked the mirror again, more closely this time, and was horrified to realize that the old man was him. The man in the mirror was gaunt and unshaven and had such dark circles under his eyes that one would have thought he was a walking corpse. His blue eyes had lost the vibrant luster that had always commanded the attention of any lady he chose to talk to, and he happened to notice the odor permeating from his skin was a foul mixture of sweat, greasy food, and despair.

Never had he felt so filthy... so utterly disgusting. He wondered how he had gotten this bad. He was virtually unrecognizable to himself, and it scared him as straight as he was apt to get without professional help.

Jack ran the hot water in the bathtub and readied himself for a good long soak, figuring he'd most likely use the entire tiny bar of soap the housekeepers left on the sink, wrapped and ready for the motel's next patron.

As the tub filled, he decided to rifle through the yellow pages that were chained to the nightstand. The thought never crossed his mind to steal the blasted thing but, obviously, it must have been a very real problem for the motel owners. He scanned the pages under the D's until he found what he was looking for. Drug rehabilitation. He almost dialed the number there on the spot but the steam from the bathroom was calling his name, and there was nothing he wanted more than a good long soak in a hot tub.

Jack left the page open on the bed, stripped down, tossed his clothes in the corner and sunk into the water. He sank as deeply as the tiny tub would allow his six-foot-tall frame to go and briefly considered staying under the water just to end it all here and now. His body, however, had other plans. Apparently, his will to live was stronger than his desire to die, so instead of slipping under the water forever, he unwrapped the bar of soap, lathered up a washcloth and went to work. The thirty minutes in the tub did wonders for Jack's appearance, smell, and overall outlook on his situation.

After he shaved and cleaned up, he inspected his job in the steamy mirror. He didn't look nearly as unkempt as he did earlier in the evening, but the bags under his eyes were still there. As he scrutinized every inch of his body, he noticed he must have lost a good thirty pounds, and he was naturally lean to begin with. It was a wonder he didn't notice it earlier. His ribcage was showing, and his once taut skin was hanging loosely from his arms and chest. The children he saw on the 'Save the Children' commercials had more substance to their bodies. He was forever hiking up his pants, but his weight loss was never self-apparent.

Wrapped only in a dingy white towel, he plopped down on the springy bed and stared at the number in the phone book. Should he, or shouldn't he?

Jack picked up the phone and listened to the dial tone ringing in his ear for what seemed forever. He dialed the seven digits without realizing it. Not until a cheery female voice at the other end picked up did he take notice of what he was doing.

"Valley View Rehabilitation Center," the perky voice said. "How may I help you?"

Jack felt as if his tongue weighed a hundred pounds, and his lips were sealed with glue. He knew he should do this. So much of his life had already been wasted, how much more was he willing to miss?

"Hello?" the voice asked.

"I... I think I need help," Jack spoke in a whispery croak.

"And what do you need help with sir?"

That voice was so unnaturally lively it almost hurt Jack's teeth from the sweetness of it. He almost hung up. He could call back tomorrow and maybe someone who had had less caffeine would pick up the phone. But he knew better. He was making excuses for something he didn't want to do, and he knew it. In the last year, Jack had lost his wife, his job, his home and even his crackhead girlfriend. It was time for a change. It was time to grow up and be a man and he couldn't do it on his own. He needed help.

"Sir?"

He took a deep breath and dove right in. "My name is Jack Harper," he told the receptionist. "I don't want to do this anymore. Please, I need help."

Chapter 10

As soon as he got off the phone, Jack packed his dirty clothes into one of the bags he brought with him. He was told to be ready as soon as possible, and not knowing exactly what that meant, he figured it was for the best that he did as he was told.

Within the hour there was a knock at the motel door. Two very large men in scrubs were standing behind a much smaller, mousy man with huge glasses and a bushy moustache.

"Jack Harper?" the little man asked.

"Yeah," Jack answered. "Who are you?"

"My name is Dr. Pine," he introduced himself without offering his hand as he welcomed himself into the room. The two bigger men stayed by the door. "These two fine men are my associates. We're from Valley View. I believe you called about our services this evening?"

"Yeah, I called but..."

"Good," Dr. Pine interrupted. "We can be on our way then. My friends here will take care of your things if you'd care to come with me."

Jack was utterly perplexed by the whole situation. Yes, he had called for help, but never in his wildest dreams did he think someone would come to take him away! For the first time in months, Claire's voice entered his head, clear as day.

If she were there to see this she would have said, "*What the hell did you think they were going to do Jack? They asked where you were right now, and you gave them the address and the god-damn room number! They asked you if you wanted to be free from your burdens starting tonight and you said yes! They even asked if you needed help getting there and you, in your infinite boneheaded wisdom, said yes! Of course, they came to take you away jackass!*"

As usual, Claire was right. Jack went back into the room and sat on the edge of the bed to slip on his shoes and Dr. Pine stepped in and sat down next to him.

"You're doing the right thing here Jack," the doctor assured him.

Jack just stared down at his shoes and nodded. So many thoughts were spinning through his head. Had he done the right thing? How had he gotten into such a situation? What would happen to him now? Then it hit him. Was this man who he said he was? How did Jack know this guy in the tweed jacket and bowtie wasn't some crazy psycho killer and his 'friends' were just his muscle? In his drug-addled brain, he didn't even consider the ridiculousness of the idea. Instead, he scanned his brain to try and remember if he owed anyone money. It was possible. There were times he had to borrow cash to score his hit for the night.

"I'd like to see some identification please," Jack said.

Dr. Pine looked at him reassuringly. "Smart man," he said as he pulled out his ID from the rehab center stating he was who he said he was.

Jack looked it over and was satisfied that this man was a doctor. He gave back the ID card and resumed lacing his sneakers.

"I have a few papers for you to sign before we go to the hospital."

"Hospital?" Jack asked.

"The center," Dr. Pine corrected. "Technically, yes, it is a hospital, of sorts, but I guess I shouldn't have called it that. I'm sorry."

Jack just shrugged and signed the forms the doctor held out to him on his clipboard without even looking at them.

Dr. Pine must have been used to these situations because he rambled off a lot of legal jargon that was in the forms Jack signed. He sounded as if he were a walking encyclopedia the way he recited everything in a monotone voice, and it was quickly lulling Jack into a sleepy stupor.

Within ten minutes of the doctor's arrival, Jack was sitting in the back of a white van with Valley View painted on the side in an elegant, flourishing script. He was on his way to a clean life. He just hoped it was worth it.

Jack's first night at the rehab center was nothing short of hell on earth. Not only was he out the fifty bucks from his hotel rental that he never even used, but he was also relieved of all his personal belongings, however meager they may be. He was escorted to a sterile-looking room with two beds, one of which was empty. On the other sat an ageless man reading a paperback novel without a cover.

"You two play nice now," the orderly told the men as he left the room, shutting the door behind him as he went.

Jack stood next to the door for a few minutes as he took in his new digs. He tossed his pile of sheets, blankets, and pillows they issued to him on the bed to his right. He noticed a bedpan under each metal framed bed and sincerely hoped they didn't expect him to use it in the middle of the night if nature happened to call.

"It's in case you puke," his roommate informed him. "You know, from the DT's."

"Oh," Jack said.

"Name's Carl," the man introduced himself with an outstretched hand.

"Jack."

On closer inspection he noticed Carl's age wasn't as diffi-cult to guess as he thought at first. He couldn't be any older than Jack was himself, which put him anywhere from his late twenties to his mid-thirties. He also noticed the book Carl was reading when Jack arrived, a battered copy of *Watership Down,* was upside-down in his hand. Jack didn't question the man. They just met after all and he wasn't keen on making any enemies during his stay, however long or short that may be, so he busied himself with making his bed.

As he pulled the fitted sheet over the thin, waterproof mattress, Jack kept tossing furtive glances in Carl's direction. He was still staring at the upside-down book and occasionally flipped a page every minute or so. After his bed was made, Jack realized just how tired he was, and that thin little mat-tress looked more inviting than anything at that moment. He crawled under the blanket and arranged his pillows just the way he liked them and almost immediately started to doze off.

Jack was in the beginning of, what promised to be, a damn good dream involving himself and the girls from *Charlie's Angels.* He was getting cozy with Kate Jackson when he was rudely awakened by a loud crash and a gust of cool night air.

Apparently, Carl was just biding his time with his inverted novel until it was lights out. Jack sat bolt upright when the door to his room swung open and three very large orderlies came rushing in. Two of them grabbed Carl's legs, which were still dangling on Jack's side of the open window, while the third pushed Jack back down on the bed and held him there easily with one meaty hand.

Within seconds the whole ordeal was over, and Jack was left alone on his cot. There was no way, he thought, he would get any sleep with the adrenaline coursing through his veins. He got up and inspected the window his roommate had tried to wriggle out of. The bars that were there when Jack arrived were gone, tossed out the window. He figured it took Carl ages to cut through the bars, and, oh, the patience it must have taken him to put them in place so no one would notice they had been cut. How long had he been here? Is that what was going to happen to Jack? Would he go crazy during his stay? He began to panic and was seriously thinking about climbing out the open window himself when a voice from behind the doorway stopped him.

"Do you really want to do that?" asked Dr. Pine.

Jack turned to look at the little man in his neatly pressed suit, clipboard under one arm. "I don't know."

"I think you *do* know Jack. Why else would you have called us?"

"I don't know why I called you," Jack admitted.

"Yes, you do," the doctor said. "You want to get yourself clean. From the look of you, you've been on the stuff for quite some time now. Am I right?"

"Maybe, but..."

"And," he interrupted, "something traumatic happened in your life recently which made you spiral out of control. Am I right about that? Of course, I am. And I'm willing to bet within the last twenty-four hours or so you finally hit rock bottom, which, from my point of view, is a good thing. It finally got you to admit you have a problem and *that* my dear Jack, is the hardest thing you'll have to do here."

Jack stared, gape-mouthed, at the man in the doorway. If admitting he had a problem was the hardest part, what exactly was he doing here?

"I know what you're thinking Jack. Just because you already accomplished the hardest part and admitted you had a problem doesn't mean you can do the rest on your own. I believe you want to be here, and I truly believe that you will work your hardest to get your life back on track, but you and I both know you need professional help to get it."

Jack couldn't deny anything the doctor said to him. He *did* want his life back and he knew he *couldn't* do it on his own. But was he strong enough? He had spent almost half of his life hooked on one kind of drug or another. Could he make it without them?

"You're right," Jack told the doctor.

"Good man," Dr. Pine said as he put his arm around Jack's shoulders and led him down the hallway to his new room; this one without a broken window, or a broken roommate.

Jack's adrenaline rush dissipated almost as quickly as it came and within minutes of climbing under the covers of his new bed, he was sound asleep. He slept the whole night through, only getting up at dawn to use the bedpan. Carl was right about the vomiting. He continued to alternate between throwing up and attempting completely restless sleep for the next twelve hours, finally waking up just before the dinner hour. He felt more pained than he ever remembered feeling. His body ached all over and he had zero appetite, but his mind was more alert than usual, and he felt as if he was ready for anything that could possibly be thrown at him. At least, that's what he thought.

Jack pulled on his slippers and headed down the hallway, having no idea where he was headed. All he knew was that he smelled coffee and, although he had no appetite, he could really use a good cup of joe. He followed his nose through corridors that seemed to go on forever before he finally found the dining hall. He was about to enter the door when a nurse called his name. She had a southern drawl and the darkest skin he had ever seen, like ebony wood in the twilight.

"Mr. Harper?"

"Umm, yeah?" Jack responded. "I was just about to get some coffee. Or do I have to wait for a certain time? I'm new here and I don't know..."

"Dinner is in half an hour," the nurse informed him, "and yes, you have to wait like everyone else. Someone should have gone over all of this with you when you checked in. But I'm not here for that. You need to come with me."

She turned and ambled back down the way she came. Jack followed obediently, watching her ample behind rise and fall with each step. He had never been an ass man, but if he was, he thought even this one might be too much to handle.

"Excuse me," Jack said, "but where are we going?"

"You have a visitor sugar."

"There must be some mistake. How could I have a visitor? No one knows I'm here. I don't even have anybody I *could* tell," he added forlornly.

"You Jack Harper?" she asked him, her deep southern accent becoming more prominent.

"I am."

"Then you have a visitor sugar. Right in there."

They arrived at a room labeled 'Conference Room B.' Jack stayed out in the hallway and tried to think who might have come to see him. The last person he saw before he came here, besides the hooker he hired at the motel, was his girlfriend, Sarah. He doubted she pulled herself out of her constant high long enough to come looking for him. Hell, he doubted she even realized he was gone or cared enough about him notice. Other than his family, who were all dead, the only person who ever cared about him was Claire and he hadn't seen her in over a year. So, when he opened the door, he was completely shocked to see Claire sitting there, alone in the big empty room, fidgeting with her necklace, as she always did when she was nervous.

"Hi Jack," she said pleasantly enough.

"Claire," he whispered. "What are you doing here?"

"You tell me. I got a phone call this morning from a Dr. Pine saying you were in the hospital. He said you put me down as your emergency contact, but you didn't have my number, so he tracked me down somehow. Here I am."

"But *why?*" Jack asked. He didn't remember putting Claire down on any of the forms he filled out but, then again, he wasn't entirely in the clearest frame of mind when he signed himself in.

Claire let out a deep sigh. "I honestly don't know Jack. When I left, it was the hardest decision I ever had to make, but once I made it, well... I felt like I could breathe again."

Jack sat down across from his ex-wife and looked at her with such a pained expression it almost made Claire break down and cry. But if living with a drug addict had given her one thing, it was strength.

"I never stopped loving you Jack," she told him. "I just can't be with you anymore. Do you understand that?"

Jack nodded. "I'm going to get better Claire. I promise you I will."

"That's good Jack. It really is. But it doesn't change any-thing."

"But what if..."

"No," she said. "I can't. Please understand, I just can't. I've gone on with my life and I want you to do the same."

"You found someone else," Jack said, more a statement than a question.

"I'd rather not go into it." She got up to leave. "I really do hope you make it this time Jack. You deserve to enjoy at least part of your life. God knows you've missed out on enough of it already."

"Claire?"

"Yes?"

"Is that the only reason you came here? To see me like this? To wish me luck?"

"No," she said. "I had something of yours I thought you should have when you get out of here. I've been holding onto it for years. I hope you finally get yourself clean so you can enjoy it."

She leaned down and kissed him lightly on the cheek. "I *do* love you, Jack Harper. I'll *always* love you."

And just like that, she was gone.

Chapter 11

The remainder of Jack's stay wasn't nearly as memorable as that first night. There were a few things that stuck out in his mind when his thoughts wandered to that horribly monotonous three months back in the mid-nineties.

Jack truly believed the one thing that kept him going during those three months was Claire's visit. He had no delusion they would ever reconcile and get back together, but just knowing she still loved him made all the difference in the world. That, and the envelope she left for him at the nurse's desk.

After Claire left that first day, Jack went directly to the check-in desk, his desire for a coffee-fix temporarily forgotten. He asked the duty nurse what Claire had left for him. She handed him a plain manila envelope. Written on the front in a scrawling script was:

Jack Winston Charles Harper

Below his name, hand printed on a plain post-it note:

DO NOT OPEN UNTIL PROGRAM HAS BEEN
SUCCESSFULLY COMPLETED

"Program?" Jack looked quizzically from the nurse to the envelope.

She just shrugged her ample shoulders. "All I was told was to hold on to this for you until the day you left. She also said, if you weren't completely clean that I should mail this back to the lawyer it came from."

"What lawyer?"

She shrugged again. "Don't know, but I suppose it's all in there."

Jack was looking at the envelope with a mixture of fear and greed and was just about to rip it open when the nurse took the choice out of his hands, quite literally, by taking back the package.

"I'm sure you'll be seeing this again Mr. Harper," she assured him. "Think of it as an extra incentive to get yourself clean."

Jack did exactly that. Any time he felt like giving up, any time the need for a hit seemed to invade his every cell, he turned his thoughts to what was waiting for him in that eight by ten packet. It seemed to work. Jack was always intrigued by the unknown. As a child, he would spend hours reading mysteries and spy novels. That envelope was the greatest mystery.

After Jack finished rehab, he consciously tried to try to rid the experience from his mind, which was easier said than done. On the rare occasion that Jack thought about his stint in rehab his mind inevitably turned to Alex. There were plenty of things he remembered about his stay, but Alex was how he defined his ordeal.

He remembered the first night, of course, with the breakout attempt by his first roommate, and he remembered his last day there and how petrified he felt to be out on his own again. He was only in Valley View for ninety days but, when that last day came around, the time felt immeasurable. Jack hadn't gotten particularly close to anyone in rehab, he hadn't allowed himself to, but there were some people there that would forever stick in his mind.

At the end of his first week, Jack was introduced to Alex. Alex was a twenty-year-old alcoholic. He had his first beer at the age of five, courtesy of his father. By the time he was twelve he was sneaking vodka to school in his thermos. He was expelled from high school in the middle of his sophomore year for showing up drunk and hitting a female teacher. He and his dad celebrated by remaining shitfaced for the entire weekend. When he woke up the following Monday, he found his dad dead in his recliner. He had drunk himself to death.

Alex was in rehab as part of a court order after he was involved with a hit and run. He thought at the time that he hit someone's cat, or possibly a dog. Instead, it was a three-year-old little girl. He found out during his sentencing that she survived the accident but would never walk or talk again. Alex was sober when they brought him in and he stayed sober when they took him to the state prison after a month of court-ordered rehab. Jack found out that Alex had hung himself in his cell just two days after he got to the prison. He supposed the young man couldn't face that little girl in his nightmares every night. He found it scarily disturbing how easily he sympathized with Alex.

There were other people who Jack found interesting or amusing or downright hysterical, but Alex always stayed with him. Alex was Jack's introduction to karma.

After Jack learned of Alex's death, he brought up the subject of karma to Dr. Pine during one of his private sessions. The good doctor, although not a believer of karma itself, entertained Jack's notions of what goes around comes around and even lent him a few books on the subject.

"Just remember, Jack," Dr. Pine said, "we can't control everything in our lives, but we can choose the good over the bad. It's not always easy and it's certainly not always fun or popular, but it at least aims us in the right direction."

"I know doc," Jack said. "It's just, well... I've done some pretty bad things in my life, and I don't want to be defined by them or who I used to be. When I die, I want to go out with a clear conscience, knowing I did everything in my power to make up for my transgressions. I refuse to be lost in perdition for the remainder of my days. It's no way to live. I know that now."

"You don't know how happy I am to hear you say that Jack. You've made some great strides since you've been here. I'd dare say you'll be leaving us soon."

Jack stared out the big picture window in the doctor's office and watched as a tiny hummingbird hovered over a flowering bush. The bird flitted from bud to bud, drinking the sweet nectar, wings moving a mile a minute. As Jack watched the bird, he wished for that type of freedom. To be able to just fly around, drinking the fruits of nature, not a care in the world... it sounded just about perfect.

"Do you think that's a good idea?" Jack asked.

"Don't you?"

Truth be told, as much as Jack hated the idea of being there in the beginning, he was now quite comfortable. He had no worries about being offered drugs, no job to be concerned with, no bills, no women to mess with his head or his heart. Life was simple. He knew where he was supposed to be every moment of the day, and even his free time was somewhat regimented.

"I like it here," he told the doctor. "There are no surprises here. It's safe."

"True, it *is* safe here," Dr. Pine agreed, "but don't you want to get on with your life? Wouldn't it be nice to have a place of your own and a job and maybe, eventually, a family again?"

"I'll never have a family again," Jack insisted.

"Why is that?"

"Because I can barely take care of myself," Jack mused with a sad chuckle. "How can I, in good conscience, take on the responsibility of taking care of another human being when I can't do it for myself?"

"Well, that's something you're just going to have to work on now isn't it."

"I guess," Jack agreed. "I still don't think I'm ready to leave yet."

"Nor do I," the doctor said. "But you will be, and sooner than you think. For now, our time is up. I'll see you tomorrow, Jack."

Jack left the coziness of the small office and went down to the cafeteria where the aroma of fish sticks filled his nose from across the room. He conceded to himself not everything here was perfect. He hated fish.

A month later, Jack was released. He was clean, in good health, back at his previous weight and no longer looked like a skeleton with a five o'clock shadow. He was also more confident than he had felt in years. If he could beat his fight with all the drugs that took over his life, he felt as if he could do anything. If only that feeling of euphoria could last.

Jack was given back all his belongings when he signed himself out, along with the manila envelope Claire had brought with her that first day. As much as he wanted to open it right at that moment, he controlled his urge and saved it for when he got to his new home. Part of the outpatient agreement stated that Jack would live in a group home for the next six months and keep a standing weekly appointment with Dr. Pine. They would help him find a job and, eventually, a place to live, but until then he was basically still a patient of the facility, he just wasn't in the actual building.

A taxi was waiting to take Jack and his belongings to the group home only half a mile away. That, too, was part of the deal. He couldn't simply walk there in case he got it into his head to just keep walking. Jack had no intention of screwing this up. Over the last three months he had become a firm believer in karma and was sometimes paralyzed with fear thinking about what might be coming his way. He vowed to stay clean and make up for every bad thing he had ever done.

When he got to the house he was immediately shown his room where he dumped his bags. It was strange not having a roommate after spending so much time with another man snoring in the bed next to his. He even had his own semiprivate bathroom which he shared with only one other person. There were rules posted all over the walls of the house in every room. Everywhere he looked he was reminded to 'wash your hands,' 'pick up your own mess,' 'don't leave dirty dishes in the sink,' and his personal favorite 'don't do drugs.' Every man had a list of chores on a rotating schedule. They took turns cooking dinner and, if the man in charge of that night's meal didn't know how to cook, another guy jumped in and taught him the basics, which meant they usually ended up eating grilled cheese sandwiches or scrambled eggs.

The purpose of the transitional home was not only to make sure they weren't simply thrown back onto the streets, but it was also there to give them the fundamentals of basic self-care, something many of them were severely lacking.

After being introduced to the rest of the household, Jack made his way back up to his room and unpacked his bags. Having put everything away, he finally sat down and opened the envelope. His hands were shaking as he slid his finger under the sealed flap and pulled out the thick pile of papers. He had to read the cover page three times before it sank in. He was rich!

Apparently, when Jack's father died, he left his entire estate, which also included Jack's mother's estate, as she passed before his dad, and left everything to him. The one stipulation was that Jack was to get himself clean and sober before he could touch the trust fund. Jack had just assumed the one-hundred-thousand-dollar life insurance policy he received after his father's death was his only inheritance, and he had used that to buy his and Claire's first home. What he didn't know was, after the funeral, Winston Harper's attorney handed an envelope to Claire with the strictest instructions that she was only to give it to Jack if he sought help on his own accord. She wasn't allowed to convince him to get help just to get the money because, according to Winston, it wouldn't have stuck.

He wanted his son to hit rock bottom before he got the bulk of his estate. That was the only way he believed his son would truly clean up his act. He was right.

Jack looked over the rest of the paperwork, which was all written in legal jargon he could only half understand, but he got the gist of it. When the trust was written up and Winston had passed away there was just over five million dollars in the account. That was twelve years ago. Jack couldn't imagine what that amount had grown to in that time.

The following day was Tuesday, and the first thing Jack did was put on his best suit, after spending most of the previous day trying to iron the wrinkles out of it. He caught the bus at the corner and made his way downtown to the main branch of Lincoln Savings and Trust. He asked to see the manager and, after waiting for ten very long minutes, was led into a stuffy office with a desk the size of his old queen bed right in the center. Behind the desk was a man nearly as large as the desk, with a bushy red walrus moustache and a bad toupee.

Jack handed the manager the pile of papers, his driver's license and his discharge papers from Valley View along with a letter of recommendation typed and hand-signed by Dr. Pine. The letter was supposed to be used for job interviews, but Jack thought it couldn't hurt to bring it along to the bank. The manager, Mr. Seyfried, looked everything over, taking his merry old time and making tutting noises every so often.

"Your license is expired Mr. Harper," he scolded.

"Is it?" Jack asked. "I've been, um, preoccupied lately."

"Mmm, I have an idea what you've been preoccupied with."

This man clearly did not like Jack, and Jack wasn't too fond of Mr. Seyfried as it was, but he kept a civil tongue to get what was rightfully his.

"I've wondered if we were ever going to see you at this bank Mr. Harper. You see, I took over as manager nearly ten years ago and when I saw the amount in this trust, I was curious as to why it hadn't been claimed. When I found out that this large sum of money was left to a drug addict, I was quite surprised and more than a little disgusted."

"Excuse me, Mr. Seyfried," Jack interrupted. "I don't see what your personal objection to me gaining control of my father's estate has to do with anything. You don't know me, and I surely would not presume to know you. Now, if necessary, I will hire an attorney to make sure you and your bank play by the rules, so to speak. As you can see I have more than enough money in that account to afford the best lawyer I can find. Will that be necessary Mr. Seyfried?"

Jack had never seen a man turn such a violent shade of purple so fast. He figured that a man such as this was used to bullying people to get his way and wasn't accustomed to having the same tactic used on him.

"Of course that won't be necessary Mr. Harper," the bank manager said through gritted teeth.

"Wonderful," Jack said. "Now, if you don't mind, I'd like a cashier's check made out to the full amount please."

"Wouldn't you rather simply open an account here sir?" he asked Jack, still not opening his teeth to talk.

"No," Jack said. "I think I would be more comfortable with an institution that didn't insult their customers."

Mr. Seyfried's face changed from bright purple to a sickly shade of green. Jack imagined the manager was thinking of how the bank's shareholders would react when they found out their top manager lost nearly ten million dollars in one day.

"The check please?" Jack prodded.

"It will take a few minutes," Mr. Seyfried informed him in a dry rasp.

"I can be a very patient man sir. Now, if you don't mind."

"Of course, Mr. Harper."

Jack felt the floor shake as the man walked across the room and out the door. For the first time in his life, Jack felt in charge. He had to remind himself to keep a clear head and remember that karma is a bitch. He made a mental note to apologize to the manager when he returned for his threat of getting a lawyer.

He sat in the stuffy office for nearly half an hour waiting for his cashier's check. Most people would have made a mental wish list of all the things they would buy or do with such a large amount of money, but not Jack. Jack was more concerned with where to keep the money and how he could keep it from ruining his newfound plans. The funny thing was, he really had no idea what those plans were yet.

"I'm sorry for the wait," Mr. Seyfried said when he came back to his office. "We don't usually deal with such large amounts of money to be honest."

"Not a problem sir. I assume there are papers for me to sign?"

"Oh, yes, of course."

The manager sifted through his files looking for the right forms for Jack to fill out. Jack noticed a renewed humbleness in the man's demeanor and wondered if he had had his ass handed to him when he went to the bank's president to sign the check for nine-million-four-hundred-fifty-two-thousand-one-hundred-twelve dollars."

"Here we are Mr. Harper." Mr. Seyfried handed the cashier's check over with a trembling hand. "As you can see, your father's money was well invested on your behalf. Just a few signatures and initials and you can be on your way. I'm truly sorry for saying anything to offend you and if there is anything I can do to win you back as a valued customer please..."

"Please, Mr. Seyfried," Jack interrupted again. "I would also like to apologize for my behavior earlier, but to be honest, I'd feel much more comfortable taking by business elsewhere. I'd like to say it's nothing personal but that wouldn't be completely honest."

"I understand," he said through gritted teeth again, the color rising to his cheeks again.

"Is that all?" Jack asked.

Mr. Seyfried shuffled through the pile of papers and gave them a quick once over. He reluctantly held out his hand to shake, indicating their meeting was officially over.

"Thank you again," Jack shook the man's beefy hand briefly and left the office.

Once he got out into the fresh air, the fact that he had such a large amount of money at his disposal hit him and hit him hard. He felt like a child again. When he was a boy, he had never wanted for anything and, if he chose, he could have that life back. Jack had to make a conscious effort to slow his thoughts and take a firm hold of his situation. Fact number one: he was a recovering drug addict with a long history of zero self-control. Fact number two: he was in a situation where he had absolutely nothing but could now afford the finest of everything. Fact number three: he didn't want his old life back, not at any cost.

Jack hopped on the next bus and headed downtown to the main branch of Midwestern Teachers' Credit Union, where he and Claire had kept their accounts. They had always been good to Harper's, and he wanted to keep doing business with them. When he presented the check to the teller the poor old woman nearly fainted. He asked to see the manager, knowing he was a much more reasonable man than Mr. Seyfried. In fact, Bob Harding was an old friend of his and Claire's.

"Jack!" Bob greeted him loudly. "Long time, no see. Where have you been man?"

"Long story Bob. Can we go to your office?"

"Sure, sure. No problem. Right this way."

Over an hour later Jack emerged with a grinning, flush-faced bank manager at his side. He had set up a long-term savings plan, an IRA, a checking account, numerous CD's and even a monthly allotment to be sent directly to Claire's savings account with the stipulation she never know where the money came from, although, Jack knew, she would figure it out on her own. He also donated a decent amount to the bank's charity of choice. The Lincoln Women's Shelter would be receiving an anonymous donation of ten thousand dollars at the beginning of the next month.

When Jack left the bank, he felt as if karma was smiling down on him.

Chapter 12

Six months can seem like an eternity, or it can fly by like no time at all, depending on the situation. In Jack's case, the time he spent in the halfway house seemed to take no more than a month. Although it was snowing in a new year when he left and when he arrived, he was wearing shorts and flip-flops.

He secured a job at the local library restocking the returned books. What he really wanted was to get back into teaching, but his counselor didn't think it was a good idea just yet.

"You need to pace yourself Jack," Dr. Pine told him on one of his weekly visits. "Your life has changed drastically in the last year. You need to give yourself time to reacclimate to normal society. Remember, you did everything before with a crutch. Now we've taken that crutch away and you basically need to learn how to walk on your own again."

"I understand," Jack said, and he did. Whether he agreed with the doctor or not, he could see his point. "Do you think I'll ever be able to teach again?"

"Oh, I have no doubt. And I believe you'll be better at it than you were before."

"How do you figure?" Jack asked.

"You've been humbled."

"I don't get you."

"Would you say you were a good teacher, Jack?"

"Sure. I mean, I always thought I was. I never really second guessed it."

"And now you are?" the doctor asked. "Are you second guessing your memories?"

Jack thought it over. He *had* always thought of himself as a good teacher, a *great* one in fact. Maybe it just seemed that way to him through the thick veil of smoke that clouded his thoughts.

"I guess I am."

"Good. Now you have something to strive for."

"And that is?"

"Greatness, Jack," Dr. Pine explained. "You've realized you're not as great as you once believed. Now when you teach others you will use that knowledge to work harder. You'll listen to your students and understand them better because you now know that you are still, in a way, a student yourself. You will always be a student of *life*. Once you accept that, you will have the tools needed to achieve your goals and *that* is what will lead you to greatness. Does that make any sense?"

Dr. Pine had always had a way of making Jack see things from a deeper level. He was more than his shrink, he was his friend, his confidant and, in a way, his hero. Jack needed saving and he didn't think he would have succeeded without Dr. Pine's help.

"It makes perfect sense."

"Now I don't want you to push yourself too hard too fast. You may not get back into the classroom any time soon, and to be honest, you might not ever again, but that doesn't mean you're not a teacher. Everywhere you go, everyone you meet, *that* is your classroom. Okay?"

"Okay doc. I got it."

That last session was one of the most profound meetings for Jack. He was quite certain the doctor didn't consciously mean to push Jack in the direction in which he ended up, but it was that last statement, the one about the whole world being his classroom, which convinced Jack he was doing the right thing.

In addition to the job at the library, Jack found an apartment on the west side of town. With all the money he had in the bank he could have afforded a nice house in one of the newer developments but, he thought, what would he do with all that space? The apartment was just the right size for a single man, easy to maintain and already furnished with a second-hand couch, recliner fully equipped with cigarette burns and a double bed that creaked every time he moved so much as his big toe.

He didn't spend much time in the apartment. He found it too dreary and lonely, and the neighbors on either side either fought loudly or partied louder nearly every night. During one of the raucous parties, Jack lay in bed trying to ignore the familiar, pungent aroma of marijuana seeping through the walls. He had been out of rehab for nearly nine months by this time and badly wanted a good high. He got out of bed, slipped on his boots and his overcoat, and headed out for some fresh air before the need overpowered him enough to go knock on his neighbor's door to ask for a hit.

Walking the streets of Lincoln sober at one in the morning was like discovering a whole new city. He had been out there many times, always stoned out of his gourd, and he just went on sheer instinct. But clean... this was a completely new experience. Jack stood on the corner and breathed in the crisp April night air and decided to let his feet take over.

He discovered parts of the town he had never seen before; parts that were ugly, parts that were scary, parts that were downright *bad* for a man with his past. He saw bums digging through trash cans, junkies shooting up in an alley, drunks staggering down the street, and young girls selling their bodies for cheap.

"Jack!"

Jack turned to the sound of his voice.

"Jack! Is that you?"

Jack stared blankly at the sallow face of a woman he barely recognized.

"Sarah?"

The scrawny woman sauntered up to Jack on unsteady legs and held her arms out to him. For one repulsive moment, Jack thought she was about to hug him. Instead, she pushed him in the chest.

"You asshole!" she yelled. "I thought you were dead!"

Jack thought back to the night he went to Valley View. He had stopped at Sarah's for a hit and a lay, but she was otherwise occupied. Back then, she still lived in her parents' basement and talked about becoming a model. The only thing she could model now was the after picture on the cigarette ads. She was only twenty now but looked twice her age. Decked out in well-worn stilettos and a stained mini-dress, Jack could only assume she had taken to prostitution. The track marks up and down her arms told Jack she had also graduated to heroin. She looked like she wanted to cry, but that one push seemed to have sapped her of all energy.

"Sarah," Jack started, "what happened?"

She looked at him with blank eyes. "What do you mean?"

"Look at you! What are you doing here?" Jack spread his arms, indicating the piteous state of the corner they were on.

The blank stare continued, and Jack could tell she was high as a kite. He pulled out his wallet and handed her two twenties and a ten.

"Here."

She grabbed the money, shoved it down her bra, and pushed Jack up against the side of a dilapidated corner market. She immediately dropped to her knees and attempted to unzip Jack's fly.

"Woah, woah, woah!" Jack exclaimed, pulling Sarah to her feet.

"What? You paid. It's all good."

"No, Sarah, I didn't give you the money for *that*. I want you to get to a safe place, ok?"

Sarah looked at him quizzically. "You don't want me to blow you?"

"No."

Her dull brown eyes darted around as if looking for a way out. She kept biting her bottom lip and wiping her nose with the back of her hand.

"Why?"

"Why what?"

"Why are you giving me fifty bucks? You don't owe me anything."

Jack sighed with the realization he *did* owe her something. It was most likely Jack's fault she ended up on the street. She was nothing more than an occasional pothead when they first met in his honors Lit class, and he had introduced her to so much more. This poor girl, this walking shell of a human, had once written beautiful poetry she had shared with him and no one else. She had potential. Now she had a death sentence.

"Please Sarah, just take it and go."

She pulled the money out of her bra and stared at it. Jack hoped she would find a safe place, but he knew she would just spend it on blow. He took her frail hand and helped her make a fist around the crumpled bills. She stared at him with empty eyes. Jack saw what he did to this girl in the sallow street-light, and it sickened him; she was dead inside. He turned and walked away before he could feel any more regret.

Jack walked until his legs ached and his eyes couldn't stay open anymore. He had no idea where he ended up until he turned the corner and came upon Carter Park. The city bus stopped right in front of the park entrance, but they didn't run this late at night and he no longer had any money for a cab. There was also no way his legs would carry him all the way back to his shabby little apartment. Just inside the archway was a row of freshly painted park benches. Jack sat down on the one nearest the entrance and mulled over his situation. He rubbed at his hands to warm them and replayed the evening over and over in his head. He had never really thought about how his addiction had hurt anyone other than Claire. How many other lives had he ruined, he wondered.

Jack was more exhausted than ever and felt as if he could just curl up right here on the bench and sleep until morning, but he wasn't too keen about sleeping out in the open. It wasn't the idea of possibly getting robbed that bothered him as he wasn't carrying even a dime; it was the possibility of being *seen*. The last thing he wanted was to be thought of as a bum.

Jack was dozing off as he sat and thought, so he got up and wandered around the park. It was your basic city park, man-made lake, landscaped gardens, and paved walkways leading to a large playground right in the center. Little did he know, this was Jack's first introduction to his future home.

The cement cylinders looked small and cramped in the moonlight, but upon further inspection, Jack found they were quite cozy. He climbed into the first tube, discovered he fit quite easily and even had enough room to turn around. The bottom was littered with fallen leaves that had blown in on the previous autumn's breeze and the smell they made when he shuffled through them took him back to his childhood days in Pennsylvania, climbing trees and jumping out into deep piles of crunchy leaves. He was asleep in record time, dreams of innocence and youth filling his subconscious.

It was late morning when Jack was awoken by a young patrolman with a nasty chip on his shoulder. Apparently, the cement tubes not only blocked out the elements, but it was also eerily soundproof as well. Once he climbed out into the bright sunlight, Jack was amazed he didn't wake sooner with all the noise from the young kids running around. One little girl, while playing hide-and-seek with her friends, happened upon Jack snoring away quite contentedly when she tried to hide in the concrete pipes. She was so scared when she found him, she ran from the playground, screaming about a bear in the tubes, making her mother run after her. After calming the little girl down and checking for herself to see if what her daughter saw was, indeed, what she saw, she flagged down the nearest police officer and told him of the situation.

Jack figured it wouldn't do any good to explain the situation to the rookie cop so he took the verbal lashing and the ticket for a fifty dollar fine with as much good grace as he could muster and was on his way.

He had to wonder, as he walked across the street and pointed himself in the direction of his apartment, what karma had in store for him. He obviously had more strikes against him than he was originally aware, and that scared him. He had stayed clean for almost a year now. He hadn't used a bit of his inheritance for anything frivolous or bad or covetous. He had, in fact, donated some of it, anonymously at that. He lived in a dump surrounded by all sorts of temptations, had a dead-end job, and hadn't had a woman since God-knew-when. He was living the clean life and nothing good had come of it yet. In fact, he felt as if he was starting to backslide, and it terrified him.

Maybe he wasn't doing enough, he thought. Maybe he needed to become even more humbled, as Dr. Pine had mentioned. Sleeping in the park had been a humbling experience and he had gotten a ticket for it.

Jack thought about all the bad things he had done in his lifetime. When he added up everything he could remember it was no wonder life kept kicking him in the balls. He was certain there was plenty more he was too high to remember, and it scared the living hell out of him. It would take him a lifetime to atone for all his transgressions, and now he had one more to add to the list. Now, all Jack had to do was figure out a way to go about making up for each one. Perdition was not a place in which he intended to stay.

On his way home he stopped at the bank and took out enough money for his loitering citation, breakfast, and a cab ride home. He could have walked the rest of the way, the weather surely wasn't an issue, but his back ached from sleeping on cement and his feet were covered in blisters. He also had a lot of thinking to do, and he couldn't think on an empty stomach.

Jack walked around the corner and entered the crowded diner. Before anything else, he went to the men's room to clean up. He felt dirty, both inside and out, from sleeping in the park, and he wouldn't allow himself to feel as dirty on the outside as he did on the inside. Once he had cleaned up, he ordered himself the largest breakfast on the menu and a cup of coffee. He watched the morning commuters passing by the diner window as he waited for his food. Businessmen hailing cabs, housewives running their daily errands, college students hurrying off to class; they all had a purpose. Then Jack spotted him; a bearded, bedraggled old man sitting on the corner across the street, his face turned toward the morning sun. He wore layers of grungy clothes, and he was leaning against a rusty shopping cart piled with random items Jack assumed were the man's meager belongings. No one took notice of the man and he seemed to prefer it that way.

In that very moment, Jack had made the most profound decision of his life. It was insane, it was completely off-the cuff, and it was the only thing he believed would work. He just had to keep himself convinced that it would work until he finally took the plunge. He was going to give up everything. Well... *almost* everything.

The enormous breakfast Jack ordered filled the gnawing hunger in his gut and his coffee cup was refilled several times. Coffee was the one thing that helped Jack to cope with the occasional urge to get high. After his fourth cup of the morning, he realized how he had replaced the drugs with caffeine and the absurdity of it all. Here he was, downing cup after cup of one of the most addictive substances on earth and no one thought anything of it. The restaurant patrons didn't look at him as if he were the scum of the earth, the cop at the counter didn't arrest him for substance abuse and was, in fact, enjoying a cup himself; the waitress regularly came to offer him free refills and, hell, even the teenagers in the next booth were drinking their fair share. There was no rehab center for coffee addicts, no twelve-step program, and no stigma attached to being a coffee drinker. Jack had found his drug, and there wasn't a damn thing anyone could do to stop him. It was the one thing he *would not* give up.

He paid his tab, left a hefty tip for the waitress, and called a cab from the pay phone on the corner. The cabbie was a pleasant enough fellow who made the typical small talk with his passenger and the ride home was short enough that Jack didn't have to engage in much of the conversation. He honestly didn't pay attention to a word the driver said, he was so lost in his thoughts.

When he got home, he noticed the smell from the previous night's party had dissipated enough that Jack could ignore the familiar odor, and spraying half a can of Lysol didn't hurt. He went through all his belongings deciding what to keep and what to donate to the needy. By the time he was done he had one big black garbage bag of things to keep and three on which he would leave a note for his landlord to toss in the donation bin in the Kmart parking lot. He gave the tiny apartment a once over with a dust rag, left that month's rent and the note in an envelope on the counter next to his keys and left it all behind.

Chapter 13

The years Jack spent on the streets of Lincoln turned out to be the most interesting, terrifying, brilliant, heartbreakingly amazing time of his life. He met some of the greatest people and had some of the worst times. He slept in shelters, in churches, on park benches and on top of heating grates. He sometimes went days without anything but coffee in his stomach.

In the early years, he often questioned his motives and seriously considered going to the bank to take out enough money to buy any house he wished. Every time he needed a reminder as to why he was punishing himself he would wander out toward the Northwest Territory and into the cozy development in which he and Claire used to live. A young couple with a little boy now lived in the tiny brown ranch home which was once his. Toys littered the lawn and a tire swing hung from the sumac tree out front. That could have been his life if he hadn't screwed it up, but this was Jack's life now, and he accepted his fate.

He had been on the street for twenty years now and he truly couldn't imagine his life any other way. Jack had the same routine for years. Every January, on the first Monday of the month, he would withdraw five thousand dollars from his account and get it all in small bills which he then placed in a bag for his daily allowance. On the same bank trip he would set up a wire transfer to the charities of his choice for the year. He always sent fifty thousand dollars to the children's ward of St. Elizabeth's hospital, and each year he chose two others to split the other fifty thousand he set aside. The year he met Kate and little Jacky he chose the 60th street shelter where he had once spent a miserable month in relative comfort when he was too sick to sleep outside, and the Lancaster County SPCA.

The previous summer he had befriended a shaggy stray that became Jack's constant companion until he was nabbed by the dog catchers. Jack went against his personal code and withdrew enough money to legally adopt the lovable terrier but by the time he got there they had already put him down. They said he was too old to put up for adoption so they put him out of his misery. That was the first time Jack had cried in years. Jack's donation was made with the stipulation that they don't put strays to sleep just because they're "too old." He didn't know if it would help or not, but at least the money was going to a good cause.

In addition to the allowance money and his yearly anonymous donations, Jack took out enough to pay for a full hot meal for a few dozen other homeless citizens.

There was a little mom and pop place on the south side of town that accommodated Jack's dinner guests; welcomed them with open arms in fact. Jack got the story from Pop about their son who ended up on the street after coming back from Vietnam without his legs. He was too proud to come home again and ended up dying of a heroin overdose in a back alley on the streets of Omaha. They had a soft spot for Jack's people and made sure they knew they were always welcome. They also agreed to never tell the patrons who their kind benefactor was. Mom and Pop didn't pretend to understand Jack, but they also knew it wasn't their place to question such kindness.

The meal was always delicious and plentiful and, sometimes, it was the only hot meal some of these men and women ate during the entire winter. Sure, they could grab a plate at the mission house or any number of homeless shelters, but what they passed as food could hardly be called as such. Mom and Pop always went overboard on the menu when Jack made his reservation. They closed the tiny diner to the public and allowed only the less fortunate. The menu usually consisted of turkey and stuffing with three different kinds of potatoes, ham, at least four kinds of vegetables, the most delicious homemade biscuits, and, oh the deserts. Pies and cakes galore. There was always plenty for seconds or thirds and everyone left every year with an overflowing plate wrapped in cellophane for later.

Saying Jack was a giving person was most definitely an understatement. He took the wellbeing of these people very personally and did everything in his power to make sure they were taken care of, hence the donations to citywide shelters and the occasional hot meals. He never let anyone know he had any money and he always preferred to live completely alone, although they all knew where he laid his head at night. He respected them and, in turn, they respected his privacy. The others never knew it was Jack who paid for their yearly feast, and he preferred it that way. Jack felt if he were to get any credit for his good deeds they wouldn't count toward his life of atonement.

Jack wasn't a religious man and didn't find God per se, but he was a firm believer of what goes around comes around. He tried to explain it once to Kate one warm, sunny day in May. Kate had just graduated from nursing school the previous weekend and she was feeling content for the first time since her divorce. She had yet to find a job, but had two interviews lined up later in the week. Kate wasn't sold on the concept of karma but was interested in Jack's reasoning.

They were walking from their usual meeting lunch spot toward the park that Jack called home. Jacky was walking between them, quietly playing with his newest Happy Meal toy.

He wasn't as chatty as usual and Kate explained Jacky was getting over a nasty flu bug. Jack had noticed the pale skin and dark circles under the boy's eyes but chalked it up to being inside during the long, rough winter. As Jacky turned the Happy Meal toy over and over in his hand, Jack imagined the boy's bedroom and how it must be filled with all the little plastic toys he's collected in his brief lifetime. He explained his views on karma as his mind wandered.

"I don't think karma works like that Jack," Kate said.

"Why not?"

"Well, do you really think God is sitting up there with a tally sheet keeping track of every good deed and every bad deed we all do just so he can decide who deserves what? What about the bad things that happen to little kids? Cancer, natural disasters, drunk drivers. Are you telling me if, God forbid, Jacky got hurt tomorrow he did something to deserve it?"

"Of course not Kate," Jack said. "I'm just trying to explain why I'm in the situation I'm in. You once asked me why I was homeless, remember?"

"I do," she said. "And I also remember your answer, which was nothing. You just shrugged your shoulders and said, 'why not?'"

"Okay, I admit I was a bit vague, but there's more to it than I felt comfortable going into at the time. I had just met you after all."

"Fair enough. You know me now though. So, explain," she said.

They had entered the playground and Jacky was tickled to death to see that he had the whole place to himself. He ran over to the swings and began pumping his little legs furiously until he got up enough momentum to give the rusty chains a good workout. Jack and Kate sat on one of the park benches that was still in good repair and watched as the little boy played.

"I wasn't always a good man," Jack started. "I *thought* I was, but I was mistaken. A long time ago I was a high school teacher. I was a son and a grandson and a husband. Once, I was *almost* a father, but she lost the baby. I was also a drug addict."

"What happened?" Kate asked.

"I let the drugs take over my life. That's what happened. You see, addiction is a sneaky thing. It creeps up on you, even lets you walk away for a spell, but then BAM! It has its hooks in you and they're too deep just to pull out on your own. I walked away for a while when we moved out here actually. I stayed away from the stuff for over a year and life was just great."

"Then why did you go back?"

Jack took a deep breath and let his gaze fix on Jacky, now merrily spinning himself on the creaky merry-go-round. "I couldn't handle it when she lost the baby."

"Oh."

"I know," Jack said. "Just when she needed me the most, I let her down. Things just got worse from there. She stayed with me for a couple more years before she finally got smart and gave up on me. I lost everything from that point and finally checked myself into rehab. I've been clean ever since."

"That's a *good* thing though," Kate told him. She reached down and took his hand in hers.

"It is," Jack agreed. "But it's not enough. I once explained to my counsellor, this was years ago. I told him I felt as if I were lost in perdition, and the only way out was to atone for my sins."

"Don't you think God, or karma, or whatever you believe in takes that into consideration? You've been punishing yourself for nearly a quarter of a century, as long as I've been alive. Don't you think you deserve better than this? You've paid your debt Jack. You need to start living for yourself again."

He gave her hand a little squeeze. "I wish it were that easy Kate. I really do."

"What you're doing to yourself here is repentance Jack, it's not karma. Maybe that's something to think about."

Jack sighed, stood up, and stretched his weary body. "Maybe you're right, but it's something I need to do. I don't know how to explain it."

Jack walked over to the teeter-totter where Jacky was trying to make it work on his own. He pressed down on his side and smiled at the boy's squeals of laughter as he rose high into the air. Jacky laughed himself right into a coughing fit. It was a deep, rattling cough that disturbed Jack deeply. He picked up the small boy and carried him to his mother. He felt light as a feather and when his tiny arms wrapped around Jack's neck, he felt how weak the boy was. He remembered how horrible he felt when he was sick and sympathized with him.

"Maybe you should take him home Kate," Jack said as he sat the boy in her lap.

She pressed her lips to his forehead and sighed. "His fever is back. I think you're right Jack. This little guy needs a nap."

Kate gathered her son and his toys and walked him back in the direction of the car. They said their goodbyes and Jack turned toward his concrete home. Kate looked back as she reached the entrance and saw him crawl into the large tubes. She assumed that was where he was living and immediately felt that her little mobile home she shared with her son was the nicest place in the world.

Chapter 14

In the few months he had known Kate, Jack noticed a change in his own demeanor. He was more cheerful, upbeat, and happier than he felt in decades. Even his appearance had improved. As the first week of June began, Jack no longer felt the need for his scraggly winter beard so, on that Wednesday morning, before he set off for their standing lunch date, Jack went down to the barber on O street and asked for a shave and a haircut. As he sat in the barber chair, he wondered if Jacky would recognize him if he showed up with no beard. At the last minute, he asked the barber to just trim the beard, so it was neat. He couldn't risk his little buddy not knowing who he was.

Jack felt like a new man as he left the barber shop. It was probably all in his imagination, but he didn't feel as if strangers scoffed at him with his new, sleek look. When he walked into McDonalds to order his breakfast, even the manager didn't give him a second look. He smiled to himself as he looked out the window, waiting for his lunch companions.

It had been three weeks since he last broke bread with them, and he missed them terribly. The first week, he was worried, and a little heartbroken, when they didn't show up after an hour of waiting. The second week he waited almost two hours before he left alone. He was starting to wonder what he did wrong when Kate found him at the entrance of Carter Park later that afternoon and explained Jacky was still under the weather and she didn't want him getting all worked up. She apologized profusely and handed Jack a picture Jacky colored for him. Jack could see the fatigue on Kate's face and felt for her. She said they would be sure to make it the following week.

As Jack turned into the park, he unfolded the picture from Jacky. It was a colorful rendition of Jack's park. There were white clouds in the bright blue sky, a rainbow curving down to the pond with little ducks swimming in a row; the swing set, merry-go-round, and teeter totter were all in the right places, and Jack's tubes were off to the side. Standing in front of it all were three stick figures of a woman, a man with a long beard, and a little boy standing between them. They were all holding hands and little hearts were dancing above the boy's head. Jack held it to his chest, knowing he would treasure it forever.

The thought of seeing Jacky after all this time made Jack feel as giddy as a kid on Christmas, and when he saw the duo walking up to the counter, his heart jumped to his throat. He fussed with his hair and ran his fingers through his shortened beard, nervous about what Jacky would think.

"Well look at you!" Kate exclaimed as she brought their tray over to the table in the corner. "Aren't you looking all dapper! Do you have a hot date I should know about?" she joked with a wink.

Jack looked down at Jacky and could tell the boy still wasn't feeling well. He was pale and still had dark circles under his eyes. He moved slower than normal and appeared to have gotten even smaller. But he didn't want Jacky to see worry on his face, so he smiled and greeted the boy the way he did every week.

"Hello there Mr. Just Jack!"

Jacky stood back and looked carefully at him. Jack didn't say anything, just smiled back at the boy.

"Jack?" the boy asked tentatively.

Jack nodded.

Jacky stepped closed and ran his little hand over the trimmed beard. "You're not as fuzzy."

Jack chuckled. "No, not quite as fuzzy. But I kept a little, just for you." He ran his palm up the side of his cheek.

Jacky's little face scrunched up in a look that was both comical and worrisome. "You don't look like Santa Claus anymore."

Jack felt he should do something to lighten the mood. He motioned Jacky forward with a crook of his finger. "You wanna know why I had to shave it?"

Jacky nodded, his mouth hanging open in anticipated wonder.

"Those darn birds at the park were starting to think I was a nest! I couldn't keep them off me!"

Jacky's face broke into a toothy grin and chuckled at the joke. He hugged Jack, walked around the table, sat next to his mom, and opened his Happy Meal bag. He put the toy aside and picked at his fries. Jacky always took the toy out to play with first, but this time, he just let it sit, unopened. He definitely wasn't feeling up to par.

They made their regular idle chit chat. Kate admired Jack's new 'do. Jack mentioned there were baby ducks at the pond and Jacky showed a moment of brief excitement, but as their lunch hour neared its end, Jacky became more lethargic, and Kate's attention waned. Before long, Jacky was sound asleep with his head on his mother's lap. Jack saw the loving way she stroked his hair and sensed the worry around her.

"Kate?"

"Hmm."

"Is Jacky okay?"

She continued to look at her son. Jack could see tears welling in her eyes. "He's been sick for a month now. Some days he seems better, but most days he's just like this. No energy, fevers, chills, aches, no appetite, and now this." She pulled up the side of Jacky's shirt to expose a greenish bruise on his stomach. "His doctor wants him to go for a bunch of tests, but my insurance isn't the greatest."

Jack let out a small gasp.

"I know what you're thinking Jack, but I would never hit my son!"

Jack was flabbergasted. He never had even an inkling of such a thought. "Kate," he started, "I would never..." He didn't know what else to say. He didn't like the look of that bruise and had his own concerns as to what it could be, but he didn't want to scare her unnecessarily. He did know she had to get him to the right doctor, and soon.

"I'm sorry, Jack. I know you wouldn't think that. It just seems to be the first thought on most people's minds when they see a kid with a bruise."

"Did you show it to the doctor?" he asked.

"Yes, and of course the first thing they did was ask if anyone hit him," Kate explained. Jack could tell she was worried he would think the same thing. He did not.

"Anyone can see what a wonderful mother you are Kate. Please don't worry about what people think. You just need to concern yourself with getting Jacky the care he needs."

"I know that, but like I said, my insurance isn't worth shit!" A tear slipped down her cheek. "Besides, I just started this new job and don't have any leave time saved yet. It's just a mess."

Jack looked her in the eyes. "We'll make sure he's ok Kate. I promise."

Kate made a sound somewhere between a laugh and a sigh. "I wish I could be as confident as you Jack."

Jack sipped his coffee while Kate drank her iced tea. The silence between them was palpable. Kate hated dumping her worries on Jack, but he was just so easy to talk to. Jack wanted to help with Jacky's medical expenses, but he couldn't find a way to bring up his financial situation without looking like a complete mental case.

"Do you have any family around to help you?" Jack asked.

"Just my mom, but we had a falling out of sorts."

"I'm sorry to hear that."

Kate shrugged. "It is what it is I guess."

"May I ask what happened?"

She sipped her tea and snagged a stray fry from the tray. "Typical mother-daughter stuff really. She thought she knew more than me, she knew what was better than I did, and I disagreed. Turns out she was right."

Jack sipped his coffee and let her go on in her own good time.

"I met Jacky's dad in high school. Marcus was the 'golden boy' and got everything he wanted. I got pregnant with Jacky right before graduation and he resented me for it; like I knocked myself up, right?" Kate chuckled sardonically, raised her eyes to Jack, and continued her story. "Anyway, he had a scholarship to UNL and took it. We got married just before his first semester in a little JP ceremony; just a couple of friends, no family. By then I wasn't talking to my mom, and I didn't invite her. I'm sure that stung more than anything. I worked as a waitress to pay the bills and took night classes when I could. He went to school full-time and cheated when he could. He left about a year ago. I signed and mailed the divorce papers the morning I met you, in fact."

"And you haven't talked to your mother since?"

"Oh, we talk, but we're not as close as we used to be. She adores Jacky and I'm sure she would do anything for him, but she's also very tight with her money, always has been. I don't know why... she has plenty of it."

"I see. Have you asked her for help recently though?"

"She bought me the trailer I live in now after Marcus left. When she signed it over to me, the entire time she rambled on and on about how she knew he was no good and she knew I would end up a single mom, just like her. Funny thing is, my dad didn't leave her for another woman. He died before I was even born. For some reason, she always seemed to begrudge him for that. She hated that I named Jacky after him."

She sat for a while, staring pensively out the window.

"Anyway, that's the last time I asked her for anything. She takes Jacky one weekend a month so I can have a break and she babysits when I need her to, but I don't ask her to watch him very often."

"Have you told her how you feel?"

Kate let out another huff. "She's not very forgiving."

"What is there to forgive? You're her daughter Kate. I can't imagine, if I had a daughter, there would be anything she could do to keep her out of my life."

She smiled warmly at him. "I appreciate that Jack. Really, I do."

They finished their drinks and cleaned up their table. Kate picked up the sleeping little boy and carried him out to her car.

"Promise me two things Kate?" Jack asked as she buckled Jacky into his booster seat.

"I'll try. What are they?"

"Take Jacky to the children's hospital at Saint Elizabeth's. They're good there. Please don't worry about the bill. I'll explain later."

"Okay, but I don't understand what you could do."

"Please, just trust me, okay?"

Kate nodded. "What's the second thing?"

"Call your mom."

Jack turned and walked away before she could argue. He couldn't put his finger on it, but he knew it was very important for Kate and her mother to reconnect. His feelings were usually spot on.

Chapter 15

Independence Day was always one of Jack's favorite holidays. His little park was perfectly situated so he could enjoy the fireworks display over the city. The bright explosions took him back to his childhood when he would run around the yard with his hands full of sparklers, waiting for the big fireworks to be set off by the river. It gave him hope knowing something so small can rise up and bloom into something big and beautiful. It made him think of Jacky and how he needs all the hope he can get right now.

July fourth was on a Wednesday this year and he was looking forward to seeing his friends for lunch. He knew Kate had taken Jacky to Saint Elizabeth's as promised, and he was hoping to hear how his appointment went. He was beginning to think of them as family and, for some reason, felt responsible for their wellbeing. The day he made Kate promise to take Jacky to the hospital, he took it upon himself to visit the billing department after he made his usual donation.

As usual, he got some strange looks as he walked through the building, but he was a man on a mission and disregarded the strangers he passed. When he found the billing department and told the receptionist why he was there, she gave him a quizzical look before having him take a seat. She disappeared into a back office for only a moment before returning with another woman who invited him to join her.

"My name is Lauren Temple," she introduced herself as she sat behind her desk, motioning Jack to take a seat across from her.

He held out his hand in introduction. "Jack Harper. Nice to meet you Ms. Temple."

She shook his hand without hesitation. Jack was impressed. She reminded him of the principal of the high school he taught at a lifetime ago. Tall and thin, sitting ramrod straight, she looked like a woman not to be trifled with. Her eyes didn't match her demeanor though; she had soft eyes. Jack knew she would help him just by looking in her eyes.

"I hear you have a rather odd request Mr. Harper. Can you please elaborate?"

Jack took a deep breath and started his story. He began with meeting Kate and Jacky and ended with his concerns for Jacky's health.

"So, Ms. Temple, I would like to set up an account to pay for any and all medical bills for the boy. I only know his name and date of birth, but I imagine you can find him with that."

She eyed him carefully, trying to figure out the best way to ask a delicate question.

"Mr. Harper," she began, "that is a very noble gesture, I admit, but... may I be frank?"

Jack nodded.

"No offense, but you hardly appear financially equipped to pay for what could possibly be a very large medical expense."

"No offense taken." Jack smiled.

"How, might I ask, do you intend to pay for these bills? *If* they accumulate that is." She punched some keys on her keyboard and looked for Jacky's name. "From what I see here, the child has no medical record at this facility."

"He'll be here. I made her promise to bring him."

"If you're so certain, then I must go back to my original question. How do you intend to pay?"

"Do you have access to private donation records?"

She squinted at him suspiciously. "I do. Why do you ask?"

"At the beginning of every year, the first Monday of January to be exact, your children's hospital receives an anonymous donation of fifty thousand dollars. This year was the twenty-first year you've received that money. According to my math, that's a little over one million dollars to date."

Ms. Temple's fingers were flying across her keyboard. She scrolled through the donations deposits and found Mr. Harper was correct.

"How did you know that?"

Jack pulled out his battered checkbook and slid it across the desk, pointing to the routing and account number on the bottom of the check.

"I believe you'll find these numbers match the ones in your system."

Her eyes grew huge and filled with tears.

"Mr. Harper," she shook his hand again. "I don't think I could thank you enough for your donations. Please, if there's anything I can do, just say it."

"Just two things," Jack explained. "One, please keep this between us. I want these donations to remain anonymous."

"Agreed."

"Second," he pulled the checkbook back, grabbed a pen from her desk, and began writing out a check, "how do I make sure this money is allotted to Jacky's care?"

Jack was in Lauren's office for over an hour ironing out the details. She found Jacky's records in another hospital from when he was two and split his chin open on a coffee table. She verified the medical insurance and discovered Kate was right; it really *was* shitty coverage. She also ran some numbers for possible tests and treatment options if Jack's suspicions were right.

"Are you sure you don't want to just pay for the tests now and go from there?" she asked. "You can't be sure he's even that sick yet."

"I'm sure," Jack replied. "I really do hope he's fine, but I like to err on the side of caution. And if he doesn't need it, the rest can be considered a donation."

"Mr. Harper, you've done so much for this hospital already."

"And I intend to keep providing what I can until the day I die."

Ms. Temple felt tears sting her eyes once more and turned away.

As Jack was leaving the office, he felt content that Jacky would get the care he needed. The director held out her hand to Jack and shook it warmly.

"Again, Mr. Harper, if there's anything you need..."

Jack just placed his forefinger and thumb to his lips and slid them across his mouth in the universal symbol of silence. "Remember, Kate can't know."

Lauren nodded and walked him to the door. As Jack walked away, she turned to her receptionist, who was watching the interaction in awe.

"That's the best man you'll ever meet right there."

A month had gone by since that day and he again found himself sitting in the corner booth at McDonalds waiting for his friends. His nerves were shot awaiting the news about Jacky's tests. Kate was good to her word and got Jacky in to see a pediatrician just a week after her promise. The pediatrician sent Jacky for bloodwork which came back with some worrisome results. They got Jacky in for more testing last week and Jack hoped Kate would have some answers by now. Jack was a realist. He always hoped for the best but expected the worst, knowing, most of the time, things fell somewhere in between. Today, when he saw Kate enter the restaurant without Jacky, he didn't feel very hopeful.

Kate sat down across from Jack without ordering any food. She wore no makeup and her hair was disheveled. She looked as if she had just climbed out of bed after a night of hard partying, but Jack knew better. He took a deep breath and asked about the results. Kate burst into tears.

He let her cry, holding back the lump in his throat while patting her shoulder, until she got herself under control.

"Let's go for a walk," he suggested. "Get you some fresh air."

Kate nodded and allowed herself to be led by the arm out into the warm summer sun. They walked toward the park in silence until they got to the bench they normally sat at while Jacky played on the playground.

"It's leukemia," Kate announced.

Jack let out a deep breath. His fears had been confirmed.

"They're sure?"

"Yes. His white cells were off the chart, so they did a bone marrow aspiration last Friday. The biopsy confirmed it."

Jack looked across the playground and let the news sink in.

"How's Jacky? Does he know?"

Kate chuckled sadly. "You know him. He's a trooper. He knows he's sick but he's too young to comprehend just how serious it is. He's with my mom today. I couldn't risk having him see me break down."

"Understandable."

"I don't know what to do Jack. What do I do?"

Kate leaned her head on his shoulder and sighed deeply. He could feel her body shake as she silently wept.

"You get him the best doctor there is. And then you hope for the best."

Jack couldn't think of anything else to say that would make her feel better. She just found out her son had cancer. Nothing can make that pain go away, and he knew it.

"I already have an appointment with a pediatric oncologist Monday morning. His pediatrician said they'll want to start treatment right away. I had to quit my job. Jacky needs me now."

"Yes, he does. You're a good mom Kate. I know he'll be well taken care of."

"I've been doing my own research. Chemo is crazy expensive. He'll probably feel even *more* sick and lose his hair. He won't be able to play with his friends. How do I explain all of this to him? He's going to go through *so* much, it's just not fair! He's only a little boy Jack. How does your *karma* do something like this to such a sweet little boy? He never hurt a soul!" Kate looked at him with a fierceness he never wanted to see again.

Jack was slightly taken aback by the sudden attack and searched for the words to try and make her understand. He was at a loss.

"I don't know Kate. I just don't know."

They sat in silence for, what seemed, ages.

"I'm glad you called your mom."

Kate shrugged. "A promise is a promise."

"Have you worked things out?"

"When I told her about Jacky she broke down and cried. She apologized for the distance between us and said she was only trying to save me from any pain. She went on and on about the pain my father caused her when he died, and even before I guess. She didn't want to see me end up in her position. I get that now. I would do anything to save Jacky from this pain. So yeah, I guess you could say we worked things out."

Jack squeezed her hand and gave her a weak smile. "Lean on her Kate. Let her be your rock. God knows you'll need one."

She sighed as she laid her head back on his shoulder. "I thought that's what you were for."

Jack wiped away the tear trailing down his cheek. Although his heart was breaking, if she wanted him to be her rock, her rock he would be.

There would be no fireworks to enjoy this Independence Day. Jack wondered if he would ever enjoy this holiday again.

Chapter 16

Jacky was a trooper and understood more than Kate gave him credit for. He knew he was very sick and resigned himself to numerous pokes and prods and trips to the hospital. He was, understandably, scared at first, but the doctors and nurses in the pediatric oncology clinic knew how to make their patients feel safe and secure.

Jacky insisted Jack come along for his first treatment. He hadn't seen Jack in weeks and missed him. Jacky was too young to explain his emotions in adult terms, but, in short, he started to look at Jack as a grandfather figure. Jacky never had a grandpa in his life to take him fishing or carry him on his shoulders or tickle him until he wet himself. He never realized how much he envied his friends when they said they were visiting their grandparents, but now that he had Jack, he felt like he had that missing piece.

Kate wasn't sure about the hospital's policy on non-family members being present, but her fears were laid to rest. The nurses said it was up to Jacky who he wanted by his side, so Jack was allowed to stay.

None of the trio knew what to expect that first treatment. Kate had researched as much as she could, but she was still surprised by the seeming simplicity of it all. Jacky sat in a big comfy chair with an IV in his arm. He watched Finding Nemo during the treatment, then he was done. Kate and Jack breathed a huge sigh of relief as they walked out of the hospital. Jacky seemed tired but in good spirits as he turned his face to the sun and let the warmth of summer envelop him.

"Mom?"

"Yes sweetie?"

"I want French fries please."

Kate was so happy to hear him request food, ANY food, she felt a lump rise in her throat. "Sounds good to me too kiddo."

They walked around the corner to McDonalds and ordered their lunches. Jacky played with his new Happy Meal toy quietly as he munched on a couple of fries and sipped his Sprite. Jack and Kate chatted about how easily the first chemo seemed to go and, before anyone knew what was happening, Jacky found himself throwing up his meager lunch. He was so embarrassed he curled up in the corner of the booth and cried. Jack jumped up to get an employee while Kate started wiping up the mess with every napkin she could find. Jack could see she was fighting back tears.

"Kate, do you want me to take Jacky to the men's room to help clean him up?" Jack asked, hoping to allow Kate time to compose herself. He knew she hated crying in front of Jacky.

She nodded. "Thanks Jack." She picked up her son and hugged him tight then handed him over to Jack.

Jacky wrapped his little arms around Jack's neck and wiped his tears and runny nose on Jack's shoulder as they made their way to the men's room. Jack sat him down on the edge of the sink and wet a handful of paper towels with warm water. He tenderly wiped the boy's pale face and hands, making sure to get him as clean as possible. As he washed him down, he assured Jacky he was not in trouble, and he shouldn't be embarrassed.

"You know Jack my boy, when I was a young man, I used to get sick a lot."

"Did you have lutemia too?"

"No, no, I didn't have leukemia. I had a different kind of sickness though and it made me feel sick to my stomach a lot. I remember one day in particular. I used to be a teacher; did I ever tell you that?"

Jacky shook his head.

"I taught big kids in high school. English Literature. The big fancy books you'll read when you grow up." Jack had a fleeting fear that this sweet little boy may never grow up to read Hamlet or To Kill a Mockingbird.

"Anyway, I was in front of my students and I wasn't feeling very well."

"Why didn't you feel good?" Jacky asked.

Jack wasn't quite prepared to answer that. "Well, it's hard to explain kiddo."

Jacky stared at him with admiration and wonder. He didn't want to burst the kid's bubble, but he also didn't want to lie to him.

"I did some things," Jack started slowly. "I made bad decisions sometimes, a long time ago, and those things I did made me sick. It was my own fault."

"Oh." Jacky didn't understand one bit and he was starting to get tired.

Jack continued to wipe Jacky down with fresh paper towels as he went on with his story. "So, I was in front of twenty teenagers and I was talking about a book called the Iliad. Most of my students were bored with the book and my lecture until, all of a sudden, I threw up all over my desk! I was so embarrassed I left the school and didn't come back for three days! So, you see Jacky, everyone has these moments. One of these days, you'll forget all about it."

"But you didn't."

"Didn't what?"

"Didn't forget. You said it was a long time ago and you didn't forget."

Jack didn't know what to say. He gave Jacky a once over, picked him up, and tousled his hair. "You're just too smart for me kiddo."

By the time Jacky was all cleaned up and Jack carried him out to his mom, the small boy was dozing on Jack's shoulder. He slid into the cleaned booth and rocked Jacky in his arms as if he had done it a million times before. He gazed out the window and let tears silently roll down his face. Kate, wanting to spare Jack any embarrassment, turned her gaze from the two of them to the passersby on the street. She contemplated the kindness of this man and the love he showed her son... something his own father couldn't even do, and her heart both broke and swelled at the thought.

Jack wiped his tears and cleared his throat. "I think this little guy needs a good nap in his own bed, don't you think?"

He stood up, handed Kate her son, and walked them to her car in a somber silence. Jacky didn't budge as she strapped him into his car seat. Jack placed his new toy on the child's lap and handed Kate an empty cup. "In case... you know, he needs it on the ride home."

Kate hugged Jack tight and kissed his bearded cheek before driving home.

Jack walked slowly across town collecting his thoughts. He considered karma and how he had spent nearly a quarter of a century assuring he would leave this world with a clean slate. Now he thought it all might be nothing but a bunch of cosmic bullshit. Kate was right. If karma worked the way Jack had assumed, what did poor little Jacky do to deserve this? The longer he walked and the more he thought about it all, the angrier he became. For the first time in more than twenty years, he yearned for the blissful void of a good high. The feeling was short-lived and, once he made it back to his park, he settled for screaming out over the duck pond at the top of his lungs. It didn't help.

Chapter 17

The summer months both dragged and sprinted forward to that strange tempo in which time often dances. Jack was reminded of an old quote by Dr. Suess... *how did it get so late so soon.* The trio stuck to their Wednesday lunch dates as often as possible, depending on how Jacky felt after his treatments. By late August Jacky's little body was acclimating itself to the chemo treatments and, although he often felt tired and his hair was starting to fall out, he was in good spirits. His birthday was fast approaching and, as he told Jack one day over lunch, he was excited to turn five because he would be a whole hand now.

The last Wednesday of August was an uncharacteristically mild day as August in Nebraska was often unbearably hot and muggy. There was a light breeze in the dry air as Jack walked to their meeting place. As always, he arrived early and ordered his breakfast, grabbed their customary table, and smiled to himself as he clutched the plastic bags he brought with him close to his side. He had made a promise to Jacky the previous week and he never broke a promise.

He was roused from his reverie by the sweet sound of Jacky's voice. "Good morning Jack!"

Kate was teaching her son the importance of manners and proper greetings at a young age, something Jack was very impressed with.

"Well good morning to you too Mr. Just Jack!" They both grinned at their long-standing personal joke. Jacky giggled and climbed onto the bench next to him.

"Do you remember what today is? You promised, remember?"

Jack rubbed his beard in a contemplative way. "Hmmm... you might have to remind me. I'm an old man after all." He winked at the boy knowing young Jacky already understood his sense of humor.

Jacky stood up on the seat and tugged at the mop of salt and pepper hair atop Jack's head. "We're getting our hairs cut today, remember?" He ran his tiny hand over his own head and a small clump of hair came out as easily as if it were blowing in the wind. Jacky didn't seem bothered by it and shook his hand nonchalantly away from the table.

"That's right!" Jack exclaimed. "I knew there was something important about today. Maybe that's why I have this bag here."

Kate joined the duo with her tray of food as Jack was passing her son the gift he had bought for him over the weekend. Jack had been finding himself playing loose with his daily allowance lately and he wasn't the least bit concerned. He was, in fact, seriously toying with the idea of living a normal life so he could spend more time with his two favorite people. Many evenings he daydreamed about buying a small, cozy home so he could have his friends over for dinner or even holidays. It was a nice dream, but just a dream, nonetheless. He had no idea what Kate would think of him if, suddenly, he was no longer a bum on the street and she found out he was, in fact, extremely wealthy. He was afraid she would be angry; that she might accuse him of lying; that she might hate him. Jack knew it had to be done, but he was still figuring out the logistics.

The gift he bought for Jacky wasn't anything elaborate or expensive, but it came from the heart. The previous week, at lunch, Kate told Jack that Jacky wanted to go to the barber and shave his head. He was starting to doze on the bench next to her and she was lightly running her fingers through his blonde hair. With every stroke, more hair fell into her hand. Jack could tell it broke her heart, but she understood and respected her young son's wishes. He wanted to do things on his terms... at least the things he could control. Jacky sleepily told Jack he wanted him to come too because, in the child's own honest words, Jack needed a haircut too. The boy wasn't wrong.

Jacky peered into the plastic bag and a huge grin spread across his face. He pulled out a baseball cap with Herbie the Husker embroidered on the front and "Just Jack" stitched in yellow on the back. Jack pulled out the other bag and showed Jacky an identical, but larger hat with "Jack too" sewn on the back. They both put their hats on and grinned over at Kate, who also had the biggest smile on her face. For the first time in weeks, they all felt happy.

After they finished their meal, they took advantage of the nice weather and walked the four blocks to the barber Jack always patronized when he felt as if he were looking too much the part of the grungy hobo. Jacky had never been to a barber as his mom always trimmed his hair and he was so excited he skipped into the shop and plopped down in the first chair before they could even say a word.

Elmer, the barber, was an elderly man and had always enjoyed chatting with Jack on the rare occasions he would visit his shop. He was surprised to see him today with the young boy and his pretty mom as he had never seen Jack with anyone before. Jack pulled him aside briefly and explained the situation. Elmer, showing a brief moment of sympathy, strode up to young Jacky, pumped up the chair which made the boy giggle in delight, and draped him in an apron.

"So there young man, what can I do ya for today?" Elmer asked.

Without a moment's hesitation, Jacky replied in his most adult inflection "take it all off please."

Elmer confirmed with a slight nod toward Kate that this was acceptable and she nodded in affirmation. By the time he was done, Jacky was as bald as a cue ball and kept running his hand over his head in wonder. After getting cleaned up a bit, he put his new hat on his head, shook Elmer's hand and thanked him as politely as any soon-to-be-five-year-old could be.

"Your turn Jack" Jacky exclaimed and pointed to the chair.

Jack sat down, Elmer draped him in the apron and asked the same question. "So there young man, what can I do ya for today?"

Jack looked over at Jacky, now sitting on his mom's lap. "Take it all off please."

"Not the beard!" Jacky exclaimed.

Jack and Elmer laughed heartily.

"The beard stays," Elmer agreed. "I'll just clean it up a bit, is that okay?"

Jacky nodded in agreement and gave him the thumbs up.

Not thirty minutes later, they walked out of the barber shop. Hand in hand, identical haircuts, wearing their matching hats. Anyone on the street would have thought they were family, and that thought made Jack smile.

Jacky was getting tired on the walk back and Jack carried him back to Kate's car for her. They talked about the weather, how good of a barber Elmer was and, briefly, about how the chemo was going. They both thought Jacky was sound asleep until he chimed into the conversation.

"Can Jack come to my birthday mommy?"

His birthday was next week and Kate had planned a small party for him with a couple of the neighbor kids this coming Saturday.

Kate glanced at Jack with a brief look of unease. "I don't know if Jack would like to be bombarded with all of your friends Jacky."

Jack assumed Kate didn't want him there because, well... he was a bum, and that wasn't something a young single mom wanted to explain to her neighbors. In fact, Kate was more concerned with Jack, feeling as if he would be required to buy Jacky a gift and how he would get from Carter Park to her place.

"PLEEEEASE mommy? PLEEEEASE Jack? Please come to my party!" Jacky hugged him tight around the neck and Jack felt tears well in his eyes.

"I'll see what I can do kiddo."

Kate buckled Jacky into his car seat and turned to face Jack. Before she could say anything, Jack spoke up. "Kate, I don't want to infringe on your family time, and I don't want you to have to explain who I am to your friends and family. I'll bring Jacky's gift with me next Wednesday and I'll think of something to tell him, okay?"

Kate looked slightly taken aback. "No, Jack, please don't feel like you need to get him anything. I know you aren't in a position to buy him a toy he doesn't need. He really just wants to spend time with you... and so do I."

It was Jack's turn to be taken by surprise. "I just figured..."

She raised her hand to stop him. "You just figured wrong. You have been more of a friend to Jacky over the last eight months... more of a *family* to us both than his own father has been. We want you there. It will only be three of the neighbor kids and their mom anyway, and I already told them about you, so... it's settled. The party starts at one, I'll pick you up at the park at noon and you can help me set up everything, ok?"

Jack was more than stunned. He was happier than he had been in ages. He also knew, in the short time he had known this young woman, not to argue with her when she had that adamant look on her face.

"Do we have a deal?" Kate asked.

Jack held out his hand. "Deal."

Chapter 18

Kate was good to her word and picked Jack up promptly at noon. He met her at the entrance to the park holding a festively wrapped gift in his hands. He had splurged at the local Walmart and bought himself a new pair of jeans and a simple polo shirt which he sported proudly, and atop his newly shaven head was his Herbie Husker baseball hat. He also bought himself new socks as his had seen better days, in case Kate didn't allow shoes on in her home. That morning he went to the YMCA and used the shower with a new bar of soap and cleaned himself up as good as he possibly could so he appeared as un-homeless as possible.

"I told you; you didn't have to get him anything" Kate admonished.

Jack shrugged. "What's a little boy's birthday party without presents? Besides, it's not all that much really."

To Jack, it wasn't much, but to Kate, his kindness meant the world. She still couldn't quite figure this man out, but she felt at ease with him and knew he meant the world to her son.

On the drive to the quaint mobile home park in which Kate and Jack lived, they discussed Jacky's diagnosis openly as he was at the neighbor's house playing while Kate was preparing for the party.

"So there's no sign of improvement yet?" Jack asked.

Kate shook her head. "No, but the doctors assure me that it's not uncommon for his symptoms to get worse before they get better. He'll be on this round of chemo for another month, then he gets a short break before they look into other options like radiation. I'm not keen on the idea, but whatever gets him better again, right?"

"Right," Jack agreed solemnly as he stared out the window.

They pulled up to Kate's place a short time later and Jack was feeling a mixture of excitement and worry. He was still concerned about how his appearance there might make others uncomfortable and how it would affect Kate, but she quickly remedied his apprehension by taking his arm and leading him up the steps to her home. She was smiling and waved at her neighbors as she did so. Jack was surprised when they smiled and waved back.

The tiny home was immaculately maintained, cozy, and felt like a home filled with love. Jack stood in the entryway and took everything in. The timeworn furniture, the large toy-box overflowing next to the entertainment center, the little wooden dining room table. He could imagine the two sharing over a bowl of spaghetti or ice cream... it was all so simple and picturesque he could feel his heart swell. Kate had decorated the living room with streamers and balloons and a "Happy Birthday" banner strung across the window. She showed Jack the cake she had hidden in the refrigerator. It was brightly decorated with toy dinosaurs and "Happy 5th Birthday Jacky" in bright orange letters. Dinosaurs happen to be his new favorite thing, recently changed from Hot Wheels.

"What do you think?" she asked.

Jack beamed at her. "I think it's perfect!"

Jack helped Kate finish setting out dinosaur printed paper plates and napkins then he hung the dinosaur pinata from the living room ceiling. There was call for an afternoon thunderstorm, so Kate planned ahead for indoor activities as Nebraska thunderstorms could turn ugly very fast. They chatted as they worked and Jack felt happy and at ease, excited to see his little buddy open the gift he bought.

"How many kids did you say were coming?" Jack asked.

"Just three, and their mom. My next-door neighbor has twins who just turned 5 and an almost-4 year old. She's a single mom too and we help each other out when we can. Her name is Jamie. She's a good woman. You'll like her."

Jack nodded. "I only ask because it looks like you bought enough hotdogs to feed a small army!"

Kate laughed heartily. "I guess I did go a bit overboard, but Marcus finally paid all his back child support. Over four thousand dollars! I splurged on the cake and stocked up on some of Jacky's favorite foods. There's not much that agrees with him lately, so we have a lot of mac and cheese, mashed potatoes, and, weirdly enough... hot dogs."

Jack wasn't quite sure what to say so he settled with "I'm glad he's stepping up."

Kate snorted out a derisive laugh. "Yeah... if stepping up is being threatened with jail time unless he paid, sure. He still hasn't seen Jacky since he left. Last I heard his girlfriend was pregnant. He has a new life now, and Jacky isn't in it."

"I'm sorry Kate. Truly I am."

Jack went about setting out the cups and pitcher of cherry Kool-Aid.

"If it's any consolation Kate," he began, "it's his loss."

Kate looked at him with watery eyes, gave him a big hug, and whispered "thank you."

Minutes later the birthday boy arrived with his three friends and their mom in tow.

"I hope we're not too early" Kate's neighbor, Jamie, announced as they walked in.

"Jack!" Jacky yelled and ran into his arms. Jack swung him up into a big bear hug and wished him a happy birthday. Jacky tugged at Jack's hat and pointed to his own on top of his tiny bald head. "We're twins!" he exclaimed, "just like Alex and Avery over there. They're twins too but they're a boy and a girl and we're both boys."

Jack could tell Jacky was already excited for his birthday, he was talking a mile a minute. It made Jack happy to see him more like himself after being so run down lately. He hoped it would last.

The small party went into full swing. The kids ran around and played, Jacky broke the pinata after a few hits by the other kids, they scarfed down hotdogs and potato chips, and made enough noise that Jack thought there was a full kindergarten class in the small home. He hadn't been to a child's birthday party since he *was* a child and, after watching Kate scurry around the house, he had a greater appreciation for everything his own mom did on his special day every year.

They sat down to open presents after they sang "Happy Birthday" and Jacky blew out the candles on his cake. He got a dinosaur play set, several coloring books, and a large box of crayons from his neighbor friends. From his mom he got a remote-controlled dinosaur that roared, new clothes which he tossed aside as most young boys would, and a new backpack for when he started school. Jack worried what Jacky would think of his gift as it was in no way associated with dinosaurs, but when Jacky tore into the small pile of books, he showed genuine excitement.

"Look mommy! New books!" he squealed in delight.

Jack had bought him some of his own favorite childhood books. He realized when he bought them, he was still a teacher at heart. He had found copies of *Where the Wild Things Are, Corduroy, Where the Sidewalk Ends, The Cat in the Hat,* and *Fox in Socks.* Jack had always believed Dr. Suess wrote the best books in which to teach a child to read. What Jack didn't know was that Kate and Jacky read together every night before bed and, when he got sick, they spent more and more time reading as he wore out too quickly to play as much as he used to.

Jacky gave him a huge hug and a big kiss on his cheek. "Thank you Jack!"

"You're very welcome kiddo."

After they ate their birthday cake, Jacky was starting to show just how tired he was becoming. The rest of the guests left and it was just the three of them in the newfound silence. Jacky brought his copy of Corduroy over to Jack, climbed into his lap, and asked him to read the story. Jack started reading about the little teddy bear's adventures when, in no time, Jacky was sound asleep on his lap. Kate was busy cleaning up after the party and Jack felt as if he should help, but he was also content to just hold the boy while he slept.

Once the kitchen was clean of cake and chip crumbs, Kate sat down on the couch next to Jack. "Do you want me to take him? He'll be out for a while and your arm will go numb holding him like that" she joked playfully.

"I suppose I ought to let you put him to bed so I can be on my way."

"Don't be silly, I'll drive you back."

"Kate, he's asleep and you said he will be for a while. The bus stop is two blocks from here and I have a pass."

"Are you sure?" she asked as she picked up her son.

"I'm sure. I'll help you clean up before I go though."

She shook her head. "No need, it's pretty much cleaned up as it is. I just need to take down the decorations but that can wait until tomorrow. Jacky likes the balloons anyway."

"If you're sure..."

She held up one hand, "I'm sure."

Jack stood up then realized just how much of the cherry Kool-Aid he drank. "Could I use your bathroom before I go?"

"Of course." She motioned to the door in the hallway on her way to Jacky's bedroom.

Jack walked down the short hallway and stopped short of the bathroom door. Something caught his eye and he had to backtrack. Surely his eyes were playing tricks on him. There's no way he saw what he thought he saw... but there it was. Among the wall full of photographs was an old photo of a young couple. It had the faded tinge of photographs from the 1980's but it was unmistakable. There, looking back at him, was Claire, and next to Claire was a young, handsome, and clean version of himself. He was looking at his wedding photo.

Chapter 19

Jack excused himself and left Kate's place without using the facilities. The old photo on the wall made him forget his overfull bladder and replaced that urgency with the need to breathe... and to think. He bid Kate a hasty "good-bye," quickly made his way to the bus stop and kept walking. Too many thoughts were racing through his head, and he needed to sort them out. He wanted to get back to his park so he could sit in silence and think things through.

He hadn't seen that picture in almost twenty-five years, just before Claire had left. She took their wedding album with her when she left. They had a small justice of the peace wedding with just a few close friends, but they still dressed the part. Kate had on a frilly white dress she found at a local thrift store. She spent a week cutting and sewing and adding on custom frills to make it her own. When she met Jack at the courthouse, he couldn't help falling in love with her all over again. She was stunningly beautiful; her auburn hair braided to one side, a white lace bow clipped above her ear, and a single sprig of baby's breath peeked out from behind the bow. Jack had rented the finest tuxedo he could afford. He was freshly shaven and his normally shaggy hair was slicked back in a striking pompadour. They were a beautiful couple.

It was clear that Kate was Claire's daughter... why else would she have that picture on her wall? She even resembled Claire, now that he thought of it. But was Kate his as well? He supposed it was possible that Claire had remarried; he had always assumed she had, in fact. But why would Kate hang a picture of her mom and her first husband on her wall? No... that made no sense. And then there was Jacky. He remembered the conversation they had at their first lunch together. Kate had told him Jacky was named after her father, to which Jacky had chimed in stating his grandpa was dead.

His head was reeling, and he felt as if he were going to have a panic attack. He sat on a bus bench nearly a mile from Kate's place, closed his eyes tight and tried to clear his head. The faces of Kate and Jacky kept popping into his mind. They came into his life by pure chance. By the kindness of a little boy, a kindness only a young child could show to a raggedy-looking old man like Jack. He didn't know why, after all these years, karma brought them together. He wasn't about to let them out of his life.

As he was catching his breath, the bus appeared before him. Jack climbed on and took a seat in the back. As he stared out the grimy and graffitied window, he thought about how much he had missed because of his addiction. He had a daughter; he had a grandson; and he couldn't tell them what he knew.

Jack got off the bus three blocks away from Carter Park. He was so lost in thought he had missed his stop. As he trudged toward his makeshift home, he stopped to grab a cup of coffee, knowing it would help clear his head. He made his way to the creaky bench at the edge of the pond, sipped his coffee as he watched a brood of ducklings paddling behind their mother. Jack imagined Claire taking a young Kate to such a pond to feed the ducks and his eyes welled with tears. He closed his eyes and pictured Jacky and Kate in his mind. How could he have missed it? Kate looked like her mother, but she had Jack's eyes and, when she raised her eyebrows, her forehead wrinkled just like his. Jacky not only had his name, but he also had

Jack's eyes and, as he reminisced, he realized Jacky also had his hair, down to the cowlick that stuck up in back, as well as Jack's smile.

He pondered the concept of karma. Was he finally getting something good in his life? If that's what it was, Jack thought, it was pretty shitty karma because he couldn't do anything about it. He was not about to walk up to Kate and say, "Hey, I saw my old wedding picture on your wall and realized I'm your dad... surprise!" He tried to imagine what it would be like for Kate to suddenly find out her supposedly dead father was, in fact, alive. Not only was he alive but he was the bum on the street her son had befriended. He imagined she would either think he was crazy, or was trying to get something from her, or even worse, that he knew all along and had abandoned her. No... he couldn't do that to her. He couldn't say a thing, it wasn't his place; it was Claire's.

He sat and pondered for hours. How would he get Claire to tell Kate the truth? How could he even find her to let her know he knew? *Should* he even try to find her? What would Claire think when she saw him like this? Would she pity him? Would she be disgusted by him? Would she use his position as an excuse to *not* tell Kate? Too many questions with too many possible scenarios were cluttering his mind.

The sun began to set and the pond changed from orange to red to dusky purple. Jack was mentally and emotionally exhausted. He was happy and sad, angry and confused... he felt both broken and whole and he couldn't explain why. He knew he had to talk to someone about it, but he had no real friends other than Kate and Jacky.

As he climbed into the cement tubes to settle in for the night, he assumed he wouldn't get a wink of sleep, but shortly after he nestled into his sleeping bag, he was dead to the world.

Jack awoke with a start. He had only been asleep for an hour but the throbbing in his bladder had plans other than a good night's sleep. He climbed out of the tube to relieve himself at the edge of the playground next to a large pine tree.

"Pine," Jack whispered into the dark. "Dr. Pine."

Jack had not seen Dr. Pine since he finished rehab and hadn't thought about him in ages. He wondered if he was still in the area and practicing. Jack had felt a bond with Dr. Pine and trusted his advice. He made a mental note to look for him in the phone book first thing in the morning.

As he settled in for the second time that night, Jack thought about how many times epiphanies happened at random times... as he was falling asleep, as he walked down the street, even as he relieved himself. He wondered if it was like that for everyone and assumed it was. He tossed and turned with too many thoughts swirling in his head. Jack knew he had to find a way to keep Kate and Jacky in his life and he wanted them to know who he was, but he had to do it just the right way. He needed help.

The last time he asked anyone for any kind of personal help was when he hit rock bottom and called the rehab center. It was funny, he thought, as he finally drifted off to sleep... he was addicted again. He was addicted to those two wonderfully brilliant, sweet, caring people who entered his life so suddenly and, instead of needing help to rid himself of his addiction, he needed help to keep it.

Chapter 20

Dr. Emmett Pine was still practicing in Lincoln but transitioned into private practice. He still helped addicts, but now he worked with his patients in a more long-term situation. After years as the lead counsellor at Valley View, he realized he was only doing so much for his patients in the short term and desired a change.

Jack found him easily enough in the yellow pages and called the office first thing Monday morning from the local library. He gave his name to the receptionist, told her he used to be a patient of Dr. Pine's, and indicated it was urgent he see him. She squeezed him in for an emergency appointment after hours that evening. The good doctor worked with all sorts of addicts, so she was aware of how important it was for them to be seen quickly, especially if they call in a tizzy. When Jack hung up, he realized Dr. Pine might be upset with him as his situation was probably not something the doctor would deem as urgent, but Jack didn't much care. His head had been spinning since Saturday and he physically felt ill after finding out he had a family in which he was denied for so many years. He hadn't felt this way since he was detoxing... it was the closest thing he could think of to describe the pain and unease he felt.

As he waited for his evening appointment, Jack wandered the streets thinking. He pondered every possible scenario he could come up with to get Kate to understand that he did not just abandon her and that he was clearly not dead, as her mother had apparently told her. Would she want a homeless father in her life? Would she want him in Jacky's life anymore? She was already going through so much with her son's illness, the last thing he wanted to do was to add to her stress. No... Jack had to do this carefully, and he had to make plans for his future. For the first time in almost three decades, Jack looked forward instead of back.

On his way to the doctor's office, he stopped by the credit union and spoke with the manager, Bob Harding, who was an old friend. Jack usually only came by the bank once a year, but there were a few things he wanted to discuss with Bob. An hour later he came out feeling more positive about what was to come. It was all part of his plan.

By five in the evening, Jack was sitting across from Dr. Pine in a cozy office barely a mile blocks from his park. It had been over twenty years since they had seen one another, and Jack was surprised to see how much the doctor had aged. He supposed Dr. Pine thought the same about him.

"So, Jack" he started, "you said it was urgent you see me. Are you using again? I haven't seen you in a very long time."

Jack slowly shook his head. "No, I haven't touched a single drug since I left Valley View... I'm not using."

"Ok, so why the urgency?"

Jack went into the story about everything... the money, his donations, how he's been living on the street by choice, how he met Kate and Jacky and that they had befriended each other, and what he recently discovered at Jacky's birthday party. Jack was growing manic as he talked about how he wanted Kate and Jacky to know the truth and how much they meant to him. He also told the doctor about the money and what he had done at the bank earlier that day.

When Jack was done, Dr. Pine looked at him over tented fingers. "You're one hundred percent certain she's your daughter?"

Jack nodded. He was a smart man. He did the math. He came to the conclusion Claire was pregnant when she left him... she was probably afraid he would get even worse if she lost this baby too. He wasn't wrong.

"How do you think she'll react when she finds out who you are?"

"I just don't know doc," Jack sighed. "I ran every possible scenario in my head; good, bad, and indifferent, and I just don't know. All I know is I don't want to lose them."

"You know it's not your place to tell her, right?"

Jack nodded.

"When was the last time you spoke to Claire?"

"The day she brought me that letter in rehab. I haven't seen her since."

"Do you think Claire would be receptive to sitting down with you and Kate to clear the air?"

Jack thought about it. "I just don't know. She could be a very different woman now. She never liked confrontation; I can tell you that. I think, if I try to reach out to her, it might put her defenses up. Right?"

Dr. Pine shrugged. "It's very possible if you give her a heads up as to what you suspect she might become very defensive, but she also might be relieved. It depends on her relationship with her daughter and how she feels about you. At this point, I would recommend against trying to meet up with Claire. It's ultimately your decision but please remember what's important. Your daughter and grandson are in a very fragile place right now. The last thing you want to do is break them."

Jack nodded again. "I never want to hurt them, that's for sure. What do I do?"

"I think you go about your routine as normal... for now at least. Talk to Kate. Ask her questions about her mother, about her childhood, but don't be probing. Just make conversation. Continue to be there for her and her son. Keep your lunch dates, be there when Jacky wants you to be there, help him get well. It's going to take time and patience, but eventually, I believe the right time will present itself. Is that something you can do? Can you be patient and let the pieces fall where they may?"

Jack sighed deeply. He knew the doctor was right. Jacky's health was the most important thing right now and Jack knew it.

"Jack?"

"Yes. I can be patient."

Dr. Pine nodded. He liked Jack from the moment he met him. He was a smart man, an educated man, and essentially a good man. He had no false delusions this man would do the right thing.

Jack stood up and shook the doctor's hand. "Thank you for everything doc. I really appreciate all you've done for me."

"You're a good man Jack. What you're doing here... this penance you've been subjecting yourself to for all these years... I think it's time you stopped. You've paid your dues."

"Have I?"

Jack turned and walked out the door. He would not see Dr. Pine again, but he would take his advice about his family. He was right... Jack's feelings didn't matter now, but when the time came, they would know the truth. Until then, he would focus on getting to know his daughter better and making sure his grandson got the best treatment possible. He would make sure they were comfortable and cared for and loved.

Chapter 21

Jack made a promise to himself to keep his newfound knowledge secret... for the time being, but he realized the longer he kept it from Kate, the more it became a lie. He didn't like the idea of lying to his daughter. He also knew Kate had enough on her plate with Jacky, and he wasn't about to cause her any more stress. Jack did, however, keep to his weekly lunch date and, while it wasn't easy at first, he learned to just enjoy the time he had with them.

In the month following Jacky's birthday, Jack kept busy making plans for his future. He met with his banker and made arrangements for both Kate and Jacky, to which they were as of yet unaware. He found a small furnished apartment halfway between the McDonalds in which they lunched every Wednesday and Kate's home. He was moving in following weekend and was excited to tell Kate the news. He also secured a part time job at the local library stocking shelves. It was the same job he held after his stint in rehab. It was an easy gig, and he never lost his love of books, so there was that bonus. He felt like he could explain his ability to afford an apartment, even a small efficiency such as his, to Kate if he had a job to pay the rent.

Jack sat in his usual seat with his breakfast and a large coffee while he waited for his family to arrive. He loved the thought of having a family. It was such a long time since he had one, the feeling warmed his heart, even if they didn't know. Jack noticed he no longer got uneasy stares from the patrons. Even the manager who used to give him flack had stopped harassing Jack and had resorted to simply ignoring him as he did any other customer. It didn't hurt that Jack had started keeping himself groomed better and his clothes no longer appeared to have been fished from the bottom of the dumpster.

He was sipping his coffee when a very excited-looking Kate sat across from him with Jacky sliding in next to her.

"Good morning" Jack beamed at them. "You look like the cat who ate the canary!"

Jacky giggled at the thought of his mom eating Tweety Bird.

"Oh, it's just a good day is all. Right Jacky?"

"Right!" Jacky grinned from ear to ear.

"Do tell," Jack insisted.

"Well, we had our appointment this morning with the oncologist and he said, based on the last tests, Jacky's numbers are getting better!"

Jack couldn't be more thrilled. "That's wonderful! How are you feeling young master Jack?"

Jacky gave Jack a thoughtful gaze, mouth twisted to one side, his tiny chin cupped in one hand and said in his best Tony the Tiger voice, "I'm GRRREAT!"

They all laughed at his little joke and ate their lunch together among smiles and more laughter. Kate excused herself to the ladies' room and Jacky moved over to sit next to Jack. He had his dinosaur backpack with him and pulled out one of the books Jack gave him for his birthday.

"Jack?" he asked, "can I tell you something?"

"Sure kiddo, what's up?"

Jacky looked ashamed, his eyes darting from the restrooms to the table in front of him. "I don't feel great."

Jack pulled the boy into his lap. "What's wrong?"

"Mommy was so happy at the doctor and he said I should feel better but I'm still tired and I still feel sick in my tummy a lot. I don't want mommy to worry about me Jack. Please make her not worry about me."

Jack hugged his grandson. "Oh Jacky... sweet, sweet boy... your mom will *always* worry about you. It's what all good mommies do. I can't stop that I'm sorry to say. But I'll tell you this... you can *always* tell your mommy the truth and she will *always* take care of you, no matter what. And it's okay that you don't feel great right away kiddo. It's going to take some time for all that yucky stuff to get out of your body but, someday soon, you *will* feel better, and you'll forget what it was like to feel so icky."

"You promise?"

Jack smiled. "I promise."

"Can you read to me please?" Jacky asked and handed him Where the Wild Things Are.

Kate returned to Jack reading to her son, perched upon his lap. She was reminded of just how much children know how to love without prejudice. She hoped Jacky never lost that kindness. She sat across the table and listened to the story, and it brought back memories from her own childhood. There were few things she had from her father, but his collection of books was one thing her mother kept for her. She had an old beat-up copy of this particular book in a box, still in her mother's attic. She noticed years ago that her father had written his name on the cover of every single one of his books and she always enjoyed seeing how his signature evolved from chunky block writing to a beautiful script. She made a mental note to dig out those books the next time she visited her mother. She was sure Jacky would enjoy some of the kids' books and, eventually, work his way up to Harper Lee, Irwin Shaw, and even Stephen King. Her dad had a very eclectic collection of books, and she inherited his love of reading.

"There should be a place where only the things you want to happen, happen" Jack read as Jacky dozed on his lap.

His eyes were beginning to glaze over but he sat up long enough to ask, "where is that?"

"Where is what kiddo?" Jack asked.

"The place where only the things you want to happen, happen."

Jack looked at Kate and she shrugged.

"Well..." Jack started, "I think the only place you can find it+ is in your dreams. Only in your dreams can you be anything you want. You can fly without wings, you can run as fast as a cheetah, you can roar like a T-Rex!"

Jacky giggled and let out a small, tired roar. "Is it a place that you never die?"

Kate suddenly looked concerned. She and Jacky had shared very little conversation about death, but she knew his illness was serious. He saw several other sick kids in the hospital, so she knew he was aware of the concept of death.

Jack just sighed. "Yes Jacky. In dreams you live forever, that's why they're so magical."

His answer must have sufficed because Jacky settled back into his lap and let him finish reading the story.

After story time was over, Kate gathered their things and they all walked out into the late summer sun. Jack realized he never had a chance to tell Kate his news and Jacky was getting tired, so he made it quick.

"Kate, I wanted to show you something."

"What's up?"

He pulled out a small flip phone from his pocket. "I broke down and got one of these blasted things. It's nothing fancy but I thought... well... if you need anything, you have a way to get ahold of me now."

Kate smiled at him, took the phone, and added her number to his contacts... something Jack would not have known how to do on his own, so he was highly grateful.

"There," she said, "now you have my number."

"Great!" Jack smiled at her. "There's something else too."

He proceeded to tell her about the part time job and the efficiency apartment. He was worried she would question his motives or how he came across the job or even why, after all these years, he decided to get his life in order, but she just congratulated him with genuine exuberance and a big hug. They both knew why he was pulling it together and that reason was falling asleep in the back seat of Kate's car.

"I'm happy for you Jack. Truly I am," Kate told him as she climbed behind the wheel and drove her sleepy son home for his afternoon nap.

Jack watched them drive away and wished more than anything Jacky would find his place where only the things he wants to happen, happen.

Chapter 22

Summer turned to fall as Jack settled into his cozy little apartment. Jacky's leukemia officially went into remission shortly before Halloween and all he could talk about was going trick-or-treating and he wanted Jack to come with them. Now that he had his own place and had started getting his life together, they started spending more than just once a week together. They still kept their weekly McDonalds lunch date, but Jack also had Kate and Jacky over to his apartment on a few occasions. Kate insisted on bringing him a housewarming gift. It was some sort of houseplant she insisted anyone could keep alive, which was good because Jack had never owned a plant in his life. She also helped him decorate his place, which came furnished, but had nothing colorful on the walls.

"Jacky made these just for you." Kate was carefully hanging framed paintings and crayon drawings on Halloween morning after she dropped Jacky off at kindergarten.

Most of the pictures were of the three of them holding hands under sloppily drawn rainbows with a playground or a pond in the background. They all had big smiles and Jacky was always in the middle. Kate told Jack she wouldn't be offended if he didn't want a bunch of kids drawings on his walls, but Jack had insisted on covering one whole wall with Jacky's artwork. He would not want to disappoint the boy by not showing off his gifts. And, besides, they made Jack happy.

"Jacky has a great eye," Jack pointed out. "Did he get his artistic ability from you?"

Kate laughed. "Me? No. I can barely draw a stick figure. My mom is a pretty good artist though. He must have gotten it from her."

Kate rarely talked about her mom and Jack respected her privacy, but it still bothered him that she didn't know who he really was, so he cautiously asked her more about Claire.

"Is your mom a painter?" he asked. He had honestly forgotten about Claire's artwork. She used to sketch things in her notebook and Jack was always impressed, but, over the years, he simply forgot.

"No. My mom is actually a financial advisor. She likes to draw though... at least she used to. She was very good at it too. I think she found it therapeutic after my dad died." Kate stared at the pictures she hung on the wall and absentmindedly adjusted them as she spoke. "She didn't talk about him much."

Jack hesitated then pressed a little more. "Did she tell you anything about him?"

Kate sat on the battered but comfortable sofa and sighed deeply. "All I know is that his name was Jack Harper, he was an English teacher who had a love of books. I actually have all of his books. I got them from my mom's attic the last time I was there. She gave them to me years ago, but I didn't have the place to store them. I told her I wanted them to pass down to Jacky now that's he's in school and learning to read. She gave me an old bookshelf of hers, so I had a place to display his books in my bedroom. I've started looking through them again. He wrote his name in every single book he had... did you know that? *Every one.* I have his copy of *Where the Wild Things Are...* Jacky loves that book by the way. I showed him his grandpa's copy and the first thing he did was to get a crayon and write his name in his copy. It's funny how all kids' handwriting is similar isn't it?"

Jack could tell she was lost in thought so he didn't say anything as she spoke, but he remembered his book collection. Claire must have gone back to their house to get them after he went to rehab. He made a mental note to thank her for that someday.

"He was very handsome... I know that much. Jacky has his eyes, I think. I have a few old pictures but they're timeworn and kind of grainy. My mom told me he was very smart... 'too smart for his own good,' she used to say." She paused briefly. "He was sick. She told me he was sick and that's how he died. I asked her a few times what she meant by 'sick' but she wouldn't elaborate. I asked her again recently... you know, because of Jacky's leukemia, because I thought it might be hereditary. All she would tell me is that it wasn't cancer. She loved him very much. I think she still does but she's very closed off about him. I wish she wasn't."

That was the most Jack had ever heard Kate talk about her mom, or her dad. It was on the tip of his tongue to tell her, but he knew it wasn't his place and, quite honestly, he was scared.

"I'm sorry Kate. I really am. If it's any consolation, I have no doubt your father would be very proud of the woman you've become."

Kate smiled and patted Jack's hand. "I guess I'll never know."

She got up to leave and reminded Jack that they would start trick-or-treating at six that night. Jacky was expecting him. Jack promised he would be there with bells on.

After Kate left, Jack made himself a sandwich and sat down with an old copy of The Shining and a home-brewed cup of coffee. He couldn't focus on the words he was reading. His mind kept wandering and something was bothering him, but he couldn't put his finger on it. It wasn't until he read the line 'She had never dreamed there could be so much pain in a life when there was nothing physically wrong. She hurt all the time,' that it hit him. He was so focused on finding a way to get Kate to know who he was, and he let himself become so absorbed in his anger of losing out on his daughter's entire life, he forgot about how much hurt he caused Claire. From what Kate described, it appeared as if she was still hurting. He remembered their miscarriage and how he spiraled out of control. He remembered his affair with his student and his swan dive into his addiction. He vaguely remembered the hazy nights in which he came home to a silent wife and a cold dinner. He was a shitty husband, and he knew it. How could he blame Claire for not wanting him in their child's life? He realized she had her reasons for what she did, and they were valid, but now he wanted to make things right. He just didn't know how.

Jack felt as if he were giving himself an ulcer thinking about it. He decided to take a nap to take his mind off things before he had to get ready for Halloween night with his family. He had to pull it together because he *would not* disappoint Jacky.

He dozed off easily, but his sleep was not restful. He had the mother of all nightmares and the realness of it made him sick to his stomach. He dreamed of Claire. She was sitting in the rocking chair they had in their old would-be nursery. She was holding three blankets in her arms... one yellow, one pink, one blue. She was slowly rocking back and forth, humming a sad, sweet lullaby. Jack approached her. She looked him straight in the eyes and handed him the yellow blanket. He took it with shaky arms, and it turned to dust in his hands. She continued to stare at him with an expressionless gaze and handed him the pink blanket. It was a little girl with his blue eyes and her auburn hair. Jack held baby Kate in his arms and smiled down at her. Claire stood up, took the swaddled baby and handed him the blue blanket. He had a brief glimpse of the baby boy with chubby cheeks and white-blonde hair, but when his bright blue eyes opened, the baby and the blanket turned to dust in his hands as the yellow blanket had. Jack stared at his empty hands; a scream stuck in his throat. He was on the verge of letting out that scream when his alarm blared.

He sat bolt upright in a cold sweat; his heart pounding and he had a painful lump in his throat. Never one for pre-monitions, Jack had a hard time shaking the symbolism of his nightmare. It was all too real. Somehow, he had to forget about it by the time he got to Kate's.

Jack got up, splashed cold water on his face, put on his jacket, and walked to the bus stop in the muted light of dusk. The brisk fall air snapped him out of his daze, and he felt better as the number 9 bus pulled up to the stop. He refused to let down his grandson. They would knock on doors and say 'trick-or-treat' and collect obscene amounts of candy. They would make memories and have a good time. Jack would make sure of it.

Chapter 23

Jack was settling into the normalcy of a real life after living on the streets for so long. He had forgotten about the simple things he used to take advantage of, such as hot running water, reading by lamplight rather than firelight, and the coziness of a warm bed. As it was before his life on the street, he assumed he would shortly begin taking advantage of these luxuries again. As fall left behind Indian summer and entered full-blown early-winter, Jack had already begun to look forward to the warmth of his apartment after being outside for any length of time.

It was just a few days before Thanksgiving and he was making plans at the local shelter to provide and help serve a hearty dinner for Lincoln's most vulnerable citizens. He remembered several years' worth of holiday meals at the shelter and, this year, he planned on being on the other side of the serving line. Jack met with the woman who ran the shelter. She was a jolly woman about his age named Susan. When Jack came in, she barely recognized him. He was clean, his clothes were new, and his beard was neatly trimmed. Jack wrote her a check as a donation for the meal and volunteered his time.

"I'm not much of a cook, I'm afraid," Jack smiled warmly, "but I can serve plates and clean up after. If you need more help, that is."

She was looking at the check in her hand with a stunned expression.

"Susan?"

"Uh, oh, yeah," she was shaken out of her shock at his dona-tion. "Yes, of course! We could always use more volunteers. But Jack... how?"

Jack looked down at his hands clasped between his knees. He didn't like having to explain his situation, especially to someone he hardly knew, but he felt as if she deserved at least part of the truth.

"I inherited some money a while back," he explained. "I just want to do the right thing Susan. I know what these people are going through, and they deserve a good Thanksgiving, don't they?"

"Of course they do." She took Jack's hands in hers. They were timeworn, but soft and warm against his rough hands. "Thank you, Jack. I can't say anything else but, thank you."

Jack nodded, shook her hand, and turned toward the door.

"Be here by 10 am on Thursday!" Susan yelled across the room.

Jack raised his hand in acknowledgement. He would be there.

He wasn't concerned about disappointing Kate or Jacky this Thanksgiving. Kate already told him they would be in Omaha having Thanksgiving with her mom. She was more than apol-ogetic that she couldn't invite him to join them, but since it wasn't her home she felt it wasn't her place to invite a stranger to her mother's house. Jack inwardly chuckled at the term 'stranger' but he kept it to himself. He could just pic-ture Claire's face if he walked into her home carrying a bowl of sweet potato casserole. *That* would be a Thanksgiving to remember. Jack assured her it was perfectly okay because he would be volunteering at the shelter. She promised to bring by leftovers the next day if he wanted some and Jack accepted.

Thursday morning came around and Jack was pleased to see it was a bright, sunny day. Although the wind cut through him like a knife, he was glad of the good weather for Kate to make the drive to Claire's.

While Jack was busy setting tables, serving food, and washing dishes, Kate and Jacky were enjoying some quality time with Claire. Claire's sister, whom she hadn't seen in years, and her husband flew in from Arizona as well. Jacky was doted on by all the adults, but he bored of their attention quickly. He was smart enough to understand the difference between being talked *to* and being talked *with*. He busied himself at the kitchen table with his crayons and drawing tablet. He also brought some of his favorite books and a handful of toy dinosaurs in his backpack. Jacky still tired quickly and the new chemo pill he was on made him queasy if he didn't eat before he took them, but it wasn't as bad as the old chemo treatments. His mommy told him about "remission" and what it meant. He knew he was still sick, but he wasn't getting sicker, which made his mommy happy. Jacky just didn't want to be sick at all anymore.

He was drawing a picture of a big turkey using his hand as a guide. His teacher, Mrs. Paget, showed the class how to do it and Jacky thought it was the neatest thing ever. While he was filling the fingers in with different colors, his grandma Claire sat down beside him.

"What a beautiful turkey!" she exclaimed.

"Thank you," Jacky smiled at her. "My teacher taught me. It's my hand...see?" He placed his hand over the outline he drew.

"Well, isn't that clever" Claire said with a wink. "Can I put that on my refrigerator when you're done?"

"This one is for Jack, but I'll make one for you next."

Claire's heart leapt in her throat. Although her grandson shared the name of her ex-husband, any time she heard someone say Jack's name, she faltered a bit.

"Who's Jack sweetie? Is he a friend from school?" Claire asked.

Jacky giggled at the thought of Jack sitting in the tiny chairs in his kindergarten class. "No grandma," he continued to chuckle. "Jack is too old for school! He's old like you."

Oh, the innocent truth that spills out of the mouths of babes, Claire thought.

"Old like me huh?"

Yeah, but he looks older, I think. Kinda like Santa Claus. Actually," Jack began, "when I was four and just a little kid I thought he *was* Santa when I met him. But I was just a little kid then and he had a big beard then. Now he has a short beard and I'm five now so I know he's not really Santa, he just kinda looked like Santa. Plus, he has happy eyes and a good smile."

Jacky talked about Jack as he colored in his turkey. He told his grandma how they met at McDonalds and how Jack gave him a Happy Meal toy. He told her that he used to live in a park but now he had a new place that Jacky liked much better but they would still go feed the ducks at the park when they came back in the spring. He told her a lot about Jack, but the most important thing Jacky said was "he's my best friend."

Claire kissed her grandson on the top of his head. His blonde hair was beginning to grow back, and it felt like peach fuzz. She wanted to know more about this Jack person, but she was afraid to ask Claire. She was afraid to open Pandora's box.

Dinner was wonderful, as all Thanksgiving meals are. They ate too much, talked a lot, and even laughed a bit. Kate enjoyed spending time with her aunt and uncle, whom she hadn't seen since she was a child. They travelled the world and had lots of interesting stories. They were instantly smitten with Jacky, but, then again, everyone was. He was just one of those kids that people just love.

Kate and Claire cleared the dishes and Jacky fell asleep on the couch.

"Turkey coma," Kate joked as she pointed to her sleeping son. It was what her mom always said after every Thanksgiving... that she was going to slip into a turkey coma from all the food.

"He looks like a little angel Katie-bug."

Kate never liked her mom's pet name for her, but she always let it slide.

Claire noticed a brightly drawn turkey hanging up in her fridge as she was putting leftovers away. 'JACK' was scrawled across the top and 'GRAMA' was written at the bottom.

"He's getting very good at sounding out words."

Kate looked over at the picture Claire was admiring. "He really is. He loves to read books and has started reading simple ones on his own now."

"He gets that from his grandpa," Claire sadly stated.

Kate rarely, if ever, heard her mom talk about her dad, especially unprompted.

"I know he liked to read. Thank you for giving me his books. I really do appreciate it."

Claire turned to her daughter and smiled thinly. "He'd want you to have them."

"Is everything ok mom?"

Claire nodded and busied herself with washing dishes. "Turkey coma," she half-heartedly joked.

She had gotten herself all worked up over a man with the same name as Kate's father. It was a coincidence, she told herself... nothing more. There were a million Jack's in the world and there was no way her Jack would have ever stooped so low to live in a park. He had millions of dollars at his disposal after all. She was certain he was living it up in some fancy house somewhere tropical. That's what she always told herself anyway. He was born with a silver spoon in his mouth and there was no way the Jack she knew and loved would ever give that up. She told herself to forget all about Jacky's 'best friend' and to just get on with her life as she always had. This was no time to bring up Jack. In her mind, there would never be a good time for that discussion.

Chapter 24

More pictures were added to Jack's collection on the wall. Next to the turkey Jacky had made him on Thanksgiving was a drawing of a snowman and a painting of a Christmas tree with piles of brightly colored presents and a bright yellow star on top.

It was nearing Christmas and Jack couldn't remember feeling such anticipation since he was a boy. Kate had invited him to share Christmas with them at her place and Jack had gladly accepted the invite. He already had a couple of presents for Jacky and one for Kate wrapped and placed neatly under the little plastic tree sitting on the end table.

Jack kept himself busy working at the library and volunteering at the shelter when asked. Any time he saw a young child return a book he made a point to ask how they liked it and kept a mental list of books Jacky might enjoy. He became a regular fixture at the library and easily moved from stocking shelves to helping students with research to occasionally taking over story time in the children's library. Once his boss learned of Jack's teaching experience, he was more than willing to let him take on new tasks and he quickly became well-liked among the regular patrons.

Christmas Eve arrived in no time. Jack was helping to close the library early so the employees could spend time with their families. As he walked the few short blocks to his apartment it began to snow. It was his favorite kind of snow too, the big, soft, fluffy flakes that fell so slowly one could follow each flake's descent like a dandelion seed dancing on the breeze. Each flake that touched his face felt like a small, cold kiss on his cheek. He smiled up at the sky, thanking the universe for sending a white Christmas for his family. Their first Christmas together, he thought, should be a white Christmas.

When he got home, he turned on the television and *It's a Wonderful Life* was on. That had always been his favorite movie and, over the past year, he felt he understood George Bailey on a deeper level.

As he sipped his coffee and watched the classic movie, his phone rang. It was Kate.

"Jack... it's Jacky" Kate spoke softly into the phone. She sounded as if she were choking on her words. "We're at St. E's. Please... can you come?"

"Of course Kate, I'm on my way. What happened?"

"He just... collapsed... fainted... I'm not sure exactly. They're running tests. Please come."

"I'm leaving now. I'll be there as soon as I can. It'll be okay Kate. It'll be okay."

Jack never felt so uncertain of anything in his life, but he kept saying to himself on the bus ride to the hospital 'he'll be just fine... just fine... he'll be just fine.'

The ten-minute ride to the hospital felt like an hour. Kate told him what room they were in. They transferred Jacky from the ER to the children's wing once they pulled his file. The doctors and nurses there were great at remembering patients and their family members. They took no notice of Jack as he walked through the halls as he had been seen with Kate and Jacky at numerous chemo treatments and tests. Jacky had always insisted Jack be there. Jacky was awake but groggy when Jack entered the room. Kate was pale and looked scared but was trying to hide it from her son. She was holding his hand and talking about Santa coming for Christmas when she noticed Jack in the doorway.

"Hi Jack" Jacky welcomed him in a small, tired voice.

"Hi kiddo," Jack choked back his feelings. "What happened buddy?"

Jacky started crying. "I don't know!" he wailed. "I got up to go to the bathroom and everything got dark and I woke up in the amblance."

"Shhh... Jacky, it's okay sweetie," Kate soothed her crying son.

"Santa won't come if I'm not at home mommy," he continued to cry. "I want to go home."

"Oh, baby, Santa will come, I promise!" she assured him. "We'll just open presents a little later, that's all."

Jacky sniffled. "Are you sure he'll come?" He looked between his mom and Jack for reassurance.

"I promise," Kate told him.

"Jack?"

Jack approached the bed and knelt down. "I promise you Jacky, Santa would NEVER forget to visit you."

Jacky stopped crying, wiped away his tears, and looked out the window.

"I s'pose you're right," he stated. "He's magic, right?"

"Right," Kate and Jack both whispered.

Jacky dozed off and was snoring lightly, so Kate and Jack moved to the doorway to talk. She never took her eyes off of her sleeping son as she spoke.

"There's no news yet, the tests take time, but his doctor thinks he might be relapsing. He told me this could happen Jack, I just didn't want to believe it. Why is this happening to my son?"

Jack pulled Kate into a tight hug. "I don't know Kate... I really don't know."

He let her cry softly before she composed herself. He was always impressed with her strength and her ability to pull herself out of a dark place quickly. He knew she did it for Jacky, but it was still moving.

"Did they say what the next step was? *If* it's a relapse that is," Jack asked her.

Kate sighed heavily. "He mentioned a lot of things, but I don't think I understood them all. There's more chemo, radiation... they mentioned the possible need for a bone marrow transplant. They're already checking to see if I'm a match."

"What about his father... does he know?"

She snorted derisively. "Marcus? I have no clue where he is. He must have changed his number and I have no idea where he lives now. Good riddance in my opinion. Jacky is better off without him."

"Fair enough. What about Christmas? Jacky was so concerned with Santa not coming. Do you need me to do anything?"

She shook her head. "No, thank you though. I called my mom. She is going to stop by the house and put out all the Santa gifts so they're all there when I take him home. We can't let him lose his Christmas spirit now, can we? He needs to believe in magic as long as possible."

"Yes, he does," Jack agreed. "What about you Kate? Do you need anything? A cup of coffee maybe?"

She smiled at him for the first time that evening. "A coffee would be great."

Jack made his way down to the café on the first floor to get two coffees. He took the long route, needing time to clear his head and ponder life, karma, whatever higher power that would allow this sweet little boy to fall sick on Christmas Eve of all days. He was so lost in thought he didn't even see the woman running toward the elevator as the doors closed between them.

Kate was back at Jacky's side when Jack came in with her drink.

"Any news?" Jack asked hopefully. It had only been fifteen minutes, so he already knew the answer.

"Nothing yet. We probably won't hear anything until to-morrow."

They sipped their coffee in silence, watching little Jacky sleeping peacefully, when the woman Jack had not noticed at the elevator came into the room.

"Katie-bug."

Claire rushed to her daughter and hugged her tightly.

Jack's heart pounded in his chest. This was not the time nor the place for Claire to see him. He slowly stood up and quietly headed for the door.

"Jack, where are you going?" Kate asked.

Jack kept his back to the two women.

"I... umm... thought you could have some alone time with your family. I'll leave you two alone."

"Don't be silly." Kate grabbed his arm and pulled him over to Claire. "Mom, this is Jack. He's a good friend of ours. Jack, this is my mom, Claire."

Chapter 25

Jack held out his hand as he looked into the eyes of the with which he once shared his bed. He felt a hitch in his throat when he said her name. "Claire."

She couldn't hold his gaze and quickly looked at the floor as she briefly shook his hand. "Jack."

The tension was palpable. Even Kate could feel it, but her thoughts were focused on her son as Jacky stirred in his sleep. Claire quickly composed herself and turned away from Jack.

"Katie," she spoke nervously. "I was in such a hurry to get here I left your spare key at home. I came to get yours."

"Oh, yeah, sure. No problem." Kate fumbled in her purse. "You can stay in my room tonight. I'm not leaving Jacky. If you could bring me a few things from home, I'd appreciate it. I made a list. Oh, and can you grab Mr. Bear from Jacky's bed? He'll want him when he wakes up."

"Sure, anything you need sweety." Claire glanced sideways at Jack. "I'll be back in a couple of hours, okay?

Kate nodded. Her eyes never left Jacky. "Sounds good," she whispered.

Claire hugged her again and left the room without acknowledging Jack.

"Kate?" Jack spoke up.

"Hmm?"

"I, uh... I think I'm going to go grab a bite to eat. Can I bring you anything?"

She shook her head. "No, thank you. I'm good."

"If you need anything, just call, okay?"

She just nodded and proceeded to hum a little song Jack couldn't place as she held her son's tiny hand.

Jack left the room and ran down the hall hoping to meet up with Claire. He reached the closing doors in just enough time to slide his way into the elevator next to his very shaken-looking ex-wife. Jack couldn't keep his eyes off her. Claire couldn't look at him.

"Does she know?" Claire whispered.

"No."

She looked him in the eye for the first time. "How long have you known?

"Since Jacky's birthday. Kate has our wedding picture on the wall."

The elevator doors opened on the ground floor and Claire quickly stepped out. Jack kept pace with her to the front door.

"Claire," he grabbed her arm so she would look at him. "Can we talk? Please?"

"I can't. I'm sorry, I need some time."

Jack felt anger rising in him for the first time in a very long time. "Time?" he spat out. "You've had twenty-four years of time. You owe me."

"I *owe* you?" she spat back.

"You owe me an explanation, that's all."

She glared at him in a display of defiance, but even she knew it was false. She *did* owe him an explanation; she just didn't know where to start.

"There's a diner on the corner," Jack pointed out. "I'll buy you a cup of coffee and we can talk. Please?"

Claire agreed. They walked in silence to the little diner that was all but empty on Christmas Eve. They took a booth in the back corner, ordered two coffees, and sat quietly until Claire broke the silence.

"You said you found out at Jacky's birthday party?"

Jack nodded.

"And you didn't have any idea about who they were before that?"

"Why would I?"

Claire eyed his suspiciously. "It just seems funny that out of all the people in the world you would just *happen* to come across your daughter and grandson, become friends with them, and simply *not know*."

Jack took a deep breath. She was deflecting and he knew it. "Claire, think about what you just said. I had no clue she even existed. You never told me you were pregnant. How would I even think I had a long-lost child out there? And more to the point, you told her I was *dead*!"

"Better dead than a drug addict," Claire mumbled.

Her words cut him like a knife. "You really mean that, don't you."

She just shrugged and let her gaze drift to the window.

"I haven't touched anything stronger than an aspirin since I went to rehab Claire."

She still wouldn't look at him, so Jack continued.

"I was a shitty husband. I knew that years ago. You deserved so much better. I was a shitty husband, a horrible friend, and a lousy human being. But I'll never know if I would have been a good father, because you never gave me that chance."

She briefly turned her gaze to him, her mouth opened as if she had something to say, but then she turned back to the window.

"You see that hospital there?" he pointed across the street to St. Elizabeth's. "That's where you had the miscarriage. I've been going there every day for more than twenty years. Every day I walk in and put whatever money I have in my pocket into the donation box. Every day I say a little prayer for our lost child... and for you. Every year, once a year, I make a sizable donation to the children's hospital. I've been paying penance every day since I got clean. I've been living on the street, taking shelter where I could, living off of a small allowance and nothing more. I once told my doctor I felt as if I were lost in perdition and I was tired of being lost, so I atoned the only way that made sense to me. I'm sure it doesn't make sense to anyone else, but that doesn't matter. I left it all behind. You know how I grew up, so yes, it was difficult. I was tempted to buy a house, a nice car, live a good life on several occasions, but I promise you this... I was never tempted to touch a single drug. Not once in more than twenty years."

Claire listened as she watched the snow fall slowly on the bare streets. She was fighting back tears. She wanted nothing more than to leave the diner and walk out into the peace of the snowy evening, but she realized she needed to get this out. She had been holding on to this horrible lie for so long she never realized how much it was eating her up inside.

"What more do I have to do to get my soul right Claire? What do I need to do to prove that I'm worthy to be in their lives?"

"Jack," she started, "I didn't really mean what I said... about dead was better than a drug addict. I was hurt... surprised... you caught me off guard. I had always assumed you took all that money and were living a good life far away from here. I truly hoped that was what you were doing. It was just easier for me to tell her you had died than to tell her the truth."

Claire sighed, sipped her coffee, and told her side of the story.

"Kate was five when she first asked about you. She had just started kindergarten and she saw all the other kids with their dads and she asked why she didn't have a daddy. It just about broke my heart. How do I tell a five year old... she was Jacky's age... how do I tell her that you didn't know she existed because I never told you? How do I explain to a child the horrors of drug abuse and how it ruins lives? How do I tell her I just wanted to keep her sheltered from that pain and disappointment? How Jack? Tell me how you would have done it!"

Jack just shook his head. "I don't know."

He was aware of his actions and just how much pain he caused her, so he tried to be empathetic. He imagined a little Kate asking her mom why she didn't have a daddy and it broke his heart. But he was still angry about the loss of all those years. He understood it, but he didn't like it.

"Claire," he spoke softly, "I can't pretend to know what it was like to raise her alone, to have to answer those questions, but," he sighed deeply, "I think the past is the past. What do we do now?"

"What do you mean?" she asked, a scared expression on her face.

"I think you know I have no intention of abandoning Kate and Jacky. Whether you like it or not, and whether they know it now or not, they are my family. They deserve to know."

Claire shook her head vehemently. "No, Jack... no. You can't tell her. She's in a fragile state right now. Jacky is sick. She's stressed beyond words. You can't dump this on her now. You just can't!"

"Claire," he reached across the table and squeezed her trembling hand. "I have no intention of telling Kate who I am."

Claire exhaled and let her body relax.

"It's not my place to tell her," Jack explained. "It's yours."

Chapter 26

Claire sat in stunned silence for what felt like ages. She always feared this day would come, but she never considered how she would handle it. She knew she had been harsh with Jack but she was caught entirely off guard and her fight or flight response leaned heavily to the fight side. There was a time in which she would have kowtowed to his wishes, but years of finding herself changed her. She was a strong woman; a force to be reckoned with, but she was still a kind woman at heart and she didn't want to hurt her daughter or her beloved grandson. She had to go about this the right way.

"Jack," she started. "You're right. It *is* my responsibility to tell Kate. And I will. I just need some time to find the right way to do it. And it needs to be the right time. She is in no place right now to deal with more stress, I think we can both agree on that point?"

"Agreed."

Claire sighed and sipped at her coffee. She grimaced at the lukewarm temperature and beckoned the waitress over for a refill. She took the time to compose her thoughts. She was a successful financial planner and, after spending years at the bank, she was excellent at negotiation tactics. But this was not the boardroom and Jack was not a client. She still had a hard time looking at him. He was still handsome but his face was weathered from years on the streets. He didn't look like a bum and that somehow bothered her.

"Can I ask you something?"

"Of course."

"You look remarkably clean for someone who lives on the streets." Claire eyed him somewhat suspiciously. She was looking for any indication he might be lying to her. He had done it on so many occasions in the past it used to be second nature to him, but she always saw through his bullshit. "How is that possible?"

Jack explained to her that he had indeed lived on the streets for several years but, after getting to know Kate and Jacky, specifically once he figured out who they were, he decided to get his life back in order.

"I have a small apartment, I bought new clothes, I even have a job at the library," explained. "I'm there whenever they need me, Claire. They are my priority."

For the first time since they were reintroduced, Claire willingly touched him. It was brief, but that small grasp of his hand was enough for Jack. He knew she didn't hate him after all these years, as much as she had every reason to.

"I'm glad you got it together Jack, really I am." She was still stalling, trying to figure out what to do next. "Jacky clearly adores you. He talked about you over Thanksgiving but I didn't put two and two together very well, did I."

"How could you have? It's not like 'Jack' is an uncommon name."

"Still," she said. "I did have a moment of panic, but it passed quickly. To be honest, any time I hear your name, I feel it."

"I'm sorry Claire. I don't know how else to say it, but I'm sorry."

She sipped her freshened coffee. "I'm sorry too."

"So, you'll tell her?" Jack asked.

Claire sighed deeply. There was no way around it.

"I'll tell her. I need time to figure out how and when, but I'll tell her."

It was Jack's turn to eye her suspiciously. He didn't want to say what was on his mind because the thought was just so horribly unpleasant, but he couldn't think of any other way to explain his need for Kate and Jacky to know.

"Jacky's really sick," he stated.

"Yes, he is," Claire agreed.

"I'm his grandpa."

"Yes, you are."

Jack sighed deeply. "I need him to know who I am Claire. I don't want him to... it wouldn't be fair to him to never know..." Jack just couldn't voice his fear that Jacky wouldn't live long enough to get to call Jack 'grandpa.' That fear left a lump in his throat and the tears welled in his eyes. He quickly wiped them away and swallowed the painful lump.

Claire was also tearing up at the thought of her sweet grandson never growing up to have a family of his own.

"I'll do it, Jack. I promise."

Jack nodded and looked away into the darkening night of Christmas Eve. He left a twenty on the table and got up to leave.

"Merry Christmas, Claire." He didn't meet her eyes. He didn't want to say or do anything to ruin the agreement they had come to.

"Merry Christmas, Jack" she whispered as he walked away.

The snow had stopped falling and the sidewalks were covered with a clean blanket of white. Very little foot traffic on this holiday eve had left the snow as pristine and magical as a white Christmas should be. The city was quiet and calm. Jack would normally have felt at peace in the silent serenity of the winter night, but his mind was running wild with thoughts and his heart was filled with too many emotions to handle. He walked to clear his mind, as he often did. He passed the hospital and looked up into the warm glow of the windows. He imagined Kate reading a story to Jacky as she held him tight. His heart broke and, with it, the flood of tears broke through the dam and streamed down his cheeks. Jack was never much of a crier. He was a tough guy... sentimental, but tough. Having a family changed him. He had walked several blocks in the direction of Carter Park before he remembered he had a home to go to.

'Home' he thought. It was such a nice word. Highly under-rated and often taken for granted, but to Jack, it was now one of the best words he knew. He headed home on the number nine bus, entered his warm, cozy apartment, and climbed into his soft bed. He fell asleep to the thought of Claire. He hoped she kept her word. He hoped she kept it, and soon.

Chapter 27

Christmas came and went. New Year's Day was just around the corner. Jacky was still in the hospital and Kate rarely left his side. The day Claire went back to Omaha, Jack showed up at the hospital with his small pile of Christmas gifts for the two of them. Jacky delighted in his new box of crayons and the biggest pad of drawing paper he had ever seen. Jack also got him more books to add to his collection including *The Giving Tree, Charlie and the Chocolate Factory, Green Eggs and Ham* and *Oh, The Places You'll Go*. That was also the day Kate found out that, while she was a marrow match, she was not eligible to donate.

"They say I'm severely anemic," Kate explained over lunch in the cafeteria. Jacky was off having more tests, so she and Jack took the time to grab a quick bite. He could see Kate was looking pale and had lost weight from her already thin frame.

"You need to take care of yourself Kate. Not just for you, but for Jacky too."

"I know, it's just not the first thing on my mind, ya know?"

"So, what's the next step?" Jack asked.

"Jacky goes on the marrow donor list, and they search for a match. I have to fill out some paperwork to get him on the list, but they said it could take months to find a match... if ever. In the meantime, he's back on chemo. If they *do* find a match, he has to go through intense radiation. It's meant to kill off all his own marrow so the donor marrow can take over. Once he starts the radiation, he'll be in a sterile room for, I think they said a week before the procedure, then we wait and see. Apparently it takes time. It'll either work and he goes into remission, or his body rejects it and he's... well, it's not good. With no marrow, any little germ can... kill him," she choked out.

Jack held her hand and gave her a comforting squeeze. "Kate, that's not going to happen, okay? I promise you Jacky will beat this. He's a fighter... like his mom."

They finished their lunch in relative silence. Jack stood up and started cleaning their trays when Kate broke the quiet.

"Jack?"

"Yeah?"

"Why are you doing this?"

Jack looked down at the trays of food. "Because it's the polite thing to do?" He looked at her quizzically.

"No, not the dishes. Why are you so kind to us? Why do you come here almost every day to see Jacky? Why are you here for me?"

Jack sat back down, not knowing exactly how to explain it to her without breaking his promise to Claire.

"Do you remember the day we met Kate?"

"I do. Jacky insisted on giving you his Happy Meal."

Jack nodded and smiled at the memory.

"You and Jacky were kind to me in a world which doesn't often show compassion to people like me."

Kate sighed and looked down at the table. "That was all Jacky. To be honest, I didn't want him to talk to you. I was afraid... protective... and wrong. I hope you understand that, Jack. It wasn't my idea; it was all Jacky's."

Jack nodded in understanding. "Kids are innocent Kate. Innocent and pure and honest, so that's what they see in the world. Jacky saw a lonely old man in need of a friend where you, and everyone else, saw a homeless old man in need of a shower and a shave. I will forever be in his debt, *and yours* for trusting the instincts of your son. I don't know if I can ever fully repay your kindness, but I'll spend my days trying to do so. I hope that answers your question."

Kate smiled weakly, nodded, and squeezed his hand. She wiped her tears and they headed back to Jacky's room. On the way there, Jack spotted the oncologist in charge of Jacky's care.

"I'll be right there Kate. I need to make a pit stop."

Kate continued down the hall while Jack grabbed the doctor's attention and introduced himself.

"Dr. Hamlin? My name is Jack Harper. Can I have a moment of your time please? I promise, it won't take long."

Dr. Hamlin was a tall, bespectacled, handsome man around Jack's age. He spoke softly and his eyes were the kindest Jack had ever seen. His presence was comforting and he seemed like a man who truly wanted to make a difference.

"Yes, I've seen you around here," the good doctor shook Jack's hand warmly. "How can I help you?"

"I was wondering about bone marrow donation. Specifically, how can I get tested to see if I'm an eligible donor."

Dr. Hamlin looked Jack over. "How old are you?" he asked.

"Fifty-one."

The doctor sighed slightly. "We generally like donors to be under forty but sixty is the allowable limit. Bone marrow begins to degrade over time so we want the healthiest sample possible. Of course, there are other factors such as general health. Do you have high blood pressure, high cholesterol, STD's, any autoimmune diseases, drug use?"

"Full disclosure," Jack admitted, "I was an addict many years ago, but I've been clean for almost twenty-five years. You can run whatever tests you need. I just need to do this. Please."

"Our marrow is constantly regenerating, it's part of what keeps us healthy. Any substances you took that long ago should have no bearing on your ability to donate now, but I must warn you, if there is even a hint of illicit substance detected, you're automatically ineligible."

"I'm clean doc. Promise."

Hamlin pulled Jack aside. "I can see this is important to you. Can I ask why?"

Jack was impressed with the care this man had been giving Jacky and, he could tell he cared for his patients. It would be an insult, and possibly detrimental to Jacky's health, to lie to him.

"I'm Jacky's grandfather."

The doctor looked him over again carefully then wrote something down on a notepad and handed it to Jack. "The lab is on the third floor. Take this to them. They'll run all the tests needed."

"Thank you," Jack shook his hand firmly. "Thank you so much!"

"Mr. Harper?" the doctor called to him as he walked away. "We always prefer donations from direct family members. There's a better chance of acceptance from the recipient. I really hope you're a match. Good luck."

"Thanks doc. Oh, and please don't say anything to Kate." Jack didn't know how tell this kind man that Kate didn't know who he really was, so he just said "I don't want her to get her hopes up too soon."

Hamlin nodded in understanding then turned to make his rounds.

Jack made his way down to the third floor and subjected himself to multiple blood draws, blood pressure monitoring, cheek swabs, breathing tests, and even more blood draws. As far as he was concerned, they could take every last drop if it would help Jacky.

"How long will it take to get the results?" he asked a pretty young technician.

"Some of these test results will be ready later today but others can take up to two weeks. You're looking to donate marrow, is that right?"

"That's right. I'm hoping to find out sooner rather than later."

"I understand. Unfortunately it's not a quick process unless any of these tests come back disqualifying you from donation. We just need to wait and see and hope for the best. What you're doing is a good thing, Mr. Harper. I wish more people would register."

Jack rolled down his sleeve and left the lab after bidding the technicians a good day. He would just have to be patient and hope for the best, like the young girl said, but it would be hard.

Chapter 28

The new year came in without any fanfare or celebration other than the fact that Jacky came home from the hospital. He continued his chemo on a regular basis and Kate tried her best to stay strong for her son. His little body didn't handle it as well as it did the first time around. He was always tired, but he kept in good spirits, especially when Jack came around to visit. Kate had to pull him out of school to keep him away from the plethora of germs that plagued every elementary school in the winter. She knew, when the time came and a donor was found, Jacky had to be as healthy as possible. Jack made regular visits to read to Jacky and to give Kate a break from time to time. He made sure to always call first as he didn't want to overstep his bounds. Claire had still not confided in Kate about who Jack was and, although Jack was losing his patience, he remembered his promise to let Claire handle it.

It had been almost a month since Jack was tested for everything under the sun and, while most of his bloodwork came back stating he was healthy as a horse, the important one, the one that would tell him if he was a match, was still out there. Jack was becoming increasingly impatient, but he kept his feelings at bay as he walked into the cozy little trailer Kate and Jacky shared.

Jacky was sitting on the couch watching an animated movie with characters Jack vaguely recognized. Jack sat down next to the boy and, without thinking, Jacky curled up in Jack's lap and popped his thumb into his mouth. Jacky had taken to sucking his thumb after the incident over Christmas, a habit Kate had told him, Jacky had broken when he was two.

"What are you watching kiddo?"

"Ice Age," he mumbled around his thumb.

Jacky crawled across the couch and pulled out from under a blanket, the McDonald's toys he got when Jack first met him.

"See? There's Manny and Sid and Diego. They're bestest friends."

"I see that," Jack agreed.

Kate was tidying up the house and sat down across from them with a basket of laundry.

"Anything I can help with?" Jack asked.

"You already are," Kate smiled.

It was a rare warm January day. It was nearing fifty degrees out, the sun was shining, and the icicles were melting in flowing rivulets rather than drips. Kate had the curtains open to let the sunlight in and it fell on his skin like a warm blanket. Jacky was dozing in the sunlight when Jack's phone rang. He carefully lifted Jacky off his lap, laid him on the couch and covered him with a blanket before excusing himself.

"Mr. Harper?" a man's voice asked at the other end.

Jack stepped outside and sat on the creaky wooden step to Kate's makeshift deck.

"Speaking."

"This is Dr. Hamlin, from St. Elizabeth's. How are you today?"

Jack's heart leapt to his throat. "You tell me doc."

The doctor laughed heartily. "That's fair I suppose. I'm sorry for the wait, truly, but we had to run every test to make sure. With your age and all, we really had to do our due diligence. I'm happy to tell you that you're an excellent candidate for marrow donation for your grandson."

Jack lowered his head. He began to laugh and cry simultaneously.

"Mr. Harper? Are you there?"

Jack sniffled and wiped his eyes. "Yes, I'm here" he choked back more tears. "That's excellent news! Just excellent!"

"Yes, yes it is" the doctor agreed. Jack could tell by his voice he was smiling. "I'm going to need you to come in for some paperwork and we need to do regular testing before we can continue with the donation. I'll explain it all to you when you come in. Does tomorrow at noon work for you?"

"Absolutely! I'll be there any time you say doc. And thanks again!"

"Thank *you*, Mr. Harper! You have a very lucky grandson there."

Jack hung up the phone and fought with all his might to keep from yelling out to the heavens. He settled for a "thank you God" under his breath. He took a few minutes to compose himself before walking back into the house.

"Everything okay?" Kate asked. She was sitting next to Jacky, who was sound asleep, and reading a beat-up old copy of Stephen King's *It*. Jack recognized it as one of his own. He could tell by the dog-eared pages and the bent spine. He was an avid reader, but he was always rough on his books, especially the ones he really liked, and he was always partial to King's works.

"Everything is great," Jack smiled at her. "Stephen King fan?"

"Oh yeah," she smiled back at him. "I read *Carrie* when I was twelve, to the horror of my mother, but I was hooked ever since."

"That one there," Jack pointed to the book, "that was always one of my favorites. The kids were so strong. They saw what needed to be done and they did it, adults be damned."

Kate laughed at his description. "Kids are a lot smarter and stronger than most people give them credit for." She was absentmindedly stroking the peach fuzz on Jacky's head as she spoke. "This little guy, for example. He knows exactly what's going on at all times, he just doesn't have the vocabulary yet to say what he really wants to say."

"He'll get there," Jack assured.

"You know what?" she asked. "I think you're right."

They made more small talk about their favorite books and authors before Jacky woke up, ran to the bathroom, and got sick. Kate followed behind and did her best to soothe her crying son. Jack was becoming an old hat at helping when Jacky felt sick. While Kate was cleaning him up, Jack got out a bottle of orange Gatorade and poured it into Jacky's favorite dinosaur cup. He set the drink on the coffee table next to a stack of saltines and a small cup of applesauce. It was the current snack of choice after chemo made him sick. Jack knew his grandson well.

Kate carried Jacky back to the couch where he sat between the two adults whom he loved more than anything in the world. He sipped his drink and took small bites of his snack before he fell asleep again on Kate's lap.

Jack excused himself quietly. He had a few errands to run before his appointment with Dr. Hamlin the next day. He wanted to make sure, no matter what happened, his family was taken care of. Just as young Jacky felt, Jack loved the two of them more than anything in the world.

Chapter 29

Jack met with Dr. Hamlin the next day. Jack filled out a mountain of paperwork while the doctor discussed the prep time, the actual procedure and the risks involved to both him and Jacky. From what Jack gathered, there was very little medical risk on his end, but, if he were being honest, he would have done it regardless of the risks. The doctor told him to expect joint and muscle pain in his hip for a few days or weeks after the procedure and he might feel tired for a short time. Nothing Jack couldn't handle. After sleeping in a cement tube for years, he was used to joint pain.

"We will have to do regular tests over the next seven to ten days to make sure you don't come down with any virus or bacterial infection before we retrieve your marrow" Hamlin explained. "I'm afraid that means making daily trips here for blood tests."

Jack considered his situation and was concerned he might inadvertently pick up a cold or flu in the meantime.

"I live alone, and I can take time off work to avoid contact with people, but I take a bus here and, well... there's a lot of people crammed into those buses. I could pick up a cold pretty easily, couldn't I?"

"True, there is always a risk, but the bloodwork is necessary."

"I understand that," Jack agreed. "I just can't risk any chance that this won't work."

Jack sat back and thought about his options.

"How long will Jacky have to be here before the transplant?" Jack asked.

"A week. He will have to undergo intense chemo and radiation to kill off all his existing marrow so yours can take its place. Once we extract your marrow and it's deemed healthy, he'll start his treatments and stay in a sterile room so he doesn't get sick. No marrow essentially means no immunities. He will be very high risk during that time. We prep your marrow and store it until he's ready to receive it. After that... well, it's a waiting game. But I have high hopes that this will work Jack. I'm not just being reassuring here. I've seen many excellent results from these procedures, especially in children."

"So would you agree that the best chance for me to stay healthy during this time would be to be admitted here?"

Dr. Hamlin gave him a concerning look. "Well, yes, in theory. But Jack, there is no insurance plan I have ever seen that would cover a patient-requested hospital stay. It's just not possible."

"What if I paid for it out of pocket?" Jack knew he was sounding crazy. He could see it in the doctor's eyes. But if it would better Jacky's odds, he would do it. It's not like he didn't have the money after all.

"That," the doctor explained carefully, "would be *very* expensive."

"I'm aware." Jack stated firmly.

"Mr. Harper."

"Jack, please."

"Okay, Jack. I don't mean to offend, but I've watched you come in here with Kate and Jacky for months now and, while it's none of my business, you don't strike me as a man who can foot the bill for a voluntary hospital stay."

Jack smiled at the man's honesty.

"Do you know Lauren Temple?" Jack asked.

The doctor thought for a moment. "The billing manager? *That* Lauren Temple?"

"That's the one. Can you please call her?"

Hamlin hesitantly picked up the phone and dialed billing.

"May I?" Jack asked, his hand held out for the receiver.

The doctor handed Jack the phone, confused yet intrigued by the situation.

"Ms. Temple? It's Jack Harper. We met a few months ago... yes, *that* Jack. I'm here with Dr. Hamlin in pediatric oncology and we're trying to make something work and I thought you might be able to help. Can I put him on to explain? Thank you... yes, it was good talking to you too!"

Jack handed the receiver to the doctor and let him explain Jack's proposition and the upcoming procedure. It took less than two minutes for Lauren to explain that Jack was good for the bill. Based on the doctor's expression, Jack was under the impression that she had mentioned the large donations Jack had given the children's hospital over the years. Hamlin hung up the phone and looked at Jack as if he were a different man. Jack supposed, in a way, he was. He wasn't just a concerned grandfather; he was a very *wealthy* concerned grandfather, and now the doctor knew it.

"Umm, can you be here tomorrow morning Mr. Harper?"

"Jack, please."

"I'm sorry, yes, Jack."

"Tomorrow morning will be just fine," Jack agreed.

"Good... great... I'll make sure everything is taken care of."

"Thank you for your time doc. I appreciate everything you do. Not just for Jacky, but for all these kids."

Jack turned to leave the office.

"Mr. Harp... sorry... Jack," Hamlin was coming around his desk to meet Jack at the door. "Thank you for everything *you've* done! Truly. You're a good man and it's a pleasure to have met you."

Jack shook the good doctor's hand and left his office feeling better than he had in quite some time.

On his way home, Jack pondered the irrationality of human interactions. He was surprised and somewhat disheartened with the power money holds over peoples' perceptions of others. Any time he had used his wealth for good and was open about it, he was met with open arms, hearty handshakes, and sincere kindness. On the other hand, when he was looked at as just another bum on the street, no one gave him a second glance; and if they did, it was one of disgust or pity.

As he sat in the back of the bus on the ride home, Jack found himself people watching again. It was always one of his favorite pastimes. He watched a businessman in his fancy suit and luxury overcoat pass by a working man in a flannel work shirt and well-worn industrial coat. He watched a young mother pushing a stroller hurriedly past an elderly woman with a walker struggling to avoid the puddles of winter slush. He saw a homeless man... ageless, weary, and hopeless, hop up to help the elderly woman across a particularly sloppy section of the street. The woman accepted his kindness and didn't even notice when the man slipped her wallet out of her purse as he crossed back to the other side of the street. It's no wonder the general population saw the homeless as an infestation if this man was representative of the whole.

Jack was disgusted with the man's actions and got off several stops early. He walked briskly to the alley where he last saw the man enter. The homeless man was sitting behind a dumpster going through the old woman's wallet. He pocketed the cash and tossed the wallet into the dumpster without noticing he had company.

"I don't think that belongs to you," Jack stated.

He towered over the filthy man who was still crouched down behind the dumpster.

"The fuck," the man slurred. "Who you think you are?"

He sounded drunk but Jack saw him moments ago hop up to 'help' the lady cross the street, so he had to assume it was an act. He had seen men like this on the street for years. They took what they could from anyone they could, and they didn't care a whit about anyone but themselves.

"You heard me," Jack continued. "I saw you take that wallet from the lady you helped cross the street. It doesn't belong to you. I suggest you give it back."

The man stood up and, although he was still ageless to Jack, he was clearly younger and bigger than Jack had first thought. He was also fast on his feet. He lunged at Jack and pushed him hard before he sprinted down the alley. Jack stumbled briefly; he wasn't prepared for the shove, but he quickly regained his footing and followed him as fast as he could go.

While the homeless man was initially fast, he had little stamina, Jack caught up with him less than half a block away. He grabbed the man, spun him around, and slammed him up against the brick wall. Anger seared through Jack's body. He had spent so many years on the street doing what he thought was right in the name of karma. He had never stolen a thing in his life, even when he was living on stale coffee and the crackers he left in his pocket for the ducks. He wanted to hit the man, knock some sense into him, but then he thought of Jacky and the kindness a little boy showed him one cold winter day, and his heart softened.

Jack loosened his grip on the man but didn't let go completely. He was hoping to talk to him. To show him there was a better way.

"Have you ever heard of karma?" Jack asked.

The homeless man's body was shaking, his eyes darted in every direction trying to find a way out of this man's grasp.

Jack shook him sharply. "I asked you a question. Have you ever heard of karma?"

The man's body loosened as he turned his head slowly toward Jack and met his gaze.

"Yeah, I have," the man stated through gritted teeth. "I heard she was a bitch."

Jack had no time to notice the stiletto the man palmed as Jack was shaking him. He slid it quickly into Jack's stomach and ran away before Jack realized what had happened.

Chapter 30

While Jack was people-watching on the bus, Dr. Hamlin was making a phone call to Kate; a call he was very excited to make. Many doctors leave the clerical work to their nurses or office personnel, but Hamlin liked to be the one to give his patients any important news, good or bad. His bedside manner was always a selling point when parents were looking for the right physician for their children. His success rate with cancer patients was excellent, but his personality and rapport with the children made him extraordinary. He could have worked at any number of top-notch hospitals and was even approached by Children's Hospital of Philadelphia and St. Jude's, but Lincoln was his home and he intended to stay.

"Hello, Ms. Bennett?"

"Speaking," Kate said.

"It's Dr. Hamlin. How are you and young master Jack doing today?"

"We're actually having a good day today! Jacky is feeling pretty good."

"That's great! I'm calling because I have some very good news to share with you. I won't drag it out. We found a match for Jacky!"

Kate sank slowly into the recliner and stared at her son. He was sitting at his little table coloring a new picture filled with dinosaurs and puffy clouds while one of his favorite movies played in the background. She was too stunned for words.

"Kate?" the doctor asked. "Are you still there?"

"Oh, uh... yeah. I'm still here," she assured him in little more than a whisper. "How?"

"Pardon?"

Kate asked again. "How is that possible? I thought you said it could take months... if ever. How did you find someone so fast?"

"Oh, well, I can go over everything when you come in to sign some forms. We need to go over the game plan for Jacky and figure out the timeline to get him admitted and prepped. Can you come in today? I know it's short notice, I apologize, but the sooner we get started, the better."

"Of course! We'll be there within the hour."

"Great! I'll have everything ready. And Kate?"

"Yes?"

"Congratulations."

Kate smiled to herself. "Thank you."

She bundled Jacky up warmly, packed snacks, drinks, toys, and books in his backpack to keep him busy and drove to the hospital in record time. For the first time in almost a year, she started to imagine her son all grown up, healthy, happy, with a family of his own. It was a nice thought that warmed her heart.

As Kate and Jacky made their way up to Dr. Hamlin's office, an ambulance pulled up to the emergency room entrance, lights and sirens blaring. The paramedics wheeled in a gurney and were quickly joined by more ER staff. Jack was conscious and aware of everything going on around him. The knife the homeless man used on him was still protruding from his abdomen but he couldn't tell how deep it penetrated as it was wrapped in white gauze stained red from his blood.

"Fifty-one year old male, states his name is Jack Harper, single stab wound to the abdomen, weapon remains intact, vitals are good..." the paramedic spouted off all the pertinent information to the doctor and nurses as they wheeled him down the hall.

As fate would have it, at the same time Jack was being wheeled to a triage room, Lauren Temple was leaving another room with a young protégé in tow. Lauren was a stickler for perfection so, when she hired a new intake officer for the billing office, she always made sure to train them herself. At the time, she was teaching the new girl how to input insurance information into the system. They were just leaving a room with a rather cantankerous old woman suffering from back pain when Lauren heard Jack's name.

"Stay here," she told the young girl.

Lauren followed the paramedics into the triage room just long enough to see Jack's face and the knife sticking out of his stomach.

"Umm, you go back to the office and input the patient's billing information. I'll be up in a bit."

Lauren made her way to the pediatric oncology floor and headed straight to Dr. Hamlin's office. She knew from their conversation earlier that day that Jack was vital to the well-being of one of his patients so she thought he should be made aware of the situation immediately.

She knocked on his door and, before she got a reply, she let herself in.

"Excuse me Dr. Hamlin, I'm sorry to interrupt, but this is a rather urgent matter."

Hamlin was sitting across from Kate. They had barely started their meeting and she was reviewing a stack of pamphlets while Jacky sat in the chair next to her attempting to read a colorful Dr. Seuss book. He sighed, excused himself from his office and joined Lauren in the hall, closing the door behind him.

"Ms. Temple, this is highly..." he started.

"Mr. Harper is in the ER," she blurted out.

"What? Are you sure?"

Lauren told him how she heard his name and checked to make sure it was the same Jack Harper.

"He was stabbed."

Hamlin looked at Lauren in horror. "Jesus," he whispered into his hand. "Do we know the extent of his injuries yet?"

She shook her head. "He was alert and responsive. He was in triage 2 when I left."

"Thank you for letting me know."

As he turned to go back into his office, another thought struck him.

"Lauren? One more thing." He motioned toward his door. "Does Kate know?"

"Who?"

"Kate Bennett. Her son is the marrow recipient. Jack is her father. Has anyone told her?"

Lauren shook her head slowly. "Not that I'm aware of."

"Okay, thanks. I'll handle it."

He went back into his office while Lauren returned to her own on shaky legs. She said a little prayer in the elevator. Devoutly Catholic, she was a firm believer in the power of prayer.

"I'm sorry about that," Hamlin apologized to Kate. He wasn't quite sure how to proceed. He had to make sure Jack was not in any serious condition but he also had to make sure Kate's spirits weren't crushed. "Would you mind waiting in the play-room for a while? I have a bit of an emergency I need to take care of. I'm afraid it can't wait."

Kate would normally have been frustrated, but the news of Jacky's donor still had her in a good mood. She agreed and took Jacky to wait in the brightly colored playroom where she continued to read over the information the doctor had given her.

Hamlin made his way down to triage. Jack wasn't there.

"Excuse me, nurse?" Hamlin grabbed the first person who walked his way. "Where did they take Mr. Harper?"

"Who?"

"The stab wound. Where did they take him?"

The young nurse went to the station and pulled up Jack's file. "He's in OR 3."

Before she could say another work, Hamlin was gone. He quickly made his way to the operating room, put on a gown and a mask, and entered the theater. The doctor working on Jack was an old friend of Hamlin's. Jack was in good hands.

"Paul," Hamlin greeted.

The doctor who was caring for Jack looked up from his work, surprised to see Hamlin standing across the table from him. "Ethan? What are you doing down here?"

"How is he?" Hamlin motioned to Jack.

"I think he'll be just fine," the doctor assured as he checked for any damage to Jack's vital organs. "From what I can see so far, the knife didn't go in too far. It missed the liver and the colon. There's a small nick on the gall bladder but no puncture wound. From what I hear, he was stabbed in an alley, made his way to the main road, and was found by a group of college students. They said Jack tried to pull the knife out himself, but one of them was smart enough to keep the blade in while another one called for the ambulance. He didn't lose much blood. He'll need high-dose antibiotics for a while... God only knows what was on that knife. But I don't see anything that's life threatening. Why the urgency? Is he a friend of yours?"

Hamlin exhaled deeply and shook his head. "No, not a friend. But he is a good man. He's donating marrow to his grandson... one of my patients... he's five years old. I have the mother upstairs now, I brought her in to sign the forms and make a game plan for her son. Are you sure he's going to be okay? Antibiotics I can work with, I can't have him going septic or catching anything viral."

"Like I said, Ethan. I don't see anything here that is life threatening. I can have the lab test the knife for any possible contaminants before the police take possession. That's about all I can do."

"Thanks Paul. I appreciate it. Oh, and can you make sure he's in a private room, preferably on four. Once you're done with him, he's my patient, okay?"

"You got it."

Hamlin left the OR feeling better, but now he had another hurdle to cross. He just had to hope that Jack didn't get an infection and that there was nothing on that knife that could hinder Jacky's chances. Now he had to find a way to tell Kate that her father had been stabbed and explain how that would affect everything else. He thought to himself how nice life would be if everything would just go as planned, but it rarely did. As he entered the elevator he said a little prayer on the way back to his floor. Unlike Lauren, he was not a praying man by nature, but he felt better by the time the doors opened.

Chapter 31

Hamlin still wasn't sure how to tell Kate her father had been stabbed. He had always hated that part of the job. Delivering bad news was a regular occurrence for a doctor, especially an oncologist, but he never got used to it. At least, he thought, he didn't have to tell her Jack had passed. He was stable and would be able to donate as planned, it would just take longer than expected. Hamlin was sure Jacky would be fine on the chemo for a bit longer, he would watch him carefully; but his best chance for a long, healthy life was his grandfather's marrow.

Kate was watching Jacky play contentedly with a little girl she had seen in the playroom before when Dr. Hamlin came in.

"I'm sorry about that Kate. I had to deal with a bit of an emergency downstairs. Shall we get back to it?"

"Of course! C'mon Jacky," Kate called.

"Can I please stay here?" Jacky asked. "It's boring in there."

Both Kate and Hamlin laughed. He knelt to Jacky's level. "I suppose it is pretty boring hanging out with grownups all the time, isn't it."

"Yeah, mostly. I like playing with Jack though. He's my best-est friend and he's old like you."

Hamlin laughed at the boy's honesty. He did find it odd that he called his grandfather by his given name though.

"Is Jack the man that comes to visit you here sometimes?"

"Yep. He reads me books and brings me Happy Meal toys." Jacky rattled on as children often do. "He used to look like Santa Claus cuz he had a big beard but now he just looks like a nice old man cuz he cut his beard short and got a haircut like mine."

"He sounds like a good friend," Hamlin stated. "I suppose you can stay here and play with Sarah, if it's okay with your mom, that is."

Kate agreed. "You know where Dr. Hamlin's office is, right Jacky?"

Jacky nodded as he placed more blocks on his growing tower.

"Everything okay there Sarah?" Hamlin asked his other young patient. She was a pretty little girl about Jacky's age with big brown eyes and beautiful caramel-toned skin. She was busy taking care of a baby doll while her mother read a book in the corner.

"I'm good, thank you," she replied with a smile.

Hamlin stood and took Kate by the arm. "He'll be just fine. The nurses can see the playroom from their station."

When they got back to his office, the doctor pulled out a pile of papers for Kate to sign. "Again, I'm sorry for the disruption."

"It's okay," Kate assured him. "It *is* a hospital after all. I hope everything is okay."

"Oh, it will be. Thank you."

He wasn't sure how to continue. It appeared as if Jacky was unaware that Jack was his grandfather and that concerned him greatly. He continued his discussion with prudence.

"I assume you had time to go over the pamphlets I left you?"

"I did, thank you."

"Are there any questions you want to go over now?"

Kate shuffled the pamphlets in her lap. "Not at the moment, but I'm sure I'll have plenty of questions later."

"Good, good. I still have to go over everything so please bear with me. We have a unique situation on our hands here so we must be cautiously optimistic."

"Cautiously optimistic?" Kate asked. "What does that mean?"

Hamlin proceeded carefully.

"*Normally*, once we find the donor, we keep them under observation for a week to ten days. We test them regularly for bacteria and viruses because any little thing can affect the donation. We must make sure the marrow is as pristine as possible."

He stopped to make sure Kate was following him. She didn't say anything, so he took it as a sign to continue.

"There are always risks with any procedure like this, but the fact that we found a good match and that it's a blood relative, that makes us more confident."

"Wait, what did you say?"

"About?"

"You said 'blood relative,' right?"

"I did, yes."

Kate looked at him quizzically. "I... I don't... did you find Marcus?"

"Marcus?" Dr. Hamlin flipped through Jacky's file.

"Jacky's father."

"Oh, no. No, we don't have anything on file for Marcus Bennett, sorry. No, I'm talking about Jacky's grandfather, *your* father... Jack Harper."

He could tell by the look on her face that she, like her son, was unaware of who Jack was. It broke his heart but he was down the rabbit hole, so to speak, and there was no turning back now.

"That's not possible," Kate said lowly, disbelief written all over her face. "My father died before I was born," she explained.

208 ~ SHANA MAVOURNIN

Hamlin flipped through the file folder again and showed Kate the DNA results. It was irrefutable.

"I'm so sorry, Kate. I had no reason to believe you didn't know."

Kate felt the room spin and she was certain she was going to pass out. Dr. Hamlin came around the desk, knelt beside her and held her hand.

"Kate, breathe," he instructed. "That's right. Nice deep breath in and let it out. There you go."

She closed her eyes and continued to breathe deeply. She was squeezing the doctor's hand harder than she probably should, but she needed something stable to ground her. Too many thoughts were spiraling out of control in her head, she didn't know which way was up. It took her several minutes before she felt as if she could open her eyes without feeling nauseated. When she finally did open them, Dr. Hamlin was looking at her with genuine concern. She loosened her grip on his hand and apologized.

"No need for apologies, Kate," he assured her. "In fact, I feel like I should be the one to apologize to you. That was a big shock, I can see. I'm sorry."

Kate whispered, more to herself than to the doctor, "you're not the one who should be sorry."

"I'll understand if you don't want to continue this today. We can reschedule when you've had time to process everything if you'd like."

Kate took another deep breath in and shook her head. "No, Jacky comes first. Let's get this done and over with... if it's alright with you."

Hamlin watched her carefully. She was clearly in shock and deep in thought, but she was right about one thing. Jacky comes first.

"Alright then, where did we leave off? Oh, yes... blood relatives." Hamlin started off tentatively. "As I was saying, blood relations have a higher success rate because of they have underlying traits. Jack was tested for everything under the sun and, even though he is a bit older than we would normally like, he is perfectly healthy."

"You said 'cautiously optimistic' before," Kate reminded him. She was still shaken, but that phrase stood out to her. "A 'unique situation' I believe is what you said. Please explain."

Hamlin sighed deeply. "Yes, we do have a unique situation. That emergency I mentioned earlier. It involved your father I'm afraid."

Kate was instantly on high alert. "What about Jack? What happened?"

Chapter 32

Dr. Hamlin explained the situation to the best of his ability. He made a call to find out how Jack's progress was and what room he would be admitted to once he was out of recovery. He jotted down notes as he spoke. Kate watched and listened to everything as closely as possible. She was still in shock at the doctor's news, but that shock seemed to give her a numb clarity regarding what she needed to do.

Kate has spent the entirety of her life thinking her father had died, but here she was, with irrefutable proof that he was indeed alive. Not only was he *not* dead, she had befriended him by chance nearly a year ago and she never had a clue.

As Dr. Hamlin spoke on the phone, Kate sat in awe of the situation in front of her. She made a mental note of all the questions running through her mind. First and foremost was why her mother lied to her. She would have to have a long discussion about that, and soon. Second was, how did Jack know? Did he know this whole time? Why didn't he say anything to her? Third, and it was in the back of her mind was, will Jack's injury ruin Jacky's chances of getting better? She felt somewhat guilty about that thought, what with Jack having been stabbed and all, but her son was always her priority.

Hamlin hung up the phone and focused on Kate. She was clearly deep in thought. He tried to put himself in her position but failed. He simply couldn't imagine what she was going through.

"Kate?" he calmly questioned. "Are you okay? Is there anything I can do?"

She broke herself out of her reverie. "How is Jack?" she asked.

"He's good. He's in recovery now and is starting to come around. He should be in his room in an hour or so. I can take you to him if you'd like, once he's settled in that is."

Kate nodded... then shook her head... then she just looked at him and shrugged.

"What do I do?" she asked.

"I really can't give you much advice on that Kate. Unfortunately, this situation is..."

"Unique," she finished for him.

"Yes. Very."

She sat forward and pressed her face into her hands. She needed to think. Hamlin gave her all the time she needed without interruption.

"What about Jacky?" she asked sheepishly.

"*That* I *can* answer. Jacky's transplant will be on hold... temporarily, I assure you." He explained the need for Jack to be on a round of high-strength antibiotics for several weeks to be on the safe side. He also assured her they would regularly test for any possible viral or bacterial infection that could have been transmitted by the knife.

"I'll understand if you would rather not go with Jack. We haven't taken Jacky off the recipient list yet so there is still a possibility of finding another donor, but it could take time, as I mentioned before."

"Can we keep him on the list, just in case something comes back as a... I don't know, as a problem I guess?"

"We can, of course," Hamlin agreed. "I feel the need to reiterate the importance of timeliness here though Kate. If someone shows up tomorrow as a match, it's your choice, but if Jack comes through as healthy after the antibiotics... and I have no reason to think otherwise... I highly recommend you go with the genetic match, regardless of your feelings."

"My feelings?"

Hamlin treaded lightly, he wasn't sure what her relationship with Jack was like, but they had always seemed close.

"Your feelings about Jack. I understand this was a surprise to you, but please don't let any negative emotions cloud your judgement."

"The only emotion I'm feeling at the moment right now is shock. I just want what is best for my son. If that means waiting for Jack to get better, that's what we'll do. Now, if you'll excuse me, I have to make a couple of phone calls."

"Of course." Hamlin motioned to the door as Kate let herself out.

She peeked in on Jacky. He was fast asleep on the couch in front of the television. Sesame Street was playing, and Kate was reminded of her own childhood. She was a fan of Oscar the Grouch whereas Jacky preferred Elmo. She stepped out into the hallway and made the first of two phone calls. The first call was an easy one. She made arranged for Jacky to be picked up by her neighbor, Jamie. Kate had the feeling she would be at the hospital for a while and she didn't want Jacky to see Jack in poor shape. The second call was to Claire. Kate had to steady her nerves as she pressed 'Mom' on her phone.

"Katie bug!" Claire exclaimed happily at the other end. "I didn't expect to hear from you today. Is everything okay? Jacky... is Jacky alright?

"Jacky is fine mom."

"Oh, good," she was genuinely relieved. "So, what's up?"

"We need to talk."

"Umm... okay. About?"

Kate took a deep breath and exhaled slowly.

"They found a donor for Jacky."

"That's wonderful news! Oh, and so fast!"

"Yeah, very fast," Kate agreed.

Claire noticed the tension in her daughter's voice. Kate had always spoken through gritted teeth when she was angry and, she could tell by the tone of her voice, Kate was angry. Claire's instinct kicked in. She was a very bright woman and she put two and two together very quickly.

"How did they find someone so quickly?" she asked tentatively.

"Funny you ask mom," Kate started. "You see, when the donor is a *blood relation*, they don't have to go through the registry."

"Katie," Claire whispered, knowing what was coming next.

"You knew," Kate cried into the phone. "You met him Christmas Eve and *you knew*. How could you not know?"

"Katie, please. I've been meaning to tell you. I just... oh sweetie... I just didn't know how."

Kate was silently crying in the hallway. She just couldn't find the words to tell her mom how hurt and disappointed and *angry* she was. She wanted to give her mom the benefit of the doubt; she truly did, but it was hard without hearing her side of the story.

"Kate?"

"I'm here." She sniffled and wiped at her tears. "I'll be here for a while. Are you coming?"

"Coming? Where?"

"To the hospital. That's where I'll be. Room 402."

"I thought you said Jacky was fine," Claire questioned.

"He is," she clarified. "That's Jack's... my father's room. I'll wait for you there." Kate hung up before her mom could protest. She wanted to talk to her, face to face, but first, she wanted to meet her dad.

Chapter 33

Kate bundled up Jacky and took him downstairs to meet her neighbor. Jamie has been a godsend since Jacky got sick. She would have to find a way to make it up to her someday. Once Jacky was on his way home, Kate made her way back to Dr. Hamlin's office. Jack was reportedly in his room, awake, and doing well.

Hamlin walked her to Jack's room and checked on him before he allowed Kate to enter. He was talking to two police officers about the attack. They were wrapping up their questioning when the doctor heard Jack tell the officers where they could find the old woman's wallet.

"I hope I was of some help officers. Thank you," Jack said as the uniformed men left the room.

"How are you doing Jack?" Dr. Hamlin asked. "Looks like you had some excitement today."

Jack laid back and sighed deeply. "I don't know what I was thinking doc. I was on my way home and saw this man... this homeless man, help an old lady cross the street then he took her wallet. I just saw red. I don't know if I told you before but, I used to live on the streets."

Hamlin looked at him quizzically. "But you're... you have plenty of..."

Jack held up his hand. "Yes, I know. It doesn't make sense to anyone but me. I'm aware. Anyway, seeing that man take advantage of that poor woman... well, I think I took it person-ally. Like he was giving all homeless people a black eye, ya know?"

Hamlin didn't know, but he pretended to understand.

"How much damage did I do?" Jack asked.

"I'm sure they explained to you that the stab wound was mostly superficial. No major damage. Our biggest concern is the risk of infection. A stab wound from a homeless man... I'm sure the knife wasn't exactly clean. We have you on a round of high dose antibiotics," Hamlin motioned toward the IV drip hanging behind the bed. "That should knock out just about anything possible; that's the good thing. The bad thing is, we have to wait on the marrow extraction until all tests come back negative."

Jack let out a sigh of relief, or exasperation, Hamlin couldn't tell.

"I can still help Jacky then?" Jack asked.

"Barring any unforeseen circumstances... yes."

"Good. That's good," Jack whispered through the lump in his throat.

"I'll leave you to rest Jack. That's the best thing you can do right now, okay?"

"Thanks doc."

Hamlin joined Kate in the hallway. He couldn't tell what was on her mind so he gave his two cents worth of unsolicited advice.

"Before you go in there," he advised, "just remember, this man is volunteering to help save your son. He's in a delicate position right now. Yes, physically he will be fine, but emo-tionally... just be gentle, alright?"

Kate nodded at the doctor's advice. She sat down in a chair in the hallway outside Jack's room and collected her thoughts while Hamlin made his way back to his office. She felt bad about how she basically opened fire on her mother over the phone. Claire had raised Kate on her own for her entire life and, other than a few typical mother-daughter bumps along the road, her childhood was great. Claire was a great mom; Kate knew it and would never say otherwise, but she couldn't get past such a big lie. What had Jack done that was so horrible he deserved a death sentence in her mother's eyes. She had to know both sides of the story to make sense of it all.

Kate gathered up the nerve to enter Jack's room. He was asleep, or at least appeared to be. She walked in quietly and stared at her father. She could see him for who he was now that she knew the truth. The wrinkles on his brow, the cowlick in his hair, his pale blue eyes, his smile. Jacky looked so much like his grandfather, but she never saw it.

There was a clipboard on the end of his bed. Kate looked toward the door before picking up Jack's file and opened it. She sat in the chair next to his bed and studied the first page of his chart. Jack's eyes fluttered open at the sound of the papers rustling.

"Kate? What are you doing here?"

He noticed the chart in her hands. She was looking down at her lap. He could see a tear make its way down her cheek.

"Jack Winston Charles Harper," Kate read.

"Kate," Jack whispered. "Please..."

Kate continued through the interruption. "Father of Kathryn Elizabeth Bennett, formerly Kathryn Elizabeth Harper. Grand-father of Jack Michael Bennett. Former husband of Claire Michelle Harper."

"Kate, please, I'm so, so sorry." Jack had tears welling in his eyes.

"Please tell me you didn't know this whole time. I don't think I could handle that, Jack."

Jack shook his head. "I didn't know, I promise you I didn't know."

"But you found out... how?"

Jack laid his head back and breathed deeply. "Jacky's birthday party."

Kate remembered back to that fun summer day.

"The wedding picture..." she mumbled to herself. "You saw your wedding picture in my hallway, didn't you."

Jack nodded.

"Why didn't you tell me?"

"Kate," Jack started. "What would you have thought if I came up to you and said 'hey, that's the wedding picture of me and your mom, you must be my daughter'? You'd think I was crazy! Hell, I thought I was crazy when I saw it. It was a lot to process. I never knew you existed. God, I wish I had. Truly, I wish I was there for you."

Kate could see his point, but that was months ago. "And what about the past several months? You didn't want me to know?"

"Of course I wanted you to know! How was I supposed to bring it up? Honestly, I was afraid. I was afraid you would be angry with me, or blame me, or want nothing to do with me. I was stuck between a rock and a hard place."

"Christmas Eve... you saw my mom on Christmas Eve. You both acted like... like nothing!"

Jack shook his head. "That's just not true Kate. You were rather preoccupied with Jacky. I had a long talk with Claire that evening when I left. She wasn't happy to see me, and for good reason, but we talked through a lot of things."

"She knew."

"Yes, she knew. But I promised her I would let her tell you in her own time. I'm sorry it took this long, but I'm glad she told you."

Kate rubbed her tired eyes and let out a deep sigh. "She didn't."

"What?"

"She didn't tell me anything."

Jack was confused. "Then... how did you find out?"

"Dr. Hamlin called me to tell me he found a donor. I came in to sign some papers and he let slip that it was from a blood relative. *He* told me."

"Oh Kate... I'm so sorry. Please believe me when I tell you this is *not* how I wanted you to find out. I don't know what to say."

"You can start by telling me your side of the story,"

"Are you sure?"

Kate nodded and tentatively reached out to hold Jack's hand.

"I want to know my father," she stated. "I want to know my dad."

Jack squeezed her hand tightly and dove into his story, from the time he met Claire to their miscarriage, to his dive deep into the drug abyss. He told her of rehab and Claire's visit and his decision to live on the street. He rehashed meeting Kate and Jacky for the first time nearly a year ago outside their McDonalds and how much they mean to him. He was about to tell her about the money when they were interrupted by a sheepish voice from the hallway.

"Ahem," Claire cleared her throat. "Can I join you?"

Kate and Jack shared a brief look before she got up and pulled another chair over to the other side of Jack's bed.

Chapter 34

The trio sat in silence for, what seemed, ages before a nurse came in to check on Jack's vitals.

"How are you feeling Mr. Harper?" the nurse asked.

Jack welcomed the interruption. "I'm doing fine, thank you."

"Any pain?"

"A bit," he instinctively reached for his wound.

"I can give you some pain meds if you like. Morphine should help the pain."

Jack glanced briefly at Claire. She was avoiding eye contact with him, but her face flushed when the nurse mentioned the drugs.

"No, thank you. I'm fine with Tylenol."

"Are you sure?"

Jack nodded. "Quite sure, thank you though."

Jack was in a fair amount of pain, but he knew, with his history, any narcotics could be the death of who he had worked to become over the years.

Once the nurse left, Claire finally broke the silence.

"So... what happened?"

Jack gave her a brief rundown of the stabbing. Talking to Claire was uncomfortable, but having Kate there with them made it even more so. He was trying to keep things as neutral as possible as he could see Kate was still upset with her mother. Claire must have sensed it too because she was avoiding looking at her daughter. To Jack's surprise, Claire reached over and patted his hand.

"I'm proud of you Jack," she whispered.

"For?" Jack was caught off guard.

"For turning down the pain meds," she explained. "Although... you *were* stabbed. No one would fault you for a bit of comfort."

"*I* would," Jack stated.

Jack and Claire looked at each other deeply for the first time in years. Kate sat in silence and watched her parents. She wondered what they were like together before she was born. For the first time since she was a child, she imagined what it would have been like to have both of her parents in her life. Claire, again, broke the silence.

"Why didn't you let me tell her Jack? You promised me you would let me tell her."

"I thought you did," he explained.

"What? Why?" Claire asked. "Why would you think that?"

"Because she knew who I was. And I assumed you finally told her. You *did* promise me you would tell her after all."

His words felt like a slap across the face and Claire flinched. He was right, she *did* promise; she just hadn't come up with the right way or the right time to tell Kate yet. She moved her gaze to Kate, looking for answers.

"Jack didn't tell me anything mom," Kate started. "Jacky's doctor told me."

Claire was still confused by the situation. "But... how did *he* know?"

Kate explained how Jack was tested to be a marrow donor for Jacky and that his results came back as a match. She explained how Jack had figured it out at Jacky's party and that he told the doctor of his relationship. She told her mom that Jack had never said a word to her about their relationship and that his love for them was, hopefully, going to save Jacky's life. Kate was talking faster and was becoming more manic as she told Jack's tale on his behalf. She was on the verge of tears when Jack sat up with a wince, reached over, and placed his hand on her shoulder.

"Kate, it's okay," he spoke softly.

"No, it's not," she cried. "I spent my whole life without you, and I want to know *why*!"

Kate turned her gaze back to Claire.

"Why mom? Why did he deserve a death sentence instead of child support and shared custody? Why did I deserve a life of lies instead of a chance to create my own relationship with my father?"

Tears welled in Claire's eyes. "I was scared," she croaked out softly.

"Scared of what?" Kate asked.

"Of me," Jack explained. "I told you Kate, I wasn't a good husband. All I could think about at that time was getting high."

He turned to Claire. "I'm sorry Claire. I didn't handle the miscarriage well. I should have been there for you. I should have been stronger, but I wasn't. I should have done a lot of things differently. I can't change the past. God, I wish I could, but I can't. All I can do is look forward and hope to God that I can remain in Kate and Jacky's life."

"I wasn't afraid of you Jack," Claire stated. "I was never afraid of *you*."

"Then what were you scared of?" Kate asked her mom.

"I was afraid of what would happen to Jack if I had another miscarriage. The one we had ruined him... I couldn't imagine what another lost baby would do to him, and I loved him too much to see that happen, so I left."

Claire took a deep breath and continued to tell her side of the story. "I kept tabs on you Jack. I saw you fall deeper and deeper while I grew larger with Katie here. When she was born... oh, she was just the most beautiful, perfect baby ever.

When I came to see you in rehab, she was barely three months old. I wanted to tell you about her... show you a picture... but you seemed so broken. I didn't want to make things worse. I wanted to look you up once you finished rehab, really I did, but you kind of disappeared. I assumed you took your inheritance and started a new life somewhere else. For all I knew, you were still using, and *that* scared me too. I couldn't have that around my daughter. I had some friends back in Pennsylvania look for you because I thought you might have moved back there, but no one could find you. I had *no clue* you were living on the street until you told me about it on Christmas Eve. I can't pretend to understand why you chose that life, but it's not for me to understand. Anyway, after years of looking, I just assumed you didn't want to be found and it was just easier for me to tell Kate you had died. In my mind, by telling her this... this lie... I gave her a father she could think of with love instead of having a father who just wasn't in her life. I know... it wasn't your choice, and I know I should have given you the opportunity to be there for her. I can't make up for what I did. Katie... sweetheart... you didn't deserve any of this. I just... I just didn't know what to do. And when I saw Jack at Jacky's bedside... I just panicked. No one wants to be caught in a lie; and I'm sorry, but that scared me too. I promised him I would tell you, but I just didn't know how. Please, *please* understand that everything I have ever done was out of love for you Katie. I had to protect you. I hope you can forgive me."

Kate watched her mother and, while she was still hurt, she understood every reason Claire gave her for her actions. She was a mother herself and would do anything to keep Jacky safe. She even toyed with the notion, at one time very briefly, to tell Jacky his father had died. The difference is, Marcus had chosen to not be in Jacky or Kate's life whereas Jack had no clue his daughter was ever born. Still, she thought she under-stood her mother's reasoning and, while it would take her time to rebuild her trust in Claire, she thought she could forgive her. She just hoped Jack could do the same thing.

Kate got up to hand Claire a tissue and placed her hand on her mom's shoulder. Claire instinctively grabbed Kate's hand and squeezed it tight. It was an unspoken language between mother and daughter. Claire knew then that Kate had forgiven her. Jack watched the little action with a warm heart and knew they would be fine over time.

"Jack?" Claire was looking deeply into Jack's clear blue eyes again. "Can you forgive me?"

"I've never been one to hold grudges Claire," Jack started. "I think you know that. I understand why you did what you did; truly I do. I can't say I agree with your choices but, God knows, you didn't agree with a lot of mine either. All I really want is to be in their life going forward."

Jack turned to Kate. "If you want me to be, that is."

Kate returned to Jack's side and sat down on the bed. She looked him over, lightly touched the cowlick on his forehead and ran her finger down the lines on his forehead. She was looking at all the traits her son shared with her father. She thought of Jacky and how much he loved Jack. Jacky had loved him from the get-go. She wondered if her son had some sort of sixth sense about this man sitting next to her. She couldn't allow Jack to leave her son's life, and she didn't want him to leave hers.

"Dad," she whispered and hugged him tightly around the neck.

Jack hugged her back and let the tears fall freely onto her shoulder.

"That's going to take some getting used to," he chuckled. "But I like the sound of it."

Chapter 35

Over the next few weeks, Jack was subjected to multiple pokes and prods to test for any possible viral infection under the sun. He was on a high dose of broad-spectrum IV antibiotics as promised, to knock out any potential bacterial infection. Jack was a stickler for making sure they tested for everything. He would not let his impulsivity ruin Jacky's chances for a healthy life.

Claire had gone back home to Omaha after their meeting. Kate visited Jack almost daily since then and, on one of her visits she told him she had been talking to her mom every day. Any time Kate thought of a new question, she called Claire, and Claire answered without question. Jack was glad they were working through things and he wanted to be as supportive as possible. He was developing a relationship with his daughter and, although she still called him 'Jack' most of the time, he felt at peace. He imagined it was difficult for her to call him 'dad' after spending her entire life having never called anyone 'dad' before, so he couldn't fault her for that at all. The only thing Jack was missing was Jacky. He hadn't seen his grandson in more than a month and he wasn't sure if Kate had even told him yet. She didn't want Jacky to see him early on because she was afraid Jacky would climb all over him and re-injure his wound.

"How's Jacky doing?" he asked Kate on one of her visits.

"He's doing okay. You know how he gets... good days and bad days."

Jack gave her a weak smile and ate his pudding.

"He misses you."

"I miss him too," Jack assured her. "Kate? Have you told him who I am?"

She shook her head. "Not yet. I thought it might be good for him to hear it from both of us. Maybe tomorrow? He has chemo tomorrow afternoon. I can bring him by before his appointment if that's okay with you?"

"I would love that," Jack beamed. "Do you think... how do you think he'll react?"

"He's five, Jack. He's not concerned with the logistics of things. He's going to be thrilled! He's never had a grandpa before and, well... I know he already thinks of you that way. I can see it in the way he acts around you and talks about you."

Jack hoped she was right.

Kate left after lunch to run some errands before she had to get home to Jacky. Jack spent the afternoon reading a new novel Kate picked up for him. Now that he had something to look forward to, Jack felt as if time was moving at a painfully slow pace. Tomorrow couldn't come soon enough.

He was starting to doze off when Dr. Hamlin knocked on his door.

"Jack, how are you feeling?" he asked.

"I'm good. I'll feel better once I get all these test results back."

"Well, that's why I'm here. As you know, we got the results back from the knife. We swabbed it for traces of anything viral or bacterial; meningitis, hepatitis, norovirus, tetanus... things like that. While it wasn't the cleanest knife, we didn't find anything concerning. As you *also* know, we've been testing you for anything and everything. Some diseases can take time to show up in the blood. Some STDs, for example. That's why it's taken so long. We tested everything, I promise you, and we had to make sure; not just for you, but for Jacky too. I'm here to tell you, everything has come back clean. I think we're good to go with the transfer!"

"That's wonderful news!" Jack exclaimed.

Hamlin was beaming from ear to ear. "I'll let Kate know when I leave here, and we'll set a date so we can get Jacky started on his radiation. You won't be able to see him during that time, except through a window. He'll be in a sterile room; I think we talked about this before."

"We did," Jack agreed.

"Good. We'll take good care of you here. Jacky too. I promise you that."

After Dr. Hamlin left, Jack finally fell into a much-needed nap. He dreamt of holiday dinners with his family and watching Jacky grow into a fine young man. It was a good dream, one Jack hoped would come true.

The next morning, Jack took a long shower and trimmed his beard shorter than it had been in decades. He wanted to make sure he looked his best for his grandson. Jack was feeling like a new man, just one wearing a hospital gown when Kate and Jacky entered his room. He had talked to Kate on the phone the night before. She was so excited to hear from Dr. Hamlin, she called Jack right away. Jack noticed she was carrying an overnight bag with her. Hamlin must have pulled some strings to get Jacky admitted as quickly as possible.

"Master Jack!" Jack greeted his grandson delightedly. "I've missed you! I think you grew another foot!"

Jacky giggled, climbed into Jack's bed, and threw his arms around him.

"Why are you in the hospital?" Jacky asked as he rubbed his hands over Jack's newly shaven beard. "Are you sick like me?"

"Oh, no sweetie, I'm not sick," Jack promised him.

Jack looked at Kate to read the mood. He didn't want to overstep his bounds. Kate nodded at Jack.

"Then why are you here?"

"Jacky," Kate intervened. "Do you remember what we talked about last night? About how Dr. Hamlin found someone who was a good match for your bone marrow?"

Jacky nodded.

"Well... as it turns out, Jack here is that person. He's here to make you all better."

Jacky looked at Jack with wide eyes. "You are?"

"I am," Jack stated.

Jacky gave Jack another neck-squeezing hug and kissed him on the cheek with a loud smack. "Thank you," he whispered into Jack's ear.

"Jacky? We have something else to tell you too," Kate stated.

She sat down on the bed next to Jack and held his hand.

"When the doctors ran all the tests to make sure Jack was a match for you, we found out something else."

Jack let Kate take the lead. She had clearly thought this through and decided a little white lie was the easiest way to explain their situation to a five-year-old. Jack was in no position to disagree with her decision and was, in fact, glad she found a way that didn't hurt his perception of anyone; or so he hoped.

"There's a lot of big people words to explain this but, all you need to know is this... Jack is a good match for you because he's actually... well... he's your grandpa."

Jacky looked at Kate quizzically, turned his gaze to Jack, then back and forth again. He wrapped his arms around Kate's neck and whispered something into her ear. Kate smiled over his shoulder and whispered back, "yes, he really is."

When Jacky pulled away, he was grinning largely. That same little kid grin Jack had loved from the day they met.

"Grandpa Jack?"

Jack loved the sound of that as much as he loved hearing Kate call him 'dad.'

"Yeah kiddo?"

"When I'm all better, can you take me fishing?"

"Fishing?"

"Isn't that what grandpas do?"

Jack laughed heartily. "You know what? I think that's *exactly* what grandpas do!"

Kate was right. The purity of a child's heart overlooks any possible logic. It just believes what it wants to believe.

They spent the next hour together talking and laughing. Jacky showed his grandpa how he learned to read the Dr. Seuss book *Hop on Pop.* Jack was proud of his advancement and his growing love of books. They colored pictures together and Jacky gave him a drawing of him and Jack standing by a pond with fishing poles. With some help from Kate, Jacky scrawled the words 'ME AND GRANDPA' in big block letters across the bottom. It was, by far, Jack's favorite piece of his grandson's artwork.

Kate glanced at her watch and realized it was time for them to get Jacky checked into his room. His normal chemo was cancelled so they could get started on the pre-transplant procedures. Jack got another big hug from Jacky and one from Kate as well.

"Kate?" Jack asked her as she pulled away from their embrace. "What did Jacky say to you? When you told him who I was, he whispered something to you. Can I ask what he said?"

Kate laughed brightly. "Oh, that. He told me when he saw Santa last year, he asked him if he could make you his grandpa. He said, 'Santa really is magic, isn't he.' I told him he really was. I'm beginning to think maybe he has it right."

Jack looked over at Jacky, standing in the doorway.

"Me too Kate. Me too."

Chapter 36

Jacky settled into his new routine as well as any five-year-old patient could. He wasn't thrilled with being stuck in bed for so long, but he did it with minimal complaint because he had faith in his grandpa Jack and his 'magic marrow,' as Jacky started calling it. He had no real idea what marrow was or how it was supposed to help him. The doctors and nurses and even his mom tried to explain it to him, but it was beyond the scope of his comprehension. He was allowed to have paper and crayons, his teddy bear, a few of his favorite books, and a couple of toys with him, but they had to be put in some special machine first to make sure they didn't bring in germs. If he couldn't have these things, he might have complained much more.

The radiation and chemo made Jacky feel very sick and very tired, so he slept a lot. Everyone warned him he would feel icky for a while, but it had to be this way for the 'magic marrow' to work. His mom stayed with him throughout the day. He thought she looked funny dressed in the papery yellow gown, mask on her face, what looked like his grandma's shower cap on her head, and paper booties on her feet; but, again... it was necessary to keep him healthy.

He spent the days napping, coloring, watching movies, reading books, and napping some more. When he was sleeping deeply, Kate would step out for fresh air, a bite to eat, or a quick visit with Jack. She loved spending time getting to know her father and, although her thoughts were always on her son, talking to Jack helped take her mind off things.

Five days into Jacky's treatment, Kate went to visit Jack. As always, she brought him a cup of coffee from the little café on the first floor. Jack swore the coffee they brought him from the cafeteria was from the same pot as when he was first admitted.

Jack sipped the steaming black coffee and let out a contented sigh. "So, how's our boy doing today?"

"He's tired a lot. Been sleeping more and more, but I guess that's good. You don't feel pain when you're sleeping."

Jack could see Kate was exhausted, but she kept on going. He admired that in his daughter. Not for the first time, he wondered what she was like as a child. Did she always have this tenacity?

"Dr. Hamlin came in this morning," Jack told her. "He introduced me to the 'team.' They're planning my procedure tomorrow afternoon, that way it'll be ready for when Jacky is ready."

"T-minus five days," Kate whispered, then giggled. "I feel like I should be working at NASA."

Jack chucked along with her. "I do believe, my dear Kate, you could do *anything* you set your mind to!"

"Well, it appears I come by my stubbornness honestly." She gave him a clever side-eye glance and a wink."

"I was hoping I could stop by to see Jacky after my procedure if that's okay with you. I know I can't come in, and that's fine, but if I could just *see* him... wave hello... let him know I'm still here for him? Is that okay?"

"Of course it's okay! Jacky will be thrilled to see you. They may let you in to see him if you're in all the protective gear. I don't see why not. You've been in the hospital longer than most of the doctors!"

Jack laughed at her little joke. He had been confined in this place for longer than he ever expected, but he did it for good reason.

Kate checked her watch. "I should get back to Jacky. He's probably awake by now and he'll want to read a story. You'd be so proud of how much he's learned to read, dad. He loves the books you gave him."

Jack smiled at the word 'dad,' as he always did. "I'll make sure to get him more books once I'm out of here. We'll make sure he has his own library in his room!"

Kate chucked. "I'll need a bigger house for that!"

Jack winked at her. "That can be arranged."

Kate hugged her dad and started back to Jacky's room. She chalked Jack's comment up to him wanting to be a good father and assumed it held no real substance; but then something her mother said jumped to Kate's mind and she made a sharp about face and returned to Jack's room.

"What did you mean?" she asked him from the doorway.

"About?"

Kate sat on the edge of the bed and asked again. "You said 'that can be arranged.' What did you mean?"

Jack shrugged. "Just that, Kate. We can arrange for you and Jacky to have a bigger house. You *should* have a bigger home."

"That day... when mom came here, and everything came out into the open... she said something about... about an inheritance? Is that right?"

Jack nodded slowly.

Kate looked out the window. It was a dreary late winter day; gray and rainy. Her thoughts wandered back to stories her mom would tell her about her dad. How he grew up with a silver spoon, but he never let it define him. How they would use their own earnings to make their way and that's how she wanted Kate to live... by earning what she had. Kate was putting the pieces together. The hospital donation box... no poor man living on pennies a day would stuff those valuable pennies into a box *every day*. As she thought about it, she realized she had never received a bill for a bit of Jacky's care. It was never at the front of her mind, but when she did think about it, she assumed they would send one large bill at some point.

"What kind of inheritance?" she asked sheepishly.

Jack sighed and laid back against his pillow. "The kind in which you and Jacky will never want for anything... ever."

Kate exhaled slowly. Her heart was pounding and she was trembling slightly.

"Jacky's hospital bills?"

Jack nodded his head. "Taken care of long ago. You can talk to Lauren Temple in billing if you want to."

"But... he got sick before you knew..."

"It didn't matter Kate," he patted her hand lightly. "He was a sick little kid I was very fond of; with a young mother I was also very fond of. I wanted to make sure he got the best care possible without causing you any worry."

"Jack... dad...I, uh... I don't know what to say. You didn't have to do any of this you know."

"I wanted to," he assured her.

Kate was speechless. She sat on the bed and stared at her father like he was foreign to her.

"Why were you living on the streets? If you had all this money... it just doesn't make sense."

Jack sighed deeply. He knew there was nothing he could say to make her understand. He had tried to explain it to others in the past and they just couldn't comprehend that Jack had chosen a life of perdition; of atonement for his sins.

"One day, Kate, I promise I'll explain it to you the best I can. But right now, please go back to Jacky. Trust me. I wasn't doing anything sinister or illegal. I wasn't taking advantage of any-one. It was just something I felt I had to do; to get my karma back on track. Remember, we talked about this before, at the duck pond?"

Kate nodded.

"It was just something I needed to do. But finding you and Jacky... you changed my life in so many ways. From here on out, I'm going to do better. I promise I'll tell you everything... someday."

Kate hugged him again, tighter than before.

"Promise?"

He hugged her back tightly. "Promise."

Chapter 37

Jack was prepped and ready to go for his marrow extraction shortly after noon. He was given the rundown on the risks, as minimal as they were, over and over by every person on the team. They assured him it was a very simple procedure, and he wouldn't feel a thing as he would be sedated for the duration. The only thing they expected him to have after it was done was pain in his hip because that's where the needle aspiration site would be.

Because he was still technically a patient in the hospital, they insisted on wheeling him down to the procedure room even though he wanted to walk. He wanted more than anything to just go for a long walk and stretch his legs. Being cooped up in a hospital bed for nearly a month was not Jack's style. He was an active man. Years on the street will do that to you, he supposed.

The sedative worked quickly and, before he knew what was happening, Jack was waking up in the recovery room. The aspiration took mere minutes, but Jack felt as if he slept through the night. Once he was fully awake, an orderly wheeled him back to his room.

Dr. Hamlin came to check on him while Jack was eating his lunch of spaghetti, undressed salad, and a rather delicious piece of chocolate cake.

"I pulled some strings to get you that cake," the doctor joked. "I thought you deserved a little 'thank you' for all you've done."

Jack smiled through a mouthful of fudge frosting.

"So, I'm out of here tomorrow, is that right?" Jack asked.

"That's the plan. We just want to keep you for observation overnight. It's not typical for marrow donors, but given your recent history and hospital stay, as well as your age, we are erring on the side of caution."

"Fair enough," Jack conceded. "I'm sure my houseplant is long dead by now anyway" he scoffed.

"Is there anything I can do for you?"

"Actually, if it's okay, I'd like to go see my grandson."

"I think that can be arranged," Hamlin smiled.

Half an hour later, Jack was being wheeled to Jacky's room. There was a large picture window so the nurses could see him from their station and two sets of doors going into the room. Kate explained to him previously that the first set of doors led to a small anteroom where guests could change into protective gear before they entered the main room. Jack thought it was eerie and almost a bit dystopic, but whatever was best for Jacky was just fine by him.

Kate was in the room, sitting on the bed, holding her son in her arms and reading his well-worn copy of *Where the Wild Things Are*, one of Jacky's favorites. Jack knocked lightly on the window, not wanting to startle them. The grin on Jacky's face when he saw his grandpa was more wonderful than all the money in the world, Jack realized.

"Grandpa Jack!" he squealed, although it was muffled through the window.

Kate came out of the room to greet Jack with a hug.

"How did it go?"

"Easy as pie," Jack grinned.

"Well, let's get you wrapped up in all this stuff so you can see your grandson."

Jack rose from the wheelchair with a slight wince. They weren't kidding about the hip pain. It shot down his leg into his calf and he almost had to sit back down, but it passed quickly. Kate was busy taking off her old garments to replace them with new ones, so she didn't see Jack flinch. Once she was re-dressed she helped Jack with his gown, mask, hair bonnet, and shoe covers. Jack felt as if they looked like a couple of doctors ready to take on the plague.

Jack tentatively hugged his grandson with such gentle care. He looked so pale and weak; Jack was afraid the boy would break if he touched him too hard.

"How are you doing there buddy?"

"I'm ready for your 'magic marrow' to fix me," Jack said somewhat excitedly.

"'Magic marrow?'" Jack asked Kate.

She smiled under her mask. "That's what he's been calling it, so we just go with it."

Jack held his tiny hand in his own weathered one. "I sure hope it's magic kiddo. I really do."

Jack let Jacky read to him from one of his books for a bit. After he got too tired to go on, Jack finished for him. He gave Jack a stack of pictures he drew for him. Most of the pictures were of Jack and the boy fishing together but one was Jacky's attempt at making Jack into a superhero, complete with flam-ing red cape with the letters 'SGJ' in a big star on the cape.

"SGJ?" Jack asked?

"Super Grandpa Jack!" Jacky explained.

Jack let out a hearty laugh and pulled Jacky into another hug. Within minutes, Jacky was sound asleep and snoring lightly. He carefully laid his sleeping grandson on the pillow and tucked the blanket up under his chin.

Kate walked him to the door and helped him remove all the sterile items before walking him back to his hospital issued ride. They stood outside the window, watching Jacky sleep peacefully for some time before Jack sat back in the wheelchair with another wince. This one, Kate saw.

"Are you okay?"

"Yeah, all good," Jack stated.

"You winced. And you look kind of pale."

"It's just from the aspiration. They took the marrow from my hip. They warned me I'll have some pain there for a few days. Nothing I can't handle."

Kate looked at him worriedly.

"I promise, Kate. I used to sleep in a cement tube. I'm used to a little hip pain," he joked.

Kate didn't laugh.

"So, tomorrow then?" she asked.

"Tomorrow?"

"You get to go home tomorrow, right?"

"Oh, yeah. Yep... first thing."

"I'll give you a ride."

"You don't have to do that. You should be here for Jacky."

Kate shook her head. "No arguments. I don't need you riding the bus and playing superhero again, got it?"

Jack smiled at his daughter's obstinacy.

"Okay, fine. You can drive me home. I'll call you when I'm discharged, okay?"

"Sounds like a plan."

The orderly returned to wheel Jack back to his room. Before they left, Kate leaned down and kissed her dad on the cheek.

"Jacky really loves you, ya know."

Jack smiled. "I love him too. Very much."

She turned back to the door of her son's room, stopped, and turned back to Jack.

"Dad?"

"Hmm?"

"I love you too. I just thought you should know."

Jack felt the tears prickling at the corners of his eyes.

"I love you too sweetie," he whispered.

Chapter 38

Kate couldn't sleep. She was getting used to the lack of sleep since Jacky's diagnosis and she found the best thing for it was to just get up and do something to get her mind off things. This morning, she had already cleaned the trailer from end to end and top to bottom, ran a load of laundry, and made herself a packed lunch for the day. She also packed a few new books she ordered for Jacky. Kate always loved the smell of libraries and bookstores and, on any other occasion, she would have bought her son the books from the local Barnes and Noble; but as she had very little free time, she resorted to Amazon. The box of books arrived the day before and she just knew Jacky would be thrilled.

As there was nothing left to do at her home, she showered, got dressed, and drove to the hospital early. On the way, she picked up a breakfast sandwich for herself and a large cup of coffee for Jack from the Dunkin on the corner. She found herself enjoying the drive to the hospital every day. It gave her time to think of things other than her son's care. Lately, she had naturally been thinking about the future she and Jacky would have now that she had a father and he had a grandfather. She, like Jacky, pictured the three of them fishing at the lake. She hoped Jack could teach her son things a father should like how to change a tire, fix a leaky faucet, or build a bookshelf; all things Kate knew how to do herself, but there was something special about that male bonding she wanted Jacky to have.

Kate parked her car in the visitor parking lot as she did every day for the past week. She wished a 'good morning' to the front desk attendant and made her way up to the fourth floor. She knew as soon as she stepped off the elevator, something was wrong.

Nurses and doctors were running down the hallway and 'CODE BLUE' was announced loudly over the intercom. Kate slowly made her way down the hall, making sure to keep out of the way of the scrambling medical personnel. It wasn't until she turned the corner and saw where all the fuss was taking place did shock take over.

Jack's room was filled with doctors, nurses, and medical machinery of all sorts. She wanted to run to his side but she knew it would be an effort in futility. Instead, she slid down the wall, sat on the cold tile floor, and stared into her father's room. She held his coffee to her chest as if it were the only thing she had of him, closed her eyes, and started to cry.

She lost track of the time she was sitting there before she was approached by a young nurse. Kate opened her eyes. Everything was quiet again. The doctors and nurses had departed, save one. Kate stood up on rubbery legs, coffee still clutched to her chest, and walked into Jack's room. Dr. Hamlin was hunched over Jack's body in a defeated sort of way. It looked, to Kate, as if he were whispering some sort of prayer before he raised the sheet to cover Jack's face.

"Don't, please," Kate said.

Hamlin was startled by Kate's presence.

"Oh, Kate... I'm so sorry. I'm just... so very sorry."

"What happened?" she asked quietly. She couldn't take her eyes off Jack's face.

Dr. Hamlin shook his head slowly. "We think it was an embolism, but until we do the autopsy, it's just a theory. It's a good theory," he whispered.

"He was fine yesterday. I saw him. Jacky saw him. He was fine!" Kate was starting to lose control. "*He was fine!*"

"Kate, please..."

"No!" She shook her head vehemently and pushed past Hamlin to be by Jack's side, placing her hand on his head. "No... this can't be happening. No... you're supposed to take Jacky fishing, remember? I brought new books for you to read to him. You're 'Super Grandpa Jack!' You have 'magic marrow' to make him all better! No... I just got you back from the dead! It's not fair! It's just not fair!"

Hamlin carefully put a hand on her shoulder. Kate shrugged it off before spinning around to face him.

"Tell me how this is fair!" she demanded.

"It's not," was all he could say.

Kate fell to the chair and sobbed. "It's not fair! I want my daddy back! You bring him back to me!"

She felt like a little girl having a temper tantrum all over again. All she wanted her entire life was to have her dad and, after almost twenty-five years, she got her wish. It lasted less than a month, and he was taken away from her abruptly and without warning. She had always known life wasn't fair, but she never knew how brutal and vicious it could be. Here was this great man... a man who recognized his failures and did what he could to right his wrongs... a man who did everything in his power to make sure his loved ones were cared for; but no matter what he did, death still stole him away.

Dr. Hamlin remained at a distance and kept anyone else from coming into the room. Kate had a right to grieve before they took Jack's body away. He had seen too much death in his life and, while he was usually good at compartmentalizing, as doctors are apt to do, he felt tears well in his own eyes at the passing of Jack Harper.

Kate cried herself into hysterics and, once she calmed down, she leaned over, kissed her dad on the forehead and whispered "I love you daddy" before covering him up.

She gathered her things but left his coffee on the table next to his bed. On the way out, she looked at Dr. Hamlin.

"What do I tell Jacky?" she pleaded.

Hamlin again placed his hand on her shoulder; she didn't shrug him away this time. "Jacky needs to remain as calm as possible for now. I'm not saying you should lie to him, not by any means, but if you can put it off until after we know the transplant has taken hold, I believe he will do much better."

Kate nodded solemnly.

"Do you want me to call anyone for you?" he asked.

She shook her head and walked toward the elevator. Kate didn't want to be there when they took her father away. She didn't want to think about what they would do next. What she *did* want was to talk to the only other adult who just might feel her pain.

It was a cold, rainy, miserable day that matched her mood perfectly. She could have stayed in the warmth of the hospital, but she couldn't bear the thought of having another emotional breakdown in front of complete strangers. Kate walked back to her car to make the phone call.

Claire answered on the third ring. "Katie bug, it's good to hear from you!"

Kate instantly burst into tears at the sound of her mother's voice.

"Mommy," she cried. "I need you."

Chapter 39

Dr. Hamlin's assumptions were right. Jack had suffered from a deep vein thrombosis that traveled to his heart while he was sleeping. Kate was concerned the marrow aspiration had caused it and felt such enormous guilt at the idea, but Dr. Hamlin and the other physicians overseeing his care assured her his donation had nothing to do with it. The fact that he had spent so much time in bed had caused the blood clot and it finally let go and travelled to his heart. There was nothing anyone could have done.

Three days after Jack's death, Jacky received his marrow transplant. It was easier than Kate had imagined, although they explained the process to her dozens of times. Jacky watched the IV of blood travel through the tube into his body and wondered just how 'magic' his grandpa really was. He still didn't know he would never go fishing or to a baseball game with him, although he asked for him daily.

Jack's funeral was held on the Saturday after Jacky's infusion. He was doing well enough that Kate felt comfortable leaving him for a few hours. Claire took care of all the funeral arrangements. Kate was too consumed with grief and wrapped up in Jacky's care to even consider planning a funeral. She gave Claire the key to Jack's apartment so she could find something appropriate for the funeral home to dress Jack in. Claire wasn't surprised to find not a single suit in his closet, but she did find something Kate had mentioned to look for. She left his apartment with nothing but a baseball cap and made her way to the nearest Macy's so she could buy Jack a suit.

Kate didn't expect it to be a long service considering Jack had never spoken of any friends and he had no other family, but she wanted to be there to say a proper good-bye to her dad. She was surprised when she entered the parlor to see the room filled with people. Claire was greeting people at the entrance as they signed the little book the funeral home set out for guests to leave a little note for the family. Standing next to the coffin was Dr. Hamlin and a woman Kate vaguely recognized. Lauren from the billing department approached Kate and hugged her as if she had known her for years.

"Your dad was a great man, I'm sure you already know that though. He will be greatly missed," Lauren assured her.

"Ms. Bennett?"

Kate turned to see a short, portly looking woman with a kind but weathered face.

"My name is Susan Winters. I run the shelter your father volunteered at. I just want to pay my respects and let you know he will be missed. He was just a kind, sweet, *giving* man."

"Thank you."

Kate meandered through the small sea pf people. Everyone reached out to her to give their condolences and let her know what a great man her father was. She was beginning to understand him more with each passing acquaintance.

"Kate?"

"Elmer, right?" Kate recognized the barber that cut Jack and Jacky's hair so many months ago.

He shook her hand warmly. "How is your little guy doing?"

"He just had his bone marrow transplant. Jack... I mean, my dad donated just before he passed," she choked out through tears.

"I heard he did that. Jack was one of the good ones you know."

Kate smiled briefly. "Yeah, I know."

Kate was approached by former students of her father's, an elderly couple who just called themselves 'mom' and 'pop,' the librarians Jack worked with, a couple of young high school students he had been tutoring at the library, and even a few homeless men who cleaned up for the occasion. She had no idea one man could touch so many lives and yet maintain such a low profile. Kate was beyond proud that this man was her father and she promised herself that her son would know all about him.

While Kate was being bombarded by everyone her father ever met, Claire was in a corner talking to Dr. Pine. She remembered meeting him briefly while Jack was in rehab. She liked his kind but no-nonsense approach.

"Well," Dr. Pine sighed, "I guess he found his way out."

"Out?" Claire asked. "Out of what?"

"Perdition."

Claire looked at him carefully. "Jack said something like that to me a while ago. That he didn't want to be lost in perdition. What did that mean? Is that why he did what he did? Lived on the streets? Avoided his inheritance?"

"Quite possibly, but I don't think he ever felt as if his actions were enough. We discussed this at length... karma, atonement, what have you. He insisted on making up for all his misdeeds so he could tip the scales in his favor. I don't think he realized just how much one good deed can snowball. If he could just see this now," Dr. Pine motioned to the full funeral parlor. "Maybe he would realize it wasn't all for nothing."

"I hope he can see this," Claire stated as she looked at all the people who came to pay their respects. "I really hope he can."

As Claire was discussing heaven and hell with Dr. Pine, Kate finally made her way to the coffin. She didn't know what to expect once she got there but, when she saw Jack in a brand-new suit with his Herbie Husker baseball cap on his head, she couldn't help but laugh. That laugh quickly turned into body wracking sobs. Claire rushed to her side to hold her tightly in her arms. She stroked her hair and whispered motherly words of love and reassurance in her ear. Dr. Hamlin helped Claire get Kate to her seat where she could take some time to compose herself.

"The hat," Kate choked out. "That silly hat... did you see the back?" she asked her mom.

Claire nodded. "*'Jack too.'* I wasn't sure what that meant."

"Jacky has a matching hat with *'Just Jack'* on the back. It was their own little joke."

Claire wiped at her own tears. Whatever happened to their relationship in the past, Claire would be lying if she said she ever stopped loving him. Jack, with all his faults, was a good man at heart. She knew it, Kate knew it, and Jacky knew it; and that's all that really mattered.

The funeral ended up lasting longer than Kate had imagined. Almost everyone in attendance volunteered to pay their respects with stories about Jack and all the wonderful things he did for them. There were tears and laughter and more tears. It was clear to everyone that Jack was well liked, admired, and respected. Jack himself would have been surprised by the outpouring of emotion.

As they finished up the ceremony and people made their way to their cars for the procession to the cemetery, Kate was approached by one more person.

"Kate Bennett?"

"Yes."

"My name is Bob Harding, Jr. Your father was a friend of my dad's and my client. My firm handled his estate for years. I wanted to pay my respects and give you this." He held out a large manila envelope with his business card attached. "When you're ready, please give me a call."

Kate thanked him rather quizzically before he turned to leave.

On the ride to the cemetery, Kate opened the envelope.

"What is it sweetie?" Claire asked.

Katre read and re-read the first page several times before handing it to her mother.

"Is that what I think it is?" Kate asked.

Claire smiled warmly and nodded.

"You're a good man, Jack," she mumbled to herself. "You were always a good man."

Chapter 40

Kate told Jacky about Jack's death on the last day of winter. His numbers were good, he had more color and energy. Jacky cried, of course, which made Kate relive her grief and she cried with him. Kids are more resilient than most people give them credit for. Over time, Jacky was able to talk about Jack with glee while Kate still found it painful to talk about her father.

Winter turned to spring and spring to summer. The bone marrow transplant worked wonders and, after a couple of hiccups, Jacky was allowed to go home just before Easter. They spent the holiday in their new home. Jack had kept his promise to Kate about getting a bigger house. In the envelope given to her by Mr. Harding was Jack's last Will and Testament. In it, he left nearly every penny to Kate with a sizeable trust fund set up for Jacky's education. He also left enough aside for one final donation to the hospital. His only request was that Kate do good things with her inheritance.

Kate followed her father's advice and did good things. One sunny Friday in May, Kate was taking Jacky in for a routine checkup with Dr. Hamlin. She smiled at the new sign that greeted everyone that stepped off the elevator on the fifth floor. The beautifully engraved bronze plaque read simply, "Jack Harper Children's Hospital." Modest and unassuming, just like her dad. She would be touched to know that every time Dr Hamlin walked past that sign, he raised a hand and touched it lightly, like giving Jack a symbolic high five.

On the fourth of July, Kate received the news that Jacky's cancer was, again, in remission. She was hopeful it would remain that way this time. Jacky was filled with his grandpa's 'magic marrow' after all. They decided to celebrate.

Claire moved back to Lincoln after Jack's funeral. She felt the need to be closer to her family, now more than ever. She prepared a picnic lunch and picked up Kate and Jacky so they could go to the park. One of the 'good things' Kate did with her inheritance was to have Carter Park renovated and renamed. She was amazed at how fast things could be accomplished with the right amount of funding. 'Jack's Park,' as it was now known, courtesy of Jacky's input, was filled with families having picnics next to the duck pond. Children were playing on the new equipment, couples were out in paddleboats, and a group of teenagers were enjoying a spirited game of volleyball. Kate, Jacky, and Claire found a nice shady spot next to the pond. Jacky insisted on bringing his new fishing pole with him but only half-heartedly cast the line out a few times before leaving it on the bank as he joined his family.

As Kate was doling out fried chicken and potato salad, Claire spoke up.

"Oh, I almost forgot! The cemetery manager called today. They delivered Jack's headstone yesterday. I thought, maybe, if you want... we could go see it? Your dad always liked the fourth of July," she said almost shyly.

"What do you think kiddo?" Kate asked Jacky. "Do you want to go see where your grandpa is?"

Jacky shrugged. "I suppose so."

Kate wasn't sure it would be good for Jacky to see the cemetery. He was still so young and she doubted he even had the slightest comprehension of death, but she often underestimated his understanding. It might be good for him to say a proper good-bye.

They finished their lunch and packed everything in Kate's new Camry for the drive over to the cemetery.

It took the mason so long to complete Jack's headstone because Kate and Claire chose a custom design. When they came up to Jack's plot, they were both brought to tears by how perfect it turned out. They chose a stone in the shape of an open book. The symbolism was not lost on either of them. Jack had spent so much of his life closed off to others, it made sense that death would allow those pages to open. On one side it simply had his name and his dates of birth and death. On the other side was inscribed 'Beloved father and grandfather.' Below that was 'No longer lost in perdition."

"What's that word?" Jacky pointed.

"Perdition, sweetie," Kate told him.

"What does it mean?"

"Well..." Kate started then looked to her mom for help.

Claire knelt next to Jacky and wrapped him in her arms.

"It means, your grandpa felt lost in a bad place for a long time, but now he's in a good place," Claire explained.

"Oh, like the place where only the things you want to happen, happens, right?"

Kate and Claire shared a look. Jacky understood more than they gave him credit for once again.

"That's right," Kate agreed and hugged her son.

They sat in silence for a while before Kate suggested they head back to the park so they could watch the fireworks.

"Just a minute," Jacky said. He sat down in front of the headstone and pulled off his backpack. He looked over his shoulder to his mom and grandma and the look he gave them was all they needed. He wanted some alone time with his grandpa. They stepped away and watched him from the shade of a nearby oak tree.

Jacky pulled out some items from his backpack and diligently placed everything just right.

"You promised you'd take me fishing," Jacky spoke to his grandpa as he worked.

There was so much he wanted to say but his little five-year-old mind was lacking the words needed to convey his feelings. His face scrunched up and he began to cry. Kate ran to him, wrapped him in a big hug, and rocked him like she did when he was a baby. She stroked his hair and told him everything would be okay.

"I can't say what I want to say!" Jacky bawled.

"I know sweetie, I know. It's hard to say good-bye."

"He promised he'd take me fishing!" he cried even harder.

Kate let him cry until the tears dried up. He wiped his nose on her shoulder and she carried him back to the car. She turned to look back one more time at her dad's gravesite. There, among the flowers she and Claire brought and the little American flag the cemetery staff placed at every site for the holiday was a row of Jacky's favorite toys, the ones he and Jack played with every week, lined up in front of the drawing of 'Super Grandpa Jack' Jacky had colored the day before Jack died. On top of the headstone, carefully placed, was Jacky's Herbie Husker hat with 'Just Jack' embroidered on the back.

Kate smiled at the scene. She knew, from the simple act of love and care by a five-year-old boy, that Jack was indeed no longer lost in perdition.

Printed in the USA
CPSIA information can be obtained
at www.ICGtesting.com
LVHW051316271023
762203LV00015B/433